Chas. H. Stubbs

Historic-Genealogy of the Kirk Family

Anatiposi

Chas. H. Stubbs

Historic-Genealogy of the Kirk Family

Reprint of the original, first published in 1872.

1st Edition 2023 | ISBN: 978-3-38212-817-3

Anatiposi Verlag is an imprint of Outlook Verlagsgesellschaft mbH.

Verlag (Publisher): Outlook Verlag GmbH, Zeilweg 44, 60439 Frankfurt, Deutschland
Vertretungsberechtigt (Authorized to represent): E. Roepke, Zeilweg 44, 60439 Frankfurt, Deutschland
Druck (Print): Books on Demand GmbH, In de Tarpen 42, 22848 Norderstedt, Deutschland

HISTORIC-GENEALOGY

OF

THE KIRK FAMILY,

AS ESTABLISHED BY

ROGER KIRK,

Who settled in Nottingham, Chester County, Province of Pennsylvania, about the year 1714, containing impartial biographical sketches of his descendants, so far as ascertained; also, a record of two hundred and nine of the descendants of Alphonsus Kirk, who migrated from Lurgan, North Ireland, and settled in the county of New Castle, Delaware.

BY CHAS. H. STUBBS, M. D.,

Cor. Member of the Maryland Academy of Science, &c., &c.

LANCASTER, PA.:

WYLIE & GRIEST, INQUIRER PRINTING HOUSE.

1872.

PREFACE.

On the 30th day of March, 1867, we had printed and distributed the following circular letter:

"We design compiling a record of the names, births, marriages and deaths of all the Kirks, and their descendants, from the time of the settlement in this country of our common ancestor—Roger Kirk—to a period that will include those of the latest generation.

"You will, therefore, confer a favor by sending us all the information in your possession relative to the dates of births, deaths and marriages of your ancestors and your descendants.

"Any old document of interest relating to the Kirks, if sent to the undersigned, will be scrupulously preserved and returned to the possessor.

"Considerable time and much labor will be required to accomplish this work, hence it is desirable that those who may be disposed to assist, should furnish us all information in their possession at as early a day as possible.

"Very respectfully, &c."

Since the date of the above we have collected the material found in this volume, a task assigned to the leisure hours of the last four years.

Our object in compiling this genealogy was twofold. First, to preserve in book form all that might be deemed worthy of an old established and extensively known family, and second, to arrange it in such a manner as to be of interest, as well as accessible to the present generation contained therein.

How well we have succeeded is not for us to determine.

All works of this character must of necessity be more or less incomplete, and we are well aware that this one is no exception to the general rule. To obtain correct data in all cases of families and branches of families, extending back through a long series of years (in this instance one hundred and fifty-seven), where they have been scattered over a large space of country, is a matter of impossibility. Nevertheless, we believe we have been as successful in tracing out the various ramifications of our family, extending, as they do, from Maryland to Utah, and from Ohio to Kentucky, as other genealogists who have attempted works of a similar nature, and at the same time had not the advantages of some governmental archives or records of royalty, to aid them in their undertakings.

Coöperation in the preparation of this volume we have generously received, and to the many friends who have rendered us assistance we emphatically offer our thanks for their untiring support. Among these we may mention Gilbert Cope, of West Chester, who has written and published several works upon genealogy, to whom we are under many obligations for important assistance in tracing out the Woodward branch of the family, also for the use of valuable MSS.; to Dr. L. R. Kirk, of Rising Sun, Md., formerly of the U. S. Army, for aid in securing a large amount of material and in assisting to push the work to a final completion; to Roger H. Kirk, of Pleasant Grove, Lancaster co, Pa.; Ann Kirk, of Brick Meeting House, and Alfred Kirk, of College Green, Cecil co., Md.. for old MSS. belonging to some of the earliest of the name of Kirk in the West and South, Theodore J.

Kirk, of Elmore; Issac Cope, of New Baltimore, James Kingham, of Port Clinton; Knight Kirk Winder, of Kingsville, Ohio; and Thomas B. Jones, Esq., of Popular Plains, Kentucky—all of whom have at different times furnished us with material from those residing in their respective neighborhoods.

In conclusion, we may remark that there need be no difficulty in understanding the arrangement pursued throughout this work. Among the various plans adopted in books of this kind the one selected is decidedly the most systematic.

We have arranged the dates in *plain style,* chiefly in use among Friends, not on account of any personal preference to the system, but because it is much more convenient to use where the age of any one is required. Dashes are used where names and dates were not ascertained. If to some, more space is accorded than to others, it is because the data was furnished, and not on the score of partiality.

May those into whose hands this volume finds its way, have as much pleasure in perusing its pages as we have had in writing them.

C. H. S.

Cedar Lawn, Lancaster co., Pa., Jan. 1, 1872.

INDEX.

PAGE.

INDEX TO MARRIAGES.

FAMILY RECORD.

MARRIAGES.

BIRTHS.

DEATHS.

THE KIRK FAMILY.

The old traditionary story "of having descended from three brothers," who came from England, Ireland, or some other foreign land, and settled in different localities, is told and believed by many of the descendants of the first colonists o south-eastern Pennsylvania and Delaware.

In fact, this ancient, stereotyped tradition, seems to attach itself to all our old families; and is related with an unction sufficient to make one, not cognizant of the uncertainties connected with genealogy, accept it as a historical truth.

The Kirk Family, of Nottingham, being among the oldest established in Pennsylvania, does not lack in traditionary lore as regards ancestry.

As a natural sequence we have the following:—

I. "The Kirks are all descended from three brothers: Alphonsus, who came from Ireland, and settled in New Castle, Delaware; Jacob, who settled on the rich lands of the Conestoga, and Roger, who located near the waters of North-East Creek."

II. The first who came to America was Alphonus Kirk, and from him descended *all of the name of Kirk in this country.*

After three years' patient search and inquiry, having access to many old documents of a historical nature, we have arrived at the conclusion that none of the above statements have any foundation in fact.

Prior to the arrival of William Penn, and for many years after this event, a number of persons of the name of Kirk, migrated to this country, settled in different localities, and eventually became the founders of numerous families. In all probability they came from the same region of country in the "Old World," but to tell what relation they bore to each other, is, at this late day, a matter of impossibility.

In our genealogical researches we have succeeded in tracing our family back to Roger Kirk, of East Nottingham; but no farther.

Of him little is known, save what can be learned in the different provisions of his "last will and testament." It appears that he was among the pioneers of Nottingham, and, reasoning *a priori*, are led to infer that he migrated from the north of Ireland. He located in East Nottingham, Chester county, Province of Pennsylvania,* at least as early as 1712, where, at different times, he purchased large tracts of land, situated on both sides, and extending for a great distance along, North-East Creek. By occupation, he was a weaver, and it would seem that he carried on this business together with farming.

He was married about the year 1714, to Elizabeth Richards, of Aston, of whom we have the following account:

Among the early settlers in Chichester township (now Delaware county), Pa., were Joseph Richards and his wife Jane, who doubtless came from England.

Their children were Joseph, Nathaniel, Ann, who married Anthony Weaver, and Humphrey Scarlet, and Susanna, who married James Lownes, of Springfield. The father died about the year 1710.

*Masons' and Dixon's line was not run until the year 1763. It was then ascertained that many of the early Friends who were under the impression that they resided in Penn's Province, were living on the lands of the Calverts.

Nathaniel Richards was a blacksmith, and settled in Aston township, where he died in the year 1700, leaving a wife, Mary, and four children: William, Nathaniel, Elizabeth and Mary.

From the will of Richard Mason, of Aston, who died in 1715, it would appear that Nathaniel's wife was his sister, and if so, she was the daughter of Richard Mason, who died in 1714, leaving a wife, Abigail, and children, Thomas, Joseph, Benjamin, Abraham, Richard, Mary, Sarah, Hannah, Elizabeth and Susanna.

After a time Mary Richards married again to one Thomas Rowland, of Aston, who probably came from Cheshire, England. Being Friends, but the marriage not being celebrated in the usual manner, they afterward made an acknowledgment for having acted contrary to the advice of the meeting.

About the year 1707 they removed westward, to William Penn's Manor, now New Garden township, and settled in a beautiful valley, on a tract of 700 acres, which they called "Marberry." This land extended from the present village of Toughkennamon, eastward to the line of Kennett township. Thomas Rowland died in 1708, and without having obtained a deed for the land, which was, however, confirmed to the widow within the same year. In 1712 she purchased 438 acres of adjoining land to the eastward. The Philadelphia and Baltimore Central Railroad now passes through both of these tracts. In 1713 Mary was married to a third husband, Evan Powell, a widower of Nottingham, who came to live with her on her property in New Garden. William and Mary Richards, the children of her first husband, probably died young, while Nathaniel and Elizabeth, the other two, accompanied their mother in her removal from Aston.

Nathaniel married Margaret, daughter of Allen Wiley, and *Elizabeth* became the wife of *Roger Kirk.*

Nathaniel left three sons, William, Nathaniel and Isaac. His widow married William Carpenter, an Englishman, who settled in New Garden. Thomas and Mary Rowland had three daughters, viz.: Mary, who married Joshua Hadley; Ruth, who married William Miller, and Rachael, who married Thomas Wiley. By her third husband she had one daughter, Sarah Powell, born in 1714, who became the wife of Joseph Dixon.

Mary Powell—the mother of Elizabeth Kirk—died on the 17th of 3d month (March), 1731–2, and her husband about the year 1736.

The next mention of Roger and Elizabeth Kirk is in a deed conveying a part of his estate to his oldest son, Timothy:

"This Indenture,* made the twenty-fifth day of the fifth month, in the year of our Lord one thousand seven hundred and fifty-two, between Roger Kirk, of the township of Nottingham and County of Chester and Province of Pennsylvania, *Weaver*, and Elizabeth, his wife, of the one part, and Timothy Kirk, of Nottingham aforesaid, Planter, and son of the aforesaid Roger Kirk and Elizabeth, his wife, on the second part, witnesseth that the aforesaid Roger Kirk and Elizabeth, his wife, for the consideration of twenty-five shillings lawful money of the said Province of Pennsylvania, paid by their said son, Timothy Kirk, the * * * * * * *
granted, bargained and sold and ______________________
Do give, grant, bargain and sell unto the said Timothy Kirk, a certain messuage, tennament, plantation and tract of land, ______________________________________ lying and being ______________________________
aforesaid and joining at ________________________ a line of Joseph Tremble's land, and being a corner of William

*The original papers had become so much faded that it was impossible to copy all the words.

Cole's land, thence extending north by the said Joseph Tremble's land, ______________________________ ______________ lying and being ______________ ______________ two hundred and thirty perches to a White Oak; thence south eighty-seven degrees, westerly by land of the said Roger Kirk, one hundred and forty perches to a heap of stones; thence by Joshua Brown's land twenty ______________ and Jeremiah Brown's and Isaac Brown's land two hundred and thirty perches to a Spanish oak, being another corner of the said William Cole's land; thence ______________ westerly ______________ one hundred and forty perches to the place of beginning, containing two hundred acres, be there more or less, together with all the out-houses and barns, buildings, garden, orchard, ______________________________ ways, rights, liberties, privilages, implements and appurtenances, __________ ______________________________ and the reversions, remainders thereof. To have and hold the aforesaid messuages with their appurtenances, and the said Timothy Kirk, his executors, administrators and assighns ______________ hereof, for and during the term of one year, ______________________________ to intent ______________________________ and of the statuet for transfering uses unto possession the said Timothy Kirk may be in the actual possession of the premisses with the appurtenances. ______________________________ ______________________________ Released and confirmed ______________________________ ______________________________ his heirs and assignes forever.

In witness the said partners to these presents have interexchangably set their hands and seals the day and year first above written.

Signed and sealed in the presence of
JOHN WHITE,
WILLIAM KIRK,
THOS. WOODWARD.

ROGER KIRK, [SEAL.]
ELIZABETH KIRK, [SEAL.]

On the day following the execution of this deed, 5 mo. 26th, 1752, Roger Kirk conveyed another farm, containing 340 acres, to his son, Timothy Kirk, making in all 540 acres.

In the language of the old records of the monthly meeting at Nottingham, "Roger Kirk, Sr., died at his house near North-East Creek, ye 28th day of ye 3 month, 1761."

His residence, or at least the one he occupied at the time of his death, is still standing, and in a good state of preservation. It is a small, antiquated, two-story brick, situated close on the highway (a short distance west of North-East Creek) leading from Brick Meeting House to Port Deposit, Md. It is now the property of Horace Duyckinck, who also owns the major part of the original farm once possessed by our common ancestor.

Two years before his decease, Roger Kirk made the following, "his last will and testament:"

To all Christian people to whom these presents shall come or may concern:

Know ye that I, Roger Kirk, of the Township of West Nottingham, in the County of Chester, in the Province of Pennsylvania, Weaver, being at this time weak in body, but of sound and disposing mind and memory, for which I am humbly thankfull, and calling to rememberance the uncertainty of time here, do make and publish this my last will and testament in manner and form following: That is to say, first and principally, I reccommend my spirit to God that gave it, and my body to be buried in a plain and decent manner, in Friend's burying ground, at their *publick* meeting place in East Nottingham. And as touching my worldly estate which God in mercy hath bestowed upon me, I give and dispose of the same as followeth, viz.:

First. I will that all my just debts which I owe in right or concience, to any person or persons whatsoever, together with my funeral expenses, be first paid and discharged by my Executrix, hereafter named, out of my personal estate, as soon as conveniently may be after my decease.

ITEM.—I give and bequeath unto my well-beloved wife, Elizabeth Kirk, and to her assigns for, and during her natural life, and after her decease to my son Samuel Kirk, his heirs and assigns forever, without impeachment of waste, all that part of my plantation whereon I now dwell, lying north of the *Great Road*, except ten acres part thereof herein after devised to my son William Kirk, she my said wife allowing unto my son Samuel, one-half of the grass which shall grow in the big meadow for hay, only; he my said son Samuel at all times maintaining one-half of the fence round the said meadow.

I also give, unto my said wife, during her natural life, the North end of the Frame House in which I now dwell, and the northern part of the cellar; one half of the Orchard, half the gardens and privilages of the draw-well and the oven; as also the north end of the barn, and the use of the floor of said barn for thrashing, &c., and the shop, called the Weaver Shop, and one-half the stables, together with free, peacable, and undisturbed way and passage into and out of the house, barn, stables, orchard, gardens, shops, &c., and also, I give and bequeathe unto my said wife for and during her natural life, my Mulatto girl, called Phillis, and my negro girl, called Jenny. I also give and bequeathe unto my said wife, my negro man, called Harry, and my Mulatto boy, called Toby.

I give, devise, and bequeathe unto my said wife and to her heirs and assigns forever, all my right, tittle and interest, which I have of, in and unto a certain tract, piece or parcel of land, situated in East Nottingham, together with appurtances, containing by computation one hundred acres, being the same lands I purchased in right of David Brown.

ITEM.—I give and bequeath unto my son, Timothy Kirk, the sum of five pounds, and unto his wife, Ann Kirk, I also give the sum of five pounds.

ITEM.—I give and bequeath unto my son, William Kirk, the quantity of ten acres of land, being part of my said plantation whereon I now dwell, joining the land of Joshua Brown and his other land, to be surveyed to him in regular and uniform manner, as soon as conveniently may be after my decease, to hold to him, his heirs and and assigns forever. I give also unto my said son, William Kirk, the sum of *five pounds*, and unto his wife, Mary Kirk, I also give the sum of five pounds. I also give and bequeath unto my said son, William Kirk, and to his heirs and assigns immediately after the decease of my said wife, my said mulatto girl, called *Phillis*.

ITEM.—I give and bequeath unto my daughter, Elizabeth Woodward, the sum of thirty pounds, and unto her husband, Thomas Woodward, I also give the sum of five pounds.

ITEM.—I give and bequeath to Matthew Aughiltree, husband to my daughter Deborah, deceased, the sum of five shillings.

ITEM.—I give and bequeathe unto my daughter, Rebecca Cook, and to her heirs and assigns, my mulatto girl, called

Violet, and also the sum of fourty pounds, and unto her husband, John Cook, I also give the sum of five pounds.

ITEM.—I give and devise and bequeathe unto my said son Samuel Kirk, and to his heirs and assigns, forever all my said plantatiou whereon I now dwell, with all and singular the hereditaments and appurtances thereunto belonging, or, in anywise appertaining; except part thereof herein before bequeathed to my said son William, and the parts, privilages herein before bequeathed unto my said wife during her natural life, which said parts and privilages herein before bequeathed to my said wife. I will my said son Samuel, his heirs and assigns, be in full possession immediatly after decease, and my said son Samuel, to be in full possession of that part of my plantation, lying south of the *Great Road*, immediatly after my decease, except the privilages before mentioned to my said wife during her natural life, on said south part of my plantation, and she my said wife to have free, peacable privilage to take off the grain on said south part of my plantation; and also I give and bequeathe to my said son Samuel, and to his heirs and assigns, three of my working horses, four cows, and six sheep, and the value of five *pounds* worth of household goods, and the sum of twelve pounds, and from and immediatly after my decease, one-half of all my implements of husbandry, such as carts, plows, harrows and their irons, and horse harness; and from and immediatly after the decease of my said wife, my said negro girl named Jenny, &c.

ITEM.—I will that the legacies herein before mentioned, I do order to be paid within two years after my decease, by my Executrix herein after appointed, in lawful money of Pennsylvania.

ITEM.—I give and devise and bequeathe unto my grandson Roger Kirk (son of Timothy Kirk), and to his heirs and assigns, forever, all that tract or parcel of land with the appurtenances, situated, lying, and being in East and West Nottingham, containing, by computation, one hundred and fourty acres, to be the same, more or less, joining the lands of the said Timothy Kirk and others.

ITEM.—I give, devise and bequeathe to my assigns forever, one full, equal, and undivided fourth part of a certain lot of land, situated in Charlestown, on North East River, together with the appurtenances.

ITEM.—I give, devise, and bequeathe the other full, equal, and undivided fourth part of the said lot, with the appurtenances, unto my grandson, Samuel Woodward, to hold to him, his heirs and assigns forever.

ITEM.—I give and bequeathe unto my grandaughter, Rebecca Woodward, one feather bed and furniture, and a pair of large chests or drawers, standing in the lower room.

ITEM.—I give and bequeathe unto my grandson, Jacob Wollison (son of Joseph and Deborah Wollison, dec'd), the sum of ten pounds, to be paid when he arrives at the age of twenty-one years.

ITEM.—I give and bequeathe unto my grandson, William Wollison, (son of Joseph and Deborah Wollison dec'd), the sum of ten pounds, when he arrives at the age of twenty-one years.

I give and bequeathe to my grandaughter, Elizabeth Wollison (daughter of Joseph and Deborah Wollison, deceased), the sum of ten pounds, to be paid when she arrives at the age of eighteen years.

ITEM.—I give and bequeathe to my grandaughter, Catharine Wollison (daughter of Joseph and Deborah Wollison, deceased), the sum of ten pounds, to be paid when she arrives at the age of eighteen years.

ITEM.—I give and bequeathe to my grandson, Joseph Wollison (son of Joseph and Deborah Wollison, deceased), the sum of ten pounds when he arrives at the age of twenty-one years; and all the rest, residue and remainder of all and singular, my goods, chattles, rights and credits whatsoever, both real and personal, of what nature and kind soever the same may be of, and not herein given or bequeathed, I give and bequeathe unto my said wife, Elizabeth Kirk, and to her heirs and assigns forever, whom I nominate, constitute and appoint whole and sole executrix of this my last will and testament, hereby revoking all former will and wills heretofore by me made. In witness whereof I have hereunto set my hand and seal the thirtieth day of the sixth month, in the year of our Lord one thousand seven hundred and fifty-nine (1759).

Signed, sealed, published, pronounced and declared by the said Roger Kirk, the testator for, and as his last will and testament, in the presence of us the subscribers, who subscribed our names in his presence.

ELISHA HUGHES,
BENJAMIN CHANDLEE, ROGER KIRK, { Locus Sigilla. }
ALEXANDER M'CASKEY.

The following were the children of Roger and Elizabeth Kirk:

Mary,	born	1715, 10, 9;	died	——, —, —.
Timothy,	"	1717, 11, 17;	"	1784, 11, 15.
William,	"	1719, 11, 25;	"	1767, 6, 30.
Elizabeth,	"	1721,-2, 5, 1;	"	1812, 1, 25.
Deborah,	"	1723, 5, 2;	"	——, -, —.
Rebecca,	"	1729, 8, 25;	"	——, -, —.
Samuel	"	1733, 9, 23;	"	176-, 7, 30.

Of these seven children it appears five were married, and

two died single. The latter were Mary, the eldest, and Samuel, the youngest of the family.

Timothy, the eldest son, was married first to Anne Gatchell, daughter of Elisha and Rachel Gatchell; and second, to Ann McLaughlin. William, the second son, married Mary Robinson. Elizabeth, the second daughter, married Thomas Woodward. Deborah married Jos. Wollison, and Rebecca married John Cook.

The descendants of all these families, save those of Joseph and Deborah Wollison, John and Rebecca Cook, have been traced out in this work, and will be found as nearly complete as a record of this kind can be made.

For the benefit of any future genealogist who may feel an interest in searching up the Cook branch of our family, we give the following as a basis from which to commence the work:—

Rebecca Kirk, married 1752, at East Nottingham, to John Cook.

Children of John and Rebecca Cook.

Elizabeth, born ——, —, —; died 1813, 5, 25. Married at London Grove, 1772, 11, 25, to Jacob, son of William and Phœbe Brown, of West Nottingham. Jacob was a carpenter. Elizabeth was interred in the family graveyard near her house.

Eleanor, born ——, —, —; married at London Grove, 1779, 5, 5, to Nathan Sidwell, of West Nottingham, son of Hugh and Ann.

John, born ——, —, —; married at New Garden, 1784, 12, 2, to Elizabeth Davis, daughter of Caleb and Margaret, of New Garden.

Timothy Kirk, designated as a planter, eldest son of Roger and Elizabeth, was a member of the Society of Friends, and married his first wife according to the discipline of this religious society. The certificate of his marriage is the oldest containing the name of Kirk found in "Nottingham Records." It may prove of much interest to those not familiar with the regulations concerning marriage as adopted by this religious denomination; we therefore insert it just as taken from the Friends' archives, kept at Nottingham.

WHEREAS, Timothy Kirk, son of Roger Kirk, and Annie Gatchell, daughter of Elisha Gatchell, of East Nottingham, in county and province aforesaid, having declared their intentions of marriage before several monthly meetings of the Christian people, called Quakers, in East Nottingham aforesaid, according to the good order used among them, and having consent of parents and relations concerned their said proposals of marriage. After deliberate consideration they appear clear of all others, were approved by the said meetings.

Now these may certify whom it may concern, that for the full accomplishment of their said intentions, this 29th day of 8th month, A. D. 1741, they, the said Timothy Kirk and Annie Gatchell, appeared in a public meeting of the said people, assembled at their public meeting place, in East Nottingham aforesaid, where they, ye said Timothy Kirk, taking the said Annie Gatchell by the hand, did in a solemn manner openly declare that he took her to be his wife, promising, with Divine assistance, to be unto her a loving and a faithful husband until it should please the Lord by death to separate them. And then and there, in the said assembly, the said Annie Gatchell did in like manner declare that she took him, the said Timothy Kirk, to be her husband, promising, with Divine assistance, to be unto him a loving and a faithful wife, until it should please the Lord by death to separate them, or words to that effect. Moreover, they, the said Timothy Kirk and

Annie Gatchell (she, according to the customs of marriage, assuming her husband's surname), did as a further confirmation thereof, then and there, to these presents, set their hands as husband and wife.

TIMOTHY KIRK,
ANNIE KIRK.

And we, being present at the solemnization of the said marriage and subscription in manner aforesaid, do as witnesses hereunto also subscribe our names the day and year first *above written:*

Mary Elgar,	Jas. Johnston,	Elisha Gatchell,
Eliza Baker,	John Jacob,	Roger Kirk,
Jane Brown,	Messer Brown,	Rachel Gatchell,
Hannah Brown,	Joseph Jacob,	Eliz Kirk,
Lyddia Day,	Joseph Wooliston,	William Kirk,
Susannah Elgar,	Will. Bristow,	M'll. Kirk,
Annie Ruddell,	William Brown,	Jon. Price,
Joseph Haines,	Jas. Lowery,	Mary Kirk,
Joshua Brown,	Jer'h Brown, Jr.,	E. Gatchell, Jr.,
Esther Brown,	John Ruddell,	Mary Winter,
David Hughes,	Joseph Richardson,	Martha Kirk,
Elisha Hughes,	Eliz. Kirk, Jr.,	Cornelius Ruddell,

Deborah Kirk, Henry Reynolds, Jr.

Soon after commencing the task of collecting material for a genealogy of our family, we became aware of the fact of there being another planted in Nottingham of the same name, whose history could be traced back to a period anterior to our own. This was the Kirk family as established by Alphonsus Kirk, who migrated from Lurgan, county of Armagh, North Ireland, and arrived in this country in the year 1688.

In the latter part of this volume will be found an imperfect record, as handed down by Rachel Price, and others, of about three hundred names of those who are descended from this settler. The narration of incidents connected with the estabment of homes in the then newly settled provinces, as there given, is not only highly interesting, but instructive.

It will be perceived that Roger, the eldest son of Alphonsus, was cotemporaneous with him who was the founder of our family.

This Roger was born in Delaware, on the 21st of 1 mo., 1694; was married at Nottingham, 9th of 12th mo., 1726, to Jean, daughter of Henry Bowen, of Cecil county, Maryland, and died 19th of 12 mo., 1762. His children were:

Abigail,	born	1727, 9, 5;	died	——, —, —.
Rachel,	"	1728, 2, 22;	"	——, —, —.
Henry,	"	1730, 3, 9;	"	——, —, —.
Margaret,	"	1731, 9, 5;	"	——, —, —.
Jean,	"	1733, 12, 1;	"	
Timothy,	"	1734, 2, 22;	"	1824, 3, 4.
William,	"	1736, 2, 10.		
Elizabeth,	"	1738, 12, 17.		
Mary,	"	1740, 12, 27.		
John,	"	1742, 12, 17.		
Hannah,	"	1744, 12, 10.		
Sampson,	"	1746, 12, 18.		
Sarah,	"	1750, 12, 13.		

What relation these two Roger Kirks bore to each other, is a problem we have been unable to solve.

Having dwelt at some length upon everything that could be ascertained of a historical nature, relative to the early settlers of the name of Kirk, and their settlements made in the counties of Chester and Delaware, Pa., and New Castle, Del., we now proceed to trace out our family to the eighth generation, adopting a form we now believe accepted by our best New England genealogists.

FIRST GENERATION.

1. Roger Kirk and Elizabeth Richards.

SECOND GENERATION.

Children of Roger Kirk and Elizabeth Richards.

2. Mary, born 1715, 10, 9; died, ——, —, —.

3. Timothy, born 1717, 11, 17; died 1784, 11, 15; married 1741, 8, 29, to Ann Gatchell, daughter of Elisha and Rachel Gatchell. Ann died 1766, 1, 8. Timothy was married 1768, —, —, to Ann McLaughlin. He was a farmer and weaver, and resided on a property in Nottingham, Md., which he inherited from his father.

4. William, born 1719, 11, 25; died 1767, 6, 30; married 1745, 10, 19, to Mary, daughter of Joseph and Elizabeth Robinson, of Christiana Hundred, Del. Mary was born 1723, 12, 5.

5. Elizabeth, born 1721–2, 1, 5; died 1812, 1, 25; married 1744, 3, 8, at East Nottingham Meeting, to John Jacobs, son of Thomas and Mary Jacobs, of Cecil county, Maryland. He was born 1715–6, 12, 6, and died 1744, 6, 2, or about three months after marriage. Elizabeth was married again 1745, 10, 26, at East Nottingham Meeting, to Thomas Woodward, son of Richard and Mary, of East Bradford, Chester county, Pa. Thomas was born 1722–3, 11, 7, and died 1785, 6, 15.

Richard Woodward, was the son of Robert, of "Rockland Manor," New Castle county, Delaware and Birmingham, Chester county, Pa. In the year 1705, he married Mary, the only heir of Henry Nayle, Esq., of Thornbury, and at his death in 1748, left seven children, viz.: Henry, John, Richard, Thomas, Deborah, wife of Wm. Bennett; Mary, wife of John Strode; and Alice, wife of Joshua Ash.

Richard conveyed to his son Thomas, "under date 1740, 12, 12," one hundred and fifty acres of land, in East Bradford. Thomas sold this in four tracts, viz.: Fifty acres to Joseph Townsend, 1744, 10, 25; fifty acres to John Townsend, 1744, 12, 12; forty-seven acres and thirty-eight perches, to Theophilus Canby, 1748, 3, 25; and nine and a-half acres to Geo. Strode, under date 1748, 3, 26.

Thomas Woodward was a Friend, and member of Concord Monthly Meeting, from which he obtained "a certificate of removal" to New Garden Monthly Meeting, dated 1749, 4, 5. This was probably about the time he settled in East Marlborough township, and became a member of London Grove Particular Meeting. His residence was on the "Street Road," one and three-fourth miles east of the meeting house. He *carried on* the business of book-binding, and was also a surveyor and conveyancer. Some of his labors as a surveyor were performed in the neighborhood of Duck Creek, in Delaware. It is related that at one time he had occasion to survey a farm, the owner of which threatened violence if he proceeded. Thomas asked if he had any objection to the survey of the adjoining properties, and receiving a reply in the negative, crossed the fence and measured around the farm without being upon it.

John Woolman, a noted preacher among Friends, and one of the most scrupulous anti-slavery men of his day, on one occasion attended Quarterly Meeting at London Grove. Here he delivered one of his powerful discourses against holding persons in bondage. At that time Friends were not all clear of this evil, though it is safe to assert that their servant swere generally treated with humanity. After meeting, Woolman, with several friends, went to the house of Thomas Woodward to take dinner. Entering the house, he observed some colored persons, and learning that they were slaves, he quietly picked up his hat and cane (he traveled on foot), and left the room and his friends. They supposed he would return shortly, but were disappointed. Thomas Woodward had a high standing in the meeting, and this incident had a great effect upon his mind, so that on awakening the next morning he told his wife he must liberate his slaves.

She asked if all must be liberated, adding, "Must Bet go too," and even burst into tears at the thought of losing her faithful servant. But the decree was made and would be carried out, for Thomas was unwilling to keep a house at which his friends could not be entertained. He was afterward appointed by the meeting one of a committee to visit such as held slaves, and endeavor to convince them "of the evil of so doing."

Elizabeth Woodward survived her husband many years, and died 1812, 1, 5.

6. Deborah, born 1723, 5, 2; died ——, —, —. Married Jos. Wollison, by whom she had five children, viz.: Jacob, William, Elizabeth, Catharine and Joseph. These are the ancestors of many of the name of Wollison, living in Chester county and Delaware. Their descendants have not been traced out in this work. Deborah Wollison, formerly Kirk, was married a second time. Her second husband was Matthew Augiltree.

7. Rebecca, born 1729, 8, 25; died ——, —, —. Married about the year 1752, to John Cooke (now spelled Cook), of Nottingham. From this John Cook descended many of the name that settled in Chester county, and in West Virginia. This branch has not been traced out.

8. *Samuel, born 1733, 9, 23; died 1776–'7, 30. Never married. At least left no descendants.

THIRD GENERATION.

CHILDREN OF TIMOTHY KIRK (3), AND ANN GATCHELL.

9. Jacob, born 1742, 3, 15; died ——, —, —. No issue.

10. Elizabeth, born 1744, 6, 18; died ——, —, —. No issue.

11. Deborah, " 1746, 7, 1, 1; " ——, —, —, No issue.

12. Esther, " 1749, 5, 28; " 1803, 4, 1. Married Job, son of Joseph and Elizabeth Haines, of Nottingham, Md. Job was born " ye 26 day of ye 8 mo., 1744," and died 1812, 10, 4. He was a farmer and resided on a tract of land near Rising Sun village, Md., now part of the farms of Marshall J. Hunt and Samuel Haines (173). The old mansion, or at least a part of it still remains.

13. Roger, 1751, 6, 5; died 1809, 3, 20. Married at East Nottingham, to Rachel, daughter of Elisha and Mary Hughes, of the same place. Rachel was born 1755, 2, 10, and died 1825, 4, at the residence of her husband, situated on North-East Creek, now the property of J. Smith Hilaman.

Roger Kirk, a man of more than ordinary ability, was ex-

*The following release, the original copy being in possession of George W. Kirk (204), No. 523 North 15th street, Philadelphia, is about all that is on record of this Kirk.

Know all men by these presents:

That I, Samuel Kirk, of West Nottingham, son of Roger Kirk, of the same place, in the County of Chester, and Province of Pennsylvania, have had and received the day of the date hereof, of and from my mother, Elizabeth Kirk, the widow and sole executrix of the last will and testament of my father, Roger Kirk, the full and just sum of twenty pounds, given and bequeathed unto me by my father, according and agreeable to his last will and testament, which sum of twenty pounds I acknowledge myself fully satisfied, and give this as a full discharge of all demands whatsoever.

Witness my hand and seal, this seventh day of December, one thousand seven hundred and sixty-nine.

SAMUEL KIRK, {SEAL.}

Witnesses Present, { ELISHA HEWES,
ARN. MCCASKEY.

tensively known among the prominent men of his time, in south-eastern Pennsylvania.

When hostilities commenced between the colonies and the mother country, he was in the prime of manhood. An ardent Whig, he joined the Continental army, and soon arose to the rank of captain.*

He continued in the service for some time and was present and took part in the principal battles fought in the Middle States under Washington.

At the close of the war, he returned home and it is related that he rode up to the door (dressed in continental uniform) of the Brick Meeting House, just in time to hear the clerk read the minute of his disownment for violating the discipline by entering the military service. This, however, is rather apocryphal. During his absence, his farms and mills became neglected, and, upon his return, required his care and attention.

Being emphatically a "*business man*," he did not remain at home long before he was elected to represent his friends and neighbors in the State Legislature. Philadelphia was then the National and State capital. Roger Kirk attended the assembly at this place, as one of the members from the county of Chester. By his urbanity and integrity, he gained the confidence of his political associates, was re-elected for several consecutive sessions, and became an influential representative.

During his term of service, he secured the passage of an act of Assembly to lay out and grade a State Road, now known as the Christiana, or "Christeen Road," a public highway, sixty feet wide, leading from the Upper Peach Bottom Ferry, a

*Until a comparatively recent period, the old commission of this, our early ancestor, was in possession of his grandson, Roger H. Kirk, of Pleasant Grove. After diligent search it could not be found. We much desired to have it printed in connection with this biographical sketch. C. H. S.

point on the eastern bank of the river Susquehanna, to the Maryland line, in the direction of the "navigable waters of Christiana creek," in the State of Delaware.

This act empowered the Governor of the Commonwealth to enter into a contract with a company, or an individual, to make this road for the sum of *five hundred dollars.* The contract was taken by Roger Kirk, the member from the district through which it mainly passed, for the faithful performance of which he gave the required bonds.

Under the impression that some of the papers relative to the making of this noted highway might prove of interest to the readers of this volume—many of them, perhaps, lineal descendants of those who constructed this road, having "hauled" grain over it in the olden time, the days of the annual trip to "old Christeen"—we shall insert a few of them in connection with this biographical sketch.*

---

*From the following report it would appear that the order to locate this road was given to Roger Kirk and others, in the year 1792; but no article of agreement or bond was made by the contractor until four years afterward:

To Thomas Mifflin, Esq., Governor of the Commonwealth of Pennsylvania:

Pursuant to your order bearing date the 30th of April, 1792, and to us directed, requiring us to lay out a road beginning at or near Peach Bottom Ferry, on the river Susquehanna, toward the navigable waters of Christiana creek, in the State of Delaware. Having, therefore, accurately examined the whole distance between the said ferry and the nearest navigation aforesaid, and accordingly laid out a road upon the most eligible ground and nearest distance, to the best of our judgment, as far as this State extends toward the navigable waters aforesaid, the courses and distances of which are as follows, viz.:—Beginning at the upper landing of Peach Bottom, called *Brown's Ferry*, and thence running down said river the different courses of the present road one hundred and fifty-four perches to *Porter's Landing*, at the *Fall Rocks;* thence leaving the river north sixty-one degrees east, fifty perches to *Porter's house;* thence north seventy-one degrees east, one hundred and forty-five perches to *Jones' house;* thence north sixty-six degrees east, one hundred and ten perches to a stake; thence north eighty-three degrees and thirty-five minutes east, two hundred and sixty perches to *Puddle Duck Run;* thence north fifty-four degrees east, one hundred and four perches to a white oak; thence north eighty-six degrees east, twelve hundred and thirty perches to a white oak; thence south sixty-five degrees east, twenty-three perches to a white oak; thence south seventy degrees east, one hundred and twenty-four perches to the north side of *Octorara Creek;* thence north seventy-six degrees east, one hundred and six perches to stake; thence south seventy-five degrees and forty-nine minutes east, three hundred and forty-two perches to a stake; thence south sixty-nine degrees and nine minutes east, eleven hundred and fifteen perches to *Kirk's Mills;* thence south sixty-nine degrees and twenty minutes east, one hundred and eighty-six perches to *Ramsey's house;* thence south seventy degrees and thirty minutes east, five hundred and eighty perches to a stake; thence south sixty-eight degrees east, forty-six perches to a stake; thence

14. Timothy, born 1753, 9, 13; died ——, —, —. No issue.

15. Elisha, born 1756, 3, 22; died ——, —, —. No issue.

16. Jeremiah, born 1758, 8, 13; died ——, —, —. No issue.

17. Eli, born 1761, 12, 2; died 183-, —, —. Married Susanna, daughter of William and Elizabeth Brown, of Nottingham. Susanna died 1821, 9, 28.

CHILDREN OF TIMOTHY KIRK (3) AND ANN MCLAUGHLIN.

18. Levi, born 1769, 9, 3; died 1817, 9, 12. Married Amelia, daughter of William and Ann Mullen. He resided near Brick Meeting House, Md., and by occupation was a farmer. He died rather suddenly in the night, while wending his way homeward from the Brick Meeting House village. His body was found next morning not far from his residence.

19. Ann, born 1772, 7, 25; died ——, —, —. Married a man by the name of Emory. (Nothing further ascertained.)

---

south sixty-eight degrees and forty-six minutes east, two hundred and fifty-six perches to a stake in the south side of *Mount Rocky*; thence south seventy degrees east, one hundred and forty perches to a stake, and south eighty-three degrees and fifty-nine minutes east, two hundred and forty perches to a stake, in intersection of *Maryland line*.

Which road, as above laid out and confirmed, and property opened 60 feet wide, we think will be of great advantage to the public in general, as it will shorten the distance five miles between said ferry and the line of Delaware State, and upon much better ground than the old road.

Given under our hand, this seventeenth day of November, one thousand seven hundred and ninety-two.

JAMES MORRISON,
JEREMIAH BROWN,
ROGER KIRK.

A true copy, taken by
JEREMIAH BROWN.

Four years after the road was "viewed" and located by the above parties, an article of agreement was entered into for making the same, as will be seen by the following document:

Article ot agreement made, &c., on the 17th day of June, 1796, between Thomas Mifflin, Governor of the Commonwealth of Pennsylvania, of the one part, and Roger Kirk, of the township of West Nottingham, in the county of Chester, of the other part. Whereas, the General Assembly of this Commonwealth did in and by entitled, "An act to provide for the opening and improving sundry navigable waters and roads within this Commonwealth," passed the 13th day of April, 1791, and one other act, entitled, "An act to appropiate certain sums of money for the laying out, opening and improving sundry roads within this Commonwealth, and for other purposes therein mentioned," passed the 11th day of April, 1793, authorize and empower the Governor to contract with individuals or with companies, among other things, for opening the State road from Peach Bottom Ferry, on the river Susquehanna, to the Maryland line, toward the waters of Christiana, and for that purpose appropriate the sum of *five hundred dollars*. Now these articles witness,

20. Mary, born 1775, 6, 11; died 1801, 3. 4. Married Levi, son of John and Rachel Rogers. They resided in Lancaster city, Pa.

21. Elizabeth, born 1777, 12, 30; died 1864, 12, 19, at the residence of her niece, Elizabeth Donohoo, in Cecil county, Md. She was married to Gideon Edgerly, and to Henry Stephenson.

22. Deborah, born 1780, 8, 16; died ——, 3–, 27. No issue.

23. Eleanor, born 1783, 6, 12; died ——, —, —. Never married.

CHILDREN OF WILLIAM KIRK (4) AND MARY ROBINSON.

24. Joseph, born 1747, 5, 25; died 1807, 12, 30. Married 1769, 10, 17 to Judith, daughter of William and Elizabeth Knight. He removed to the western part of Pennsylvania,

---

that for the consideration hereinafter mentioned, he, the said Roger Kirk, hath agreed, undertaken and contracted to and with the said Thomas Mifflin, and his successors, Governors of the said Commonwealth, that he, the said Roger Kirk, will well, and truly, and with all due dilligence, skill, judgment and economy, lay out and expend the said sum of five hundred dollars in opening and improving the said road from Peach Bottom Ferry, on the river Susquehanna, to the Maryland line, toward the waters of Christiana, agreeably to the true intent and meaning of the Legislature, or such part thereof, as it will be most for the public interest and benefit to open and improve; and that he shall, and will keep, and render to the said Thomas Mifflin, or to his successors, as aforesaid, a true, exact and faithful account of the monies so laid out and expended by the said Roger Kirk, for himself, heirs, executors, and administrators, doth covenant with the said Thomas Mifflin, his successors, Governors of Pennsylvania, &c., that he will well and truly execute his agreement and contract aforesaid. And the Governor, in these considerations, promises and agrees to pay unto the said Roger Kirk, his heirs, executors, and administrators, the said sum of five hundred dollars, to be considered as a full compensation for his expenses and services in executing this contract.

Sealed and delivered in presence of us, ROGER KIRK. (Seal.)
MAURICE KENNEDY,
LEVI HOLLINSWORTH.

True copy,
JAMES TRIMBLE,
Deputy Sec'y of the Commonwealth.

For the faithful performance of the obligation agreed to by the said Roger Kirk the following bond was given by the contractor to the chief officer of the Commonwealth. One of the witnesses and one of the surities were well-known citizens of Lancaster county, "in their day and generation"

Pennsylvania, S.S.

Know all men by these presents, that we, Roger Kirk, of the county of Chester Jeremiah Brown, of the county of Lancaster, and Levi Hollingsworth, of the city of Philadelphia, are held and firmly bound unto Thomas Mifflin, Governor of the

and located in what was known as the "Redstone Settlement," now Redstone Township, Fayette county. He resided here for a great number of years, but died in Bloomfield township. He was chiefly engaged in agricultural pursuits.

25. Benjamin, born 1748, 11, 11; died ——, —, —. (Nothing further is known of him.)

26. Abner, born 1749, 11, 1; died 1809, 4, 10. Married 1770, 10, 17 to Ann, daughter of William and Rachel Allen. Ann died 1785, 2, 4. Abner married a second time; second wife was Sarah Chandlee.

27. William, born 1751, 3, 1; died ——, —, —. Married to Ann, daughter of John and Lydia White. Ann was born 1747, 2, 9, and died 1775, 7, 7.

28. Nathaniel, born 1753, 11, 15; died ——, —, —. Married a lady, a resident of Baltimore, a city to which Nathan removed. (After patient and diligent search, we were unable to learn anything further of this member of the family, or trace out any of his descendants.)

29. Ezekiel, born 1756, 2, 22; died ——, —, —. Never married.

30. Jacob, born 1758, 7, 22; died ——, —, —. Married Rachel, daughter of William and Rachel Allen.

Commonwealth, in the sum of four hundred pounds, to be paid to said Thomas Mifflin, or to his successors in the said office. To the which payment well and truly to be made, we bind ourselves jointly and severally, for, and in the whole, our heirs, executors, and administrators, firmly by these presents. Sealed with our seals, dated the seventeenth day of June in the year of our Lord, one thousand seven hundred and ninety-six. Whereas, the said Roger Kirk hath this day entered into contract with the Governor for improving the said road from Peach Bottom Ferry, on the river Susquehanna, to the Maryland line, toward the waters of Christiana, by expending and accounting for the sum of *five hundred dollars.*

Now the condition of this obligation is such, that if the above bounden, Roger Kirk, shall and does in all things well and truly execute and perform the said contract according to the terms, stipulations, and conditions thereof, then the above obligation to be void, otherwise to be and remain in full force and virtue.

Signed, sealed, and delivered
in presence of us,
TIMOTHY HAINES,
MAURICE KENNEDY.

ROGER KIRK. (seal.)
JEREMIAH BROWN. (seal.)
LEVI HOLLINGSWORH. (seal.)

31. Elisha, born 1761, 3, 17; died 1807, 11, 20. Married Mary, daughter of William and Rachel Allen, sister of Abner and Jacob's wives.

CHILDREN OF THOMAS WOODWARD (5) AND ELIZABETH KIRK.

32. Rebecca, born, 1746, 9, 24; died 1835, 7, 14. Married 1766, 12, 25, at London Grove Meeting, to William Dixon, son of Joseph and Sarah (Powell) Dixon, of New Garden. After living some years in Chester county, they migrated with their surviving children to Fayette county, Pennsylvania, and settled in Minulin township. William died 1833, 11, 20.

33. Elizabeth, born 1748, 6, 12; died 1808, 8, 24. Married Joseph Painter, son of Samuel and Esther, of East Bradford. He was born 1748, 4, 1; died 1804, 10, 20. By trade, a fuller, and had a mill on Radley's run, in the southern part of East Bradford, now Birmingham township.

34. Samuel, born 1750, 8, 9; died 1814, 2, 29. Married 1773, 5, 12, at London Grove Meeting, to Sarah, daughter of John and Sarah Jackson, of East Marlborough. She was born 1750, 3, 4; died 1791, 10, 14. Second marriage 1799, 12, 18, at London Grove, to Hannah, widow of Peter Cooke, of London Grove, and daughter of Thomas and Sarah Starr, of New Garden. She was born 1771, 1, 10, and died 1853, 2, 3. Thomas Woodward purchased from his brother-in-law, John Cooke, a farm in London Grove, and conveyed it to his son, Samuel, who settled thereon. It is now owned by Peter Lefevre, of Chatham.

35. Thomas, born 1753, 3, 17; died 1837, 6, 2. Married 1777, 10, 15, at London Grove, to Mary, daughter of Ellis and Susanna Pusey, of West Fallowfield. She was born 1756, 3, 12, and died 1838, 8, 16. Thomas was a farmer and remained on the homestead.

36. Deborah, born 1755, 3, 19; died 1765, 8, 28.

37. Mary, born 1756, 1, 26; died 1786, 1, 2. Married 1784, 10, 20, at London Grove, to Joseph Smith, of London Grove, son of John and Margaret, of Lampeter, Lancaster county, Pa. He was born 1757, 6, 5; and died ——, —, —. He married a second time.

38. Timothy, born 1759, 10, 22; died 1760, 5, —.

39. Susanna, born 1761, 8, 7; died 1765, 9, 6.

FOURTH GENERATION.

CHILDREN OF JOB HAINES (12) AND ESTHER KIRK.

40. Jacob, born 1767, 9, 3; died ——, —, —. Never married.

41. Timothy, born, 1768, 11, 15; died 1846, 3, 7. Married 1795, 12, 3, to Sarah, daughter of Jeremiah and Hannah (England) Brown, of Little Britain, Lancaster county, Pa. She was born 1772, 3, 15; and died 1842, 2, 2. Timothy Haines moved to Little Britain soon after his marriage, and purchased a large tract of land, near the Susquehanna. He was a farmer and merchant; for many years a member and elder of Friends' Meeting at Little Britain.

42. Isaac, born 1770, 7, 7; died ——, —, —.

43. Reuben, born 1772, 5, 17; died 1811, 10, 4. Married Mary Johnson, daughter of ——— and ——— Johnson, she died 1837, 10, 1. Reuben Haines was a farmer and resided on the road leading from Brick Meeting House to Port Deposit, Md.

44. Joseph, born 1774, 3, 29; died ——, —, —. Never married.

45. Eli, born 1776, 7, 17; died 1816, 9, 25. Married Eliza-

beth Brown. Elizabeth died 1814, 7, 31. Eli Haines was a farmer. He became melancholy, and committed suicide by hanging himself to a tree.

46. Job, born 1778, 8, 22; died 1827, 10, 10. Married Prudence, daughter of —— and —— Brown. She was born 1780, 2, 5, and died 1833, 3, 15.

47. Lewis, born 1780, 11, 9; died ——, —, —. Never married.

48. Elizabeth, born 1783, 2, 16; died 1852, 6, 1. Married William Kirk (94) son of Abner and Ann Kirk. They resided near Brick Meeting House, Md.

49. Esther, born 1785, 5, 18. Married 1806, 12, to Immer Knight. Immer died 1846, 2, 19. They migrated to northern Ohio many years ago, and settled near Port Clinton, on Lake Erie. Esther is still living at an advanced age.

50. Elisha, born 1787, 9, 19; died ——, —, —. Married Hannah (120), daughter of Elisha and Mary Kirk.

51. Nathan, born 1790, 4, 26; died 1858, 7, 8. Married Rachel, daughter of Basil and Jane Williams. Rachel died 1817, 3, 3. Nathan married a second time; second wife Mary Carter. Nathan was interred in the Odd Fellows' Cemetery, Philadelphia. His first wife at Brick Meeting House, ——,

CHILDREN OF ROGER KIRK (13) AND RACHEL HUGHES..

52. Elisha, born 1775, 4, 20; died 1823, 5, 18. Married Hannah, daughter of William and Ann Mullen. Hannah died 1816, 4, 17. Elisha resided at the Brick Meeting House and was extensively known as a merchant. He died suddenly of some affection of the heart.

53. Jacob, born 1779, 5, 16; died 1841, 8, 25. Married Sarah, daughter of John and Elizabeth England, of Nottingham. She was born 1784, 7, 3, and died 1812, 4, 21. Jacob

married a second time. Second wife, Hannah England, a sister of the first. Hannah was born 1793, 12, 19, and now resides at "Kirk's Mills."

Jacob Kirk resided in Little Britain, Lancaster county, Pa., where he purchased considerable real estate and built what is now known as Kirk's Mills, a small village containing several mills, a store, post-office, &c., &c.

54. Timothy, born 1781, 3, 23; supposed to have died about the year 1839. Married 1805, 4, 25, to Mary, daughter of Jacob and Esther Reynolds. She was born 1788, 12, 18, and died 1840, 2, 5.

Timothy Kirk, for many years, was extensively engaged in business. Was a member of the State Legislature for seven sessions. He owned, at one time, half the land on which the borough of Oxford is situated. While residing in Oxford he owned a hotel, store and several farms and mills. Prior to the completion of the railroad from Philadelphia to Baltimore, the main stage road led through Oxford—this place being a station and one of the "relays." Timothy Kirk was interested in this "line of stages" and in running cars on the Pennsylvania Railroad. In the year 1837 he became pecuniarily involved. To escape trouble he departed, and finally sailed for Europe, and remained on the continent for some time. In 1839 he proposed returning, and embarked for Boston, but never reached America. In the early months of that year several sailing vessels were shipwrecked on the New England coast, all the passengers being lost. It is generally supposed that he was on board one of these vessels and was one of the ill-fated number.

55. John (twin brother of Timothy), born 1781, 3, 23; died 1853, 9, 9. Married Deborah, daughter of Jeremiah and

Hannah Brown, of Little Britain. She was born 1782, 5, 25, and died 1845, 5, 27.

John commenced business in York county, Pa., in partnership with Jas. McConkey, carrying on the business of country merchants. From York county he removed to Penn Hill, Lancaster county, where he purchased a farm, mill and store. These he superintended. He was for a number of years a member and elder of Friends' Meeting. In his youth he made a voyage to Ireland, visiting those parts of the island from whence his ancestors are supposed to have migrated. He revisited Europe in 1851, and attended the World's Fair in London. He also made a tour through Ireland, and brought a colony of emigrants to *America.* John Kirk was "well versed" in English history, and familiar with the old English poets. He was a great reader, being well informed, and possessed remarkable conversational powers.

He married a second wife—Sarah Brown—who still survives. She resides at Penn Hill, Lancaster county.

56. Josiah, born 1784, 8, 17; died 1821, 9, 8. Married Phoebe, daughter of Ellis and Ruth Passmore. Phoebe was born in 1792, 9, 16; and died in 1849, 8, 28. Josiah resided on a part of the homestead, and managed several mills, manfacturing flour and paper.

57. Ann, born 1788, 5, 20; died 1816, 9, 8. Married 1807, 5, 14, Jeremiah, son of Jeremiah and Hannah Brown, of Little Britain, Lancaster county, Pa. Jeremiah Brown was born in 1785, 4, 14; died 1858, 3, 2, and was interred in Friends' burying ground, at Penn Hill. He resided in Fulton township, Lancaster county, Pa., and possessed a large tract of land, situated in the Conowingo valley. During a long life, he was an active politician, and held many positions of "honor and trust." In 1838 it was decided by the people

of Pennsylvania to call a convention to amend the Constitution of the State. Jeremiah Brown, along with several others, was elected by the citizens of Lancaster county to represent them in that convention. In 1840 he was elected to represent his district in Congress, and re-elected in 1842. In 1851, he was elected Associate Judge of the several courts of the county, and retained this position for five years. He was married three times after the decease of his first wife.

58. Levi, born 1790, 5, 17; died 1814, 6, 20. Married Rachel (109), daughter of Jacob and Rachel (Allen) Kirk.

59. Mary, born 1792, 2, 4; died 1857, 11, 6. Married 18—, —, —, to Slater, son of Jeremiah and Hannah Brown, of Little Britain. He was born 1787, 3, 27, and died suddenly, 1855, 6, 5. He resided on the homestead in Fulton township, and carried on milling and farming. Was also engaged in operating the slate quarries at Peach Bottom. At one time he held the office of Prison Inspector for Lancaster county.

60. Lewis, born 1793, 11, 15; died 1825, 8, 22. Married Ruth, daughter of Ellis and Ruth Passmore. Ruth, born 1794, 3, 4; died 1866, 7, —, at the residence of her son in West Chester, Pa. Lewis Kirk, at one time had an interest in the several paper mills belonging to his father, and for a number of years was engaged in the manufacture of paper.

CHILDREN OF ELI KIRK (17), AND SUSANNA BROWN.

61. Esther, born 1786, 2, 7; died 1855, 2, 27. Married William, son of Jeremiah Brown, of Nottingham. William, born 1784, 11, 1; died 1837, 5, 8. He resided near Brick Meeting House, and was engaged in farming.

62. William B., born 1788, 1, 8; died 1864, 5, 2. Married Mary, daughter of ——— and ——— Williams. She died 1865, 6, 28.

63. Reuben, born 1792, 6, 13; died 1863, 1, 5. Never married.

64. Roger, born 1794, 5, 30; died 1842, 7, 5. Married 1817, 10, 15, to Ann, daughter of —— and —— Trump. She was born 1798, 8, 1; died 1848, 5, 23. They moved from Nottingham many years ago, and settled finally in Northern Ohio. Roger was a miller by occupation.

65. Timothy, born 1796, 9, 13; died ——, —, —. (Nothing further known of him.)

66. Elijah, born 1800, 9, 4; died 1811, 4, 3.

67. Elizabeth, born 1803, 4, 2. Married John Donahoo. They reside south of Nottingham Station, on the Philadelphia and Baltimore Central Railroad. John is a carpenter and has worked at his trade for a number of years. He has held the office of Justice of the Peace in his election district. P. O. address, Nottingham, Chester county.

68. John, born 1807, 1, 17; died 1851, 7, 21. Married 1830, 5, 25, to Belinda (186) daughter of Immer and Esther Knight. Belinda, born 1809, 2, 1. John removed, along with his brother Roger, to Northern Ohio, where he settled and married.

CHILDREN OF LEVI KIRK (18) AND AMELIA MULLEN.

69. Ann, born 1790, 12, 11; died ——, —, —. Married 1812, 2, 14, to Thomas, son of —— and —— Knight. They resided in Lancaster, where Ann died not many years ago.

70. William M., born 1794, 7, 19; died 1833, 12, 4. Married Ann (390), daughter of Elisha and Mary England, of Nottingham.

71. Timothy, born 1796, 11, 16; died ——, —, —.

72. Hannah, born 1799, 5, 5. Married Francis Rawlins.

They resided in Bordentown, New Jersey. (Nothing learned of their family.)

73. Roger, born 1801, 8, 5; died 1802, 11, 24.

74. Harriet, born 1803, 8, 24; died 1858, 11, 10. Married to Joseph (165), son of Reuben and Mary Haines.

75. Washington, born 1805, 12, 8; died 1864, 10, 20. Married 1834, 11, 20, to Eleanor, daughter of —— and —— Dungan. Eleanor, born, 1814, 9, 14; died 1860, 3, 1.

76. Myra, born 1808, —, —. Married Hope Blanchard. (Nothing further known of this family.)

77. Eliza, born 1810, 5, 30. Married Norris Lewis. They reside on Elk Creek, south of "Rock," Cecil county, Maryland. Post-office address: Elkton, Maryland. Norris superintends a large mill for the manufacture of flour.

78. Randolph, born 1813, 2, 13; died ——, —, —, in St. Louis, Missouri, of cholera.

CHILD OF ——— EMORY AND ANN KIRK (19).

79. Ann K., born 1792, 11, 7; died ——, —, —. Married a man named Rothwell. (Nothing further ascertained.)

CHILDREN OF LEVI ROGERS AND MARY KIRK (20).

80. Timothy, born 1798, 2, 26; died 1848, 10, 3. Married 1821, 12, 21, to Anna Mary, daughter of Joseph and ——Gibbs. Second marriage, to Jane Brown, daughter of David and Dianah, of Drumore, Lancaster county. Timothy Rogers kept a hotel on East King st., Lancaster, for many years. His second wife now resides on a farm in Drumore township.

CHILDREN OF GIDEON EDGERLY AND ELIZABETH KIRK (21).

81. Gideon, born ——, —, —; died ——, —, —. Nothing further known of this individual, except that he lived in Lancaster city, where he died. He left several children, one of whom entered the army during the rebellion, and arose to

the rank of captain. His name is Edward, and at the present time is engaged in the manufacture of carriages, under the firm of "Edgerly and Myers."

CHILD OF HENRY STEVENSON AND ELIZABETH KIRK (EDGERLY) (21).

82. Joseph, born ——, —, —; died ——, —, —.

CHILDREN OF JOSEPH KIRK (24) AND JUDITH KNIGHT.

83. Elizabeth, born 1770, 4, 9; died ——, —, —. Married Robert Lapine. They resided at "Redstone," Fayette county, Pa.

84. Sarah, born 1772, 2, 17; died 1861, 1, 16. Married 1789, 12, 10, to Isaac, son of John and Mary Cope. They resided near Brownsville, Fayette county, Pa.

85. Mary, born 1774, 1, 17; died 1849, 5, 3. Married John, son of ——— and ——— Taylor. John was born in 1770, 8, 6, and died in Crawford county, Pa., 1826, 3, 20. Mary died at New Baltimore, Ohio, the residence of her son, Abraham Taylor.

86. Judith, born 1776, 3, 18; died ——, —, —. Married David Smith. (Nothing further known of this family.)

87. Ann, born 1779, 5, 4; died 1860, 11, 2. Married James, son of —— and —— Winder. James died 1861, 2, 3. He resided in the town of Bloomfield, Crawford county, Pa.

88. Deborah, born 1781, 2, 4; died ——, —, —. Married Abraham Fernington. (Nothing further ascertained of this family.)

89. William, born 1783, 4, 17; died 1837, 10, 8. Married Elizabeth Jorden. Elizabeth died 1867, 12, 7. William moved from western Pennsylvania to Fleming county, Ky., where he died.

90. Susanna, born 1787, 7, 18; died ——, —, —. Married

1806, 6, 26, to Lewis Broomfield. They resided for some time in western Pennsylvania.

91. Rachel, born ——, —, —; died ——, —, —. Married Stephen Bloomfield. (Nothing further ascertained.)

CHILDREN OF ABNER KIRK (26) AND ANN ALLEN.

92. Rachel, born 1771, 7, 4; died ——, —, —. Married David White.

93. Mary, born 1771, 7, 4; died 1802, 2, 6. Married 1791, 5, 19, to Elisha, son of ——— and ——— England, of Nottingham, Md. They resided near Brick Meeting House, Md. Elisha was a farmer.

94. William, born 1773, 2, 4; died 1862, 12, 4. Married 1795, 6, 4, to Lydia, daughter of Daniel and Mary Job. Lydia was born 1776, 2, 14, and died 1804, 3, 10. William married a second time. Second wife, Elizabeth Haines (48), daughter of Job and Esther, of Nottingham.

William Kirk was a well-known citizen of Nottingham, Md. He was, for many years, a member and elder of Friends' Meeting. He owned and resided upon part of the land taken up by the first of his ancestors, who are generally supposed to have come from Ireland. William was a fuller or clothier.

95. Joseph, born 1774, 11, 18; died ——, —, —. He married Susan McGarrighan. Migrated from Nottingham to "Redstone Settlement," Fayette county, and from thence to Charleston, South Carolina. Is said to have left two children.

96. Hannah, born 1776, 12, 11; died ——, —, —. Married William, son of ——— and ——— Miller.

97. Elizabeth, born 1779, 3, 21; died ——, —, —. Married William, son of Samuel and Sarah Brown, of Nottingham.

98. Ann, born 1781, 3, 29; died ——, —, —. Never married.

99. Abner, born 1783, 2, 24; died ——, —, —. Married 1808, 2, —, to Sarah, daughter of John and Mary Stevenson. Sarah born 1785, 11, 30; died ——, —, —. Abner's second marriage 1815, 8, 24, to Mary, daughter of John and Jane McCrea. Mary, born 1797, 10, 8.

CHILDREN OF ABNER KIRK (26) AND SARAH CHANDLEE.

100. Benjamin, born ——, —, —, died ——, —, —. Never married.

101. Susanna, born ——, —, —, died ——, —, —. Married John Shepherd, and with him migrated to "*the West.*".

CHILDREN OF WILLIAM KIRK (27) AND ANN WHITE.

102. William, born 1771, 3, 4; died ———, —. He resided near Rising Sun, Cecil county, Md. Married 1793, 5, 16, to Elizabeth Howell. Elizabeth deceased. Married second time. Second wife, Sarah Haines. William was a vendue crier.

103. Lydia, born ——, —, —, died ——, —, —. Married Jehu Brown. They lived near Brick Meeting House. Jehu died 1839, —, —.

CHILDREN OF JACOB KIRK (30) AND RACHEL ALLEN.

104. William, born 1780, 12, 14,; died ——, —, —. Infant.

105. Mary, born 1782, 11, 27; died ——, —, —. Infant.

106. Elisha, born 1784, 8, 15; died 1868, 10, 28. Married Elizabeth Wollison. He lived south of Brick Meeting House, Md.

107. Nancy, born 1786, 6, 1; died ——, —, —, in infancy

108. Deborah, born 1788, 4, 9. Married 1807, 1, 22, to Thomas I. Slicer. They resided near the village of Farmington, Cecil county, Md. Thomas died 1851, 1, 13.

109. Rachel, born 1790, 11, 30; died 1871, 5, 12. Interred at Brick Meeting House. Married Levi Kirk (58), son of Roger and Rachel Kirk. Rachel lived at Glen Roy, Chester county, along with her son Jacob L. Kirk.

110. Roger, born 1794, 1, 17; died ——, —, —. Never married.

111. Jacob, born 1794, 8, 31; died ——, —, —. Married Sophia Brown. He was a blacksmith by occupation.

112. Hannah, born 1796, 3, 25. Married David Wright.

113. Mary, born 1798, 7, 5; died ——, —, —. Married George, son of Elizabeth and Mary England. They resided in Nottingham, Md.

CHILDREN OF ELIZABETH KIRK (31), AND MARY ALLEN.

114. Allen, born 1789, 1, 11. Married 1813, 1, 1, to Martha McCullough. Married a second time. Second wife, Deborah (455), daughter of Thomas and Rachel Slicer. Allen resides on a farm south-west of the village of Brick Meeting House. He carries on the business of farming.

115. Jonathan, born ——, —, —; died ——, —, —. Married 1815, 2, 9, to Mary Thompson. Mary died 1821, 12, 11. Aged 43 years. Jonathan Kirk moved from Maryland to Rockford, Illinois, where he died.

116. William, born 1794, 6, 25; died 1869, 11, —. Married 1822, 8, 1; to Catharine, daughter of William and Elizabeth Selheimer. Catharine died 1825, 11, 25. William married 1833, 7, 31 to Rachel Pierson. He was a farmer, and died at Rising Sun village.

117. Joseph, born 1796, 10, 22. Married Eliza Scott. Joseph is extensively engaged in agricultural pursuits. Owns several farms, on one of which, near "Kirk's Bridge," he now resides. His address is Glen Roy, Chester county, Pa.

118. Nathan, born 1802, 3, —. Married 1833, -, —, Catharine, daughter of Israel and Hannah White. Catharine was born 1815, 9, —. Nathan left Maryland, and traveling westward, located in northern Ohio, near Elmore, where he still resides.

119. Elisha, born ——, —, —; died ——, —, —. Never married.

120. Hannah, born ——, —, —; died ——, —, —. Married Elisha (50), son of Job and Esther Haines of Rising Sun, Md.

121. Rachel, born ——, —, —; died ——, —, —. Married William K. Brown. (Nothing further ascertained of this family.)

CHILDREN OF WILLIAM DIXON (32) AND REBECCA WOODWARD.

122. Susanna, born 1767, 11, 12; died 1847, 8, 31. Married 1790, 10, 6, to Abel Campbell, of Fayette county, Pa., son of William and Mary Campbell. Abel died 1846, 12, 5. He was a farmer.

123. Joseph, born 1769, 10, 7; died 1789, 5, 13. Never married. Was killed by lightning while sitting at dinner.

124. Thomas, born 1771, 8, 31; died 1771, 9, 21.

125. William, born 1773, 3, 22; died ——, —, —. Married Jane Morrison, and resided near New Salem, Fayette county, Pa. He afterward removed to St. Clairsville, Belmont county, Ohio.

126. Sarah, born 1775, 4, 8; died 1776, 4, 30.

CHILDREN OF JOSEPH PAINTER (33) AND ELIZABETH WOODWARD.

127. Lydia, born 1774, 9, 20; died 1845, 12, 26. Married 1796, 4, 21, at Birmingham Meeting, to Nathan Sharpless, son

of Joshua and Edith, of East Bradford. Nathan was born 1772, 12, 18, and died 1863, 4, 11. He was a hatter, and followed that business in Wilmington, Delaware. Several years prior to his death he removed to a farm near Concordville, where "he ended his days."

128. Mary, born 1776, 1, 30; died 1811, 8, 24. Married 1801, 9, 24, at Birmingham Meeting House, to Eli Harvey, son of Amos and Hannah, of Pennsbury, Chester county. He was born 1772, 12, 29. They resided in Birmingham, Delaware county, near Chadd's Ford. Eli married a second time.

129. Thomas, born 1778, 1, 27; died 1788, 6, 5.

130. Joseph, born 1782, 7, 5; died 1855, 8, 12. Married 1805, 9, 12, at Bradford Meeting, to Lydia Marshall, daughter of Samuel and Rachel, of West Bradford. Lydia was born 1788, 8, 2; died 1857, 5, 10. They resided for many years in East Bradford, but settled in West Chester about the year 1830.

131. Elizabeth, born 1790, 12, 25; died 1815, 12, 15. Married 1810, 4, 11, at Concord Meeting, to Isaac Peirce, of Philadelphia, son of Joseph and Sarah, of Sadsbury, Lancaster county, Pennsylvania. Isaac was born 1788, 8, 22; died 1858, 3, 11, in Ohio. He married a second time.

CHILDREN OF SAMUEL WOODWARD (34) AND SARAH JACKSON.

132. Susanna, born 1773, 8, 5; died 1806, 3, 20. Married 1801, 12, 10, at London Grove, to Benjamin Swayne, of East Marlborough, son of William and Ann. He was born 1763, 11, 1, and died 1848, 2, [illegible].

133. John, born 1775, 5, 22; died 1843, 5, 11; buried at West Grove Meeting House. Married 1805, 1, 16, at Caln Meeting, to Rebecca Coates, of East Caln. She died 1850, 3, 25, and was buried at London Grove. Had no children.

134. Samuel, born 1777, 3, 18; died 1841, 10, 4; buried at Centre Meeting House, Delaware. Married 1800, 4, 9, at London Grove, to Ann, daughter of Caleb and Mary Swayne, of East Marlborough. She was born 1775, 1, 3; died 1834, 3, 7. They settled in Christiana Hundred, Delaware, about the year 1804.

135. Sarah, born 1779, 2, 11; died 1829, 3, 23. Married 1800, 11, 12, at London Grove, to John Fell, of New London, son of John and Sarah Fell. John was born 1778, 4, 10, and died 1850, 3, 2.

136. William, born 1782, 1, 23; died 1856, 6, 13. Married 1812, 1, 15, to Sarah, daughter of Isaac Bolton. Sarah, born 1782, 9, 28; died 1856, 9, 1. They settled in Kennett township, but died in Christiana Hundred, Delaware. William was interred at London Grove, and Sarah at Centre Meeting.

137. Thomas, born 1784, 2, 15; died 1859, 7, 15. Married 1809, 12, 14, at Okesson Meeting, to Mary, daughter of Reuben and Elizabeth Barney, of New Garden. She was born 1792, 4, 9, in Kennett township. They settled in East Marlborough. Thomas died at Kennett Square, and was interred at Friends' burying ground in that place.

138. Levi, born 1786, 8, 29; died 1855, 1, 15. Married, 1816, 1, 11, at New Garden Meeting, to Phœbe Hutton, daughter of Joseph and Sarah, of New Garden. He learned the tanning business, but after his marriage became a farmer and settled on a farm near Pleasant Grove, Lancaster county about the year 1818–19. From thence he removed to York county, in 1844.

139. Rachel, born 1787, 11, 25; died 1830, 9, 7. Married 1810, 10, 17, at London Grove, to Levi Wickersham, of New Garden, son of Sampson and Elizabeth. Levi was born 1784, 12, 26; died 1865, 3, 7.

140. Rebecca, born 1790, 4, 4; died 1866, 6, 24. Married, 1824, 4, 14, at London Grove, to William Commons, of Kennett, son of John and Sarah, of Jefferson county, West Virginia. He was born 1789, 6, 5; died 1855, 5, 19. They were both interred at Kennett Square. No children.

CHILDREN OF SAMUEL WOODWARD (34) AND HANNAH STARR.

141, Lewis, born 1800, 10, 26; died 1824, 4, 5. Married 1821, 12, 12, at London Grove, to Sarah Shipley, of Marlborough, daughter of William and Orpha, of Newcastle county. He was a farmer in New Garden township. Sarah married a second time. Present husband, Ellis Allen.

142. Hannah, born 1803, 2, 2; married 1841, 3, 10, to Elisha Speakman, of Londonderry township, son of Amos and Hannah, of London Grove. Elisha, born 1801, 10, 16; died 1867, 9, 12. They resided on a farm in London Grove, just north of Chatham, part of a tract settled by his ancestor, Thomas Speakman, about 1722. Hannah now resides with a nephew in West Marlborough.

143. Elizabeth, born 1804, 9, 24. Married 1823, 11, 13, at New Garden, to Stephen Pusey, of London Grove, son of David and Naomi. Stephen was born 1801, 11, 4; died 1866, 3, 18. They lived for some years in East Marlborough and afterward in West Fallowfield township. He died and was buried at London Grove. Elizabeth resides with a daughter.

144. Lydia, born 1806, 12, 20. Lives at London Grove village. Unmarried.

145. Esther, born 1809, 8, 24. Lives at Isaac Walton's, in West Marlborough. Unmarried.

CHILDREN OF THOMAS WOODWARD (35) AND MARY PUSEY.

146. Susanna, born 1778, 10, 9; died 1853, 8, 6. Buried at London Grove. Unmarried.

147. Deborah, born 1781, 7, 25; died 1813, 12, 24. Married 1807, 10, 14, at London Grove, to Eli Swayne, of East Marlborough, son of James and Hannah. He was born 1786, 6, 10; died about 1863. He was for some time doorkeeper of the House of Representatives, and resided at Harrisburg. From thence he removed to Philadelphia, and afterward to Delaware, where he died. Deborah was buried at London Grove, Chester county.

148. Elizabeth, born 1783, 1, 20; died 1858, 3, 16. Married 1816, 4, 11, at Bradford Meeting, to Joseph Hawley, son of Joseph and Elizabeth, of West Bradford. Joseph, born 1772, 11, 12; died 1851, 12, 21. They resided on the East Branch of Brandywine creek, in West Bradford township. Both interred at Bradford Meeting.

149. Ellis, born 1784, 10, 7; died 1857, 11, 29. Married Rebecca Shur, who died 1821, 11, 19. Married second, Rachel Woodward, daughter of James and Sarah, of West Bradford. She was born 1802, 5, 31; died 1866, 6, 3, in Midway, Chester county. Ellis was buried at East Caln Meeting House.

150. Thomas, born 1788, 1, 23; died 1788, 4, 17.

• 151. Mary, born, 1789, 6, 16. Married 1819, 3, 2, to Jonathan Woodward, son of Robert and Jane, of West Bradford. He was born 1780, 9, 8; died 1834, 9, 19. She was his second wife, and after his death, married 1838, 12, 12, at Caln Meeting, Jas. Davis son of James and Mary, of Brandywine township.

152. Joshua, born 1792, 2, 9; died 1852, 12, 30. Married 1821, 10, 17, at London Grove, to Rebecca, daughter of John and Mary Nutt. She died 1822, 12, 17, and he married Rebecca, daughter of Isaac and Sarah Lewis. She was born 1797, 9, 17 and died 1833, 12, 19. Joshua's third wife,

Ellen (Todd) Matthias. She died 1853, 9, 20, and was buried at St. Andrew's Church. Joshua was interred at Lionville, Uwchlan twp.

153. Ann, born 1795, 4, 9; died 1844, 6, 4. Married 1818, 10, 21, at London Grove, to William Kent, of East Fallowfield, son of Daniel and Esther. He was born 1792, 8, 3; died 1860, 10, 15. Both died in Upper Oxford twp., and were interred at Penn's Grove.

154. Lydia, born 1797, 12, 21, died 1867, 11, 10. Interred at Greenmount cemetery, West Chester. Unmarried.

CHILD OF JOSEPH SMITH (37) AND MARY WOODWARD.

155. John W., born 1785, 10, 29; died 1833, 7, 3. Married 1811, 3, 20, to Alice Wilkinson, and removed to Ohio the same year. He was buried at Flushing, Ohio, and she at Louisville, Henry county, Indiana, where she died 1858, 12, 15. He was a tanner by occupation.

FIFTH GENERATION.

CHILDREN OF TIMOTHY HAINES (41) AND SARAH BROWN.

156. Jeremiah B., born 1797, 4, 3. Married Mabel, daughter of Joseph and Sarah Hutton, of Little Britain, formerly of New Garden, Chester county. Married second, to Sarah Thomas, daughter of Joseph and Rebecca D. Roman, of Cecil county, Md. Third marriage, to Ruthanna Newlin, daughter of Jacob and Elizabeth Taylor, of New Garden, Chester county. Jeremiah resides at Pleasant Grove, Lancaster county, where he owns several farms and a store. Of late years has been interested in the manufacture of iron near Clear Spring, Washington county, Md. Until recently has held the office of President of Conowingo Bridge Company.

Was at one time President of the Columbia and Port Deposit Railroad Company.

157. Job, born 1799, 11, 16; died 1823, 2, 27. Unmarried.

158. Edwin, born 1801, 6, 20. Married Margaret, daughter of Joseph and Sarah Hutton, of Little Britain, formerly of New Garden. Edwin has resided for many years at Rising Sun, Cecil county, Md., where he has a large farm and several mills. He is one of the Directors of the Philadelphia and Baltimore Central Railroad, of the Rising Sun Building Association, &c., &c.

159. Lewis, born 1803, 12, 1. Married Sarah, daughter of Joseph and Sarah Hutton, of Little Britain. Married a second wife—Sarah Kirk (213), daughter of Jacob and Hannah Kirk, of Kirk's Mills, Lancaster county, Pa. Lewis commenced the mercantile business, at the village of Darlington, Harford county, Md. From thence removed to Quarryville, Lancaster county, where he continued the business until about the year 1841–2; when he disposed of his interest in the store, and removed to a farm, his present residence, near Pleasant Grove, Lancaster county. He has been elected, for several terms, a Director of the Farmers' National Bank of Lancaster.

160. Mark, born 1805, 9, 11; died 1870, 9, 16. Married Mercy, daughter of William and Susan Cook, of Fulton, Lancaster county. Second marriage, to Mercy, daughter of Daniel and Jane Stubbs, of Fulton, Lancaster county. She still resides at the residence of her late husband. Mark lived on a farm—a part of the original tract purchased by his father. He died suddenly, of an affection of the heart, and was interred in Friends' burying ground, at Penn Hill.

161. Hanson, born 1807, 11, 1; died 1841, 10, 4. Never married.

162. Levi, born 1809, 7, 14; died 1834, 3, 19. Never married.

163. Sarah, born 1812, 2, 22; died 1822, 8, 20.

164. Timothy, born 1817, 8, 20. Married Rachel E (214), daughter of Jacob and Hannah Kirk, of Kirk's Mills, Lancaster county. Timothy resides upon the "old homestead," near the Susquehanna, Fulton township, Lancaster county.

CHILDREN OF REUBEN HAINES (43) AND MARY JOHNSON.

165. Joseph, born 1798, 1, 3; died 1866, 1, 23. Married Harriet (74), daughter of Levi and Amelia Kirk. Joseph resided at Brick Meeting House, Md.; carried on the mercantile business, and was extensively known throughout the county in which he lived. He died rather suddenly at Elkton, Md., while performing the duties of clerk of the county court, a position held by his son Charles, who died the same day his father did, and was interred at the same time at the cemetery, Brick Meeting House, Md.

166. Robert, born 1799, 6, 28. Married ——, —, —; settled in St. Charles, Ill, where he is said to have amassed a large fortune. He owns extensive flour mills. He has several children, one of whom died rather suddenly, while the family was sojourning at West Chester, Pa. (Nothing further was learned of this family.)

167. Moriah, born 1801, 12, 13. Married, 1819, 12, 1, to Isaac, son of John and Elizabeth England. Isaac was born 1785, 11, 23; is still living at an advanced age. He resides on a farm near Brick Meeting House, Md.

168. Esther, born 1802, 6, 30. Married 1821, 11, 1, to Samuel, son of John and Elizabeth England. Samuel was born 1799, 10, 21. He resides near Brick Meeting House.

By occupation a cabinet maker; has not worked at the business for a number of years.

169. Elizabeth, born 1804; died 1870, 1, 21. Married 1824, 4, 15, to Isaac, son of Vincent and Priscilla Stubbs, of Little Britain, Lancaster county, Pennsylvania. Isaac was born 1799, 4, 6. He lived at Peach Bottom, Lancaster county, Penn's Grove, Chester county, and now in Peach Bottom township, York county, Pennsylvania, where he owns two large farms.

170. Ann, born 1808, 1, 13; died 1841, 5, 29. Married John F. Cazier, of Cecil county, Maryland. (Nothing further ascertained of this family.)

171. Littleton, born 1808, 2, 15; died 1808, 8, 30.

172. Sarah, born 1811, 5, 16. Married Benjamin J., son of Ellis and Ruth Passmore. Benjaman was born 1807, 5, 27. He learned the trade of a tailor, and carried on the business at Nottingham, Chester county. He finally received the appointment of clerk to the board of County Commissioners of that county; removed to West Chester, and after serving the Commissioners for a time, commenced the business of a conveyancer. At the present time he is serving his second term as Associate Judge of the several Courts of Chester county.

CHILDREN OF ELI HAINES (45) AND ELIZABETH BROWN.

173. Samuel, born 1801, 2, 16. Married Mary Eliza Reynolds. Mary died 1849, 5, 2. Samuel resides at Rising Sun, and is, by occupation, a farmer.

174. Mark, born 1802, 6, 1; died 1802, 7, 10.

175. Esther, born 1803, 10, 8; died 1803, 10, 27.

176. Myra, born 805, 13, 31; died 1870, 6, 24. Married Isaac, son of Jonathan and Elizabeth Reynolds. Isaac was

born 1799, 1. 3. He resides on a farm near Rising Sun, Cecil county, Md.

177. Eliza, born 1809, 2, 16; died ——, —, —. Married —— ——, Absalom, son of Joseph and —— Roman, of Cecil county, Md. Absalom was for many years engaged with his father and brother Joseph, in the manufacture of sheet-iron, at the village of Rowlandville, Cecil county. From thence he removed to the "Eighth District," Cecil county, where he purchased a farm, and now resides. His second wife, Catharine Maxwell, daughter of Joel and Alice Jackson.

178. Eli, born 1811, 8, 6; died ——, —, —. Married Hannah, daughter of Humphrey and Mary Marshall. Hannah died 1854, 7, 16.

CHILDREN OF JOB HAINES (46) AND PRUDENCE BROWN.

179. Sarah, born 1806, 9, 11. Married 1834, 10, 3, to Thomas, son of John and Jane Huie. Thomas was born 1802, 8, 2. They reside in Yates county, New Jersey. Post-office address, Benton.

180. Esther, born 1807, 9, 7. Married 1830, 3, 23, to John C. Powley. John C. was born 1803, 1, 12. He resides on a fine farm two miles south of the borough of Oxford, Chester county. He is a farmer and agent for the Mutual Fire Insurance Company of Chester county.

181. Lucy, born 1809, 7, 21. Married Williamson McCullough. They resided near the village of Farmington, Cecil county. Williamson deceased.

182. Basil, born 1811, 5, 21. Married 1835, 10, 9, to Lydia A. Taylor. Basil resides on a farm, near Rising Sun.

183. Daniel Job, born 1815, 8, 21.

184. Eri Washington, born 1823, 9, 10. Married 1846, 9, 10, to Sarah Evelyn McKown. Eri is a dentist by profession, and resides at Newark, Delaware.

CHILDREN OF WILLIAM KIRK (94) AND ELIZABETH HAINES (48.)

Sec 94.

CHILDREN OF IMMER KNIGHT AND ESTHER HAINES (49.)

185. Naomi, born 1807, 9, 5. Married 1837, 4, 9, to Andrew Gamble.

186. Belinda, born 1809, 2, 1. Married John Kirk (68), son of Eli and Susanna Kirk. They resided at Port Clinton, Ottawa county, Ohio.

187. Nathan H., born 1810, 12, 5. Married 1836, 4, -, to Mary Lockwood. No children.

188. Hannah E., born 1812, 6, 24. Married 1845, 4, 3, to Abraham Bell.

189. Immer, born 1813, 11, 27; died 1867, 4, 19. Married 1843, 1, 11, to Eliza Merion.

190. Lydia A., born 1815, 5, 22. Married 1837, 8, 12, to James Kingham. James resides at Port Clinton, Ohio. He held a position in the United States Internal Revenue service in that place.

191. Esther H., born 1817, 6, 23. Married 1837, 10, 5, to Cyrus Moore.

192. William K., born 1819, 6, 3; died 1854, 11, 14. Married Susan J. Kirk (274), daughter of Roger and Ann Kirk. William, married a second time; second wife, Anna L. Kleinhaus. Date of second marriage, 1848, 11, 26.

193. Clarrisa, born 1821, 1, 28. Married 1843, 4, to Cyrus T. Smeed. Cyrus died 1863, 10, 1.

194. Lucinda, born 1823, 1, 5. Married 1846, 11, 15, to Theodore J. Kirk, (273), son of Roger and Ann Kirk.

CHILDREN OF ELISHA HAINES (50) AND HANNAH KIRK.

195. Kirk, born 18—, —, —. Married ——, —, —. Kirk resided in Middletown, Perry county, Pa. Learned that he

has been extensively engaged in the "lumber trade." For several years he represented this district in the State Legislature, as a member of the Senate. While in this capacity, the author of this work met him at Harrisburg, and had quite a lengthy conversation in reference to his family relations in Nottingham. While procuring material for this work, we made several attempts to gain *data* of his family, but failed of success.

CHILDREN OF NATHAN HAINES (51) AND RACHEL WILLIAMS.

196. Philip, born 1810, 2, 4. Married 1837, 1, 3, to Mary, daughter of James and Martha Miles. Philip resides at Anamosa, Iowa, and is engaged in the manufacture of marble mantles, steps, &c., &c.

197. Caroline, born 1813, 9, 6; died 1866, 10, 21. Unmarried.

198. Reuben, born 1814, 12, 31. Married 1850, 2, 21, to Miriam Robinson. Miriam was born in England, and died 1865, 10, 24. Reuben married, 1866, 12, 27, Sarah, daughter of Emmor and Deborah Bradley. By this marriage no children.

199. Rachel, born 1817, 2, 26; died 1817, 8, 11.

CHILDREN OF NATHAN HAINES (51) AND MARY CARTER.

200. Lewis, born 1826, 6, 23; died 1852, 1, 23.

201. Annie E., born 1827, 9, 22. Not married.

202. Margaretta A., born 1829, 9, 2. Married 1853, 9, 11, to Thomas Bowker. Thomas, born 1831, 7, 23. They reside in Upland, Delaware county, Pa.

203. Job, born 1831, 10, 20.

CHILDREN OF ELISHA KIRK (52) AND HANNAH MULLEN.

204. George W, born 1800, 12, 20. Married 1822, 1, 10, to Maria, daughter of William Thompson, M. D., and Mary

Thompson, of Nottingham. George kept a store at Brick Meeting House; from thence removed to Kirk's Mills, Lancaster county. Receiving an appointment as clerk in the United States Custom House, Philadelphia, he removed to that city, where he still resides. He now follows the business of a weighmaster. Present residence, 523 North Fifteenth street.

205. Rachel, born 1804, 8, 30. Married William, son of Joseph and Sarah Hutton, of Little Britain, formerly of New Garden, Chester county. William died 1854, 12, 23, and was interred in Friends' burying ground, at Penn Hill. He resided for many years in Philadelphia, where he kept a clothing store. From thence he removed to Little Britain, where he purchased a farm, north of Pleasant Grove. Rachel still resides on this place.

206. Hughes, born 1806, 10, 31, died 1843, —, —. Married Ruthanna Robinson. He removed from Cecil county, Md., to Virginia, and purchased a small tract of land. His widow is still living, in some part of the State. It is said he left two daughters and a son.

207. Amelia, born 1808, 11, 13. Married 1831, 2, 17, to John Neal, son of John and Ann Russell. John resides in Drumore township, Lancaster county; owns and manages a large farm. For many years he has taken great interest in farming operations, having pursued agriculture as a science. He ranks first among the prominent, progressive agriculturists of southern Lancaster county.

208. Ann M., born 1821, 3, 11; died 1863, 2, 15. Married 1838, 2, —, to James, son of Samuel and Rachel Morrison, of Drumore, Lancaster county, Pa. James died 18—, —. They resided near Drumore Centre, Lancaster county.

CHILDREN OF JACOB KIRK (53) AND SARAH ENGLAND.

209. John, born 1804, 1, 9. Married Ellen, daughter of ——— and ——— Bender. John resided and kept store for several years at Oak Hill, Lancaster county. He purchased and sold several farms in that vicinity. Now resides on a farm in Little Britain, on the road from Peach Bottom to Oxford. When a young man, in company with his cousin, Jacob R. Kirk, he made a voyage to England, and visited the noted localities in London and several other large cities of Europe.

210. Mary, born 1805, 4, 8; died 1826, 6, 21. Never married.

211. Roger, born 1807, 3, 30; died 1807, 6, 4.

212. Hannah, born 1809, 1, 22; died 1850, 11, 4. Married Isaac, son of Jonathan and Rachel Pierce. They resided a few years near Kirk's Mills, on the farm now owned by Henry Townsend. From this place they removed to near Cochranville, Chester county, where Hannah died. Isaac was a farmer. He is also deceased.

CHILDREN OF JACOB KIRK (53) AND HANNAH ENGLAND.

213. Sarah, born 1817, 2, 1. Married Lewis (159), son of Timothy and Sarah Haines.

214. Rachel E., born 1820, 3, 26. Married Timothy (164), son of Timothy and Sarah Haines.

215. Elizabeth, born 1822, 9, 12. Resides at Kirk's Mills.

216. Levi, born 1825, 3, 14. Resides at the homestead, Kirk's Mills, where he superintends the farm. Was formerly engaged in the mercantile business, but ceased to have an interest in the store some years ago. Unmarried.

217. Mary, born 1827, 516. Married William (634), son of Jeremiah B. and Mabel Haines, of Pleasant Grove. William has been alternately farming and keeping store for several

years. Now resides at Pleasant Grove, where he is engaged in the mercantile business.

218. Lewis J., born 1829, 11, 9. Married Adaline, daughter of James A. and Adaline Caldwell. Lewis is engaged in the mercantile business at Kirk's Mills, Little Britain; also, has an interest in several mills at this place.

CHILDREN OF TIMOTHY KIRK (54) AND MARY REYNOLDS.

219. Jacob R., born 1807, 11, 8; died 1838, 10, 24. Married Hannah B., daughter of Isaac and Hannah Stubbs. Hannah, born 1808, 5, 27. Jacob resided, at the time of his death, upon a farm, situated on North-East Creek. He owned a paper and saw-mill and store. When a young man, he made a voyage to Europe, visiting England and Ireland.

220. Rachel H., born 1813, 9 ,30. Married 1836, 2, 25, to Jeremiah B., son of Isaac and Hannah Stubbs. Jeremiah was born 1804, 4, 4, and died suddenly of angina pectoris, 1862, 7, 10. He studied medicine under direction of Dr. Vincent King, of Little Britain, Lancaster county; attended two courses of lectures at the Jefferson Medical College, Philadelphia, and graduated on the eighth day of March, 1827, at the age of twenty-three.

He commenced the practice of his profession at Rising Sun, Cecil county, Md., and remained there a period of nine years. While practicing in that State he was elected a member of the Medico-Chirurgical Society of Maryland, under date September 11, 1827.

Soon after his marriage, in 1836, he returned to Little Britain—having previously purchased the farm of John K. Sappington, M. D. Here he continued the practice of his profession until his decease. On the 14th of February, 1844, he was elected a member of the Lancaster City and County

Medical Society; was afterward chosen president of the society. Taking an active part in the advancement of his profession, he was elected a member of the American Medical Association, and attended its sessions as a delegate, in 1849, at Boston; Richmond, 1851, and New York, 1856. In 1848-9 he was elected to in part represent his county, in the State Legislature, as a member of the "lower house." While a a member of that body he was appointed on two of its most important committees—"On Banks" and "Education."

221. Esther T., born 1818, 2, 13; died 1858, 8, 15. Married Elwood M., son of Daniel and Jane Stubbs, of Little Britain. Elwood resided for a number of years in Fulton township, but disposed of his farm and purchased another near Fairfield, Lancaster county, where he now resides. Elwood married a second time. Second wife, Philena, daughter of Jesse and Mary Cutler, of Drumore.

222. Anna M., born 1819, 10, 26. Married ——, —, —, Montgomery R. Gryder, son of Christian and Hannah Gryder, of Drumore township, Lancaster county. Montgomery read medicine under direction of Edward Chandlee, M. D., and graduated at the Jefferson Medical College, Philadelphia. He commenced practice at the village of Cochranville, Chester county, but remained there only a short time. He returned to Chestnut Level, Lancaster county, where he continued his profession for a number of years. Purchasing a farm near the "Fulton House," he moved upon it and remained there until he received an appointment as one of the clerks in the Naval office, Philadelphia. His present residence is 104 Friedlander street.

223. Lewis, born 1821, 8, 9; died 1827, 7, 20.

CHILDREN OF JOHN KIRK (55) AND DEBORAH BROWN.

224. Rachel, born 1808, 2, 5; died 1814, 5, 21.

225. Deborah, born 1810, 9, 15. Married Samuel, son of Joshua and ——— Webster, of Penn Hill, Lancaster county, Pa. Samuel read medicine under Dr. John K. Sappington, and finished his studies under Sappington's successor, Dr. Jeremiah B. Stubbs. He attended two courses of medical lectures, and graduated at Jefferson Medical College, Philadelphia. He removed to Monmouth, Ill., where he practiced his profession for many years. Leaving Monmouth he went to Superior City, where he died. His wife Deborah still resides at the town of Monmouth, Ill.

226. Hannah, born 1813, 1, 4. Married Ellis P., son of Samuel and Mary Irwin, of Chester county. They resided for many years in Sadsbury township, Lancaster county. From thence removed to Philadelphia, No. ——, N. Fifteenth street. Of late years Ellis has been a "stock operator." No children.

227. Jeremiah, born 1815, 5, 24. Married 1839, 12, 26, to Eliza, daughter of William and Sarah Hatton of Fulton, Lancaster county, Pa.

Jeremiah resided for a time on the mill property of his father, near Penn Hill. Then removed to Peach Bottom, York county, where he kept a store, carried on a slate quarry and managed a farm. He disposed of all these, and went to Philadelphia, where his family still resides.

228. Rachel, born 1818, 8, 9; died 1854, 4, 7. Married 1837, 12, 28, to William C., son of Samuel and Mary Irwin. They resided at Pleasant Garden Forge, Chester county, Little Britain, Lancaster county, and finally in Philadelphia, where Rachel died. William married a second time and parted from his wife, she obtaining a divorce. Since then he

has lived in Illinois, Alabama, &c., &c. Is said to be superintending a cotton plantation near Huntsville.

229. Mercy, born 1820, 12, 9. Married 1842, 7, 12, to Alexander, son of Robert Johnson, M. D. Alexander was engaged in the mercantile business, at Penn Hill, for several years, then removed to Philadelphia, where he still resides. He is now engaged in the business of weigh-master.

230. John, born 1823, 12, 9; died 1824, 8, 16.

231. Slater, born 1825, 7, 18; died 1848, 3, 12. He resided in York county, Pa., and was engaged in the mercantile business at the time of his decease. He was interred at Friend's burying ground, Penn Hill, Lancaster county, Pa.

CHILDREN OF JOSIAH KIRK (56) AND PHEOBE PASSMORE.

232. Ellis P., born 1813, 9, 4. Married Sarah A., daughter of Jacob and Catharine Hilaman. Ellis inherited the farm belonging to his grandfather, upon which he resided several years. He disposed of this, and now lives on a farm north of Nottingham Station, Philadelphia and Baltimore Central Railroad.

233. Roger H., born 1815, 3, 16. Married Deborah, daughter of Levi and Harriet Brown, of Little Britain. After his marriage, he disposed of his farm in Nottingham, and removed to near Pleasant Grove, Lancaster county, where he now resides. While in Nottingham, Roger conducted a mill, and was engaged in the manufacture of flour. Since, his attention has been engaged in farming. Formerly he was one of the directors of the Conowingo Bridge Co., and has been, for several years, and is now, a director of the National Bank of Oxford.

234. Josiah F. born 1816, 11, 6. Married Sarah Ann, daughter of Bailey and Catharine Biles, of Blue Ball, Cecil

county, Md. Josiah F. lived for a number of years at the Blue Ball and kept a store. He departed for "parts unknown," and it appears was located in New Jersey. The last time heard from he was running a steamboat from New York to some port South.

235. Rachel A., born 1818, 7, 21; died 1871, 6, 4, Married Daniel, son of Isaac and Hannah Stubbs, of Little Britain, Lancaster county.

Daniel was born 1812, 7, 17; died 1869, 4, 29, at his residence, near Nottingham station, Baltimore Central R. R. He was interred in Friend's burying-ground, Brick Meeting House, Md.

Daniel Stubbs was engaged in the mercantile business many years. For a short time he "stood in a store" at Wilmington, Del., then entered into a partnership with his elder brother, Amer, and conducted stores at Peach Bottom and Fairfield, Lancaster county. Afterward, with his brother Joseph, purchased a farm, store, and paper-mill in Nottingham, where they continued business for a number of years. Purchasing the farm and mill of his brother-in-law, Roger Kirk he sold his interest in the farm to his brother Joseph, and removed to the mills near Hilaman's, where he erected a store building and several brick dwellings. He was elected one of the first directors of the Baltimore Central railroad, and after the completion of this road to Nottingham, he moved to the station of that name, where he had erected a fine dwelling and extensive grain depot. Soon after locating on the railroad, the disease which had been making inroads upon his frail constitution proved fatal.

Possessing fine business qualifications, he entered into all enterprises started in the section of the county in which he resided that he thought would inure to the benefit of the community in general. At the time of his death, in addition to being a director of the railroad company, he was a director of the Oxford National Bank, and the Oxford Fire Insurance company.

CHILDREN OF JEREMIAH BROWN AND ANN KIRK (57).

236. Hannah, born 1808, 7, 14. Married Samuel C., son of David and Catharine Wood. They resided for many years near Pleasant Grove, Lancaster county. They removed to Goshen, where they reside on a large farm. Samuel owns a mill and store. He is now postmaster at Goshen.

237. Rachel, K., born 1810, 4, 5. Married Allen, son of William and Susan Cook, of Little Britain. Allen died —— —, —. For a number of years after the decease of her husband, Rachel resided on a farm near Peach Bottom, Pa. She at last disposed of this and removed to Delavan, Illinois, where she still resides.

238. Kirk, born 1812, 1, 5; died 1869, 7, 27. Married 1832, —— ——, to Susanna, daughter of Joseph and Ann Hambleton. Kirk moved to "the west," but remained a short time. He then returned to Little Britain, where he lived a number of years; worked at his trade—wagon-making, and farming. Three years prior to his decease, he purchased a farm in Cecil county, Md., to which he had removed.

239. Levi K., born 1814, 6, 27. Married Hannah, daughter of Joseph and Mercy Moore, of Nottingham, Md. Levi was, for many years, a merchant; first at Goshen, afterward at Oxford and West Chester. In 1853 he returned to Goshen, where he has resided on his farm. He in now an insurance agent and conveyancer, and is often called upon to settle estates, guardian accounts, and business of that character. He is a director of the Oxford National Bank and of the Conowingo Bridge company.

240. Lewis H., born 1816, 9, 6; died 1851, 10, 31. Married 1841, 2, 16, to Elizabeth, daughter of Thomas and Rachel Bradway, of Nottingham. Lewis was a merchant, and was engaged in the dry goods business in West Chester and afterward in Philadelphia. He died while a resident of Philadelphia, and was interred in Friends' burying ground, at Fairhill, near that city.

CHILD OF LEVI KIRK (58) AND RACHEL KIRK (109).

241. Jacob L., born 1814, 1, 31. Married 1835, 12, 31, to Jane, daughter of Cyrus and Sarah Milner. Jacob keeps the hotel at Glen Roy, West Nottingham, Chester county. Jane deceased. Jacob married a second time. Wife's maiden name, Elizabeth P. Keech.

CHILDREN OF SLATER BROWN AND MARY KIRK (59).

242. Sarah, born 1811, 9, 5; died 18—, ——, ——. Never married.

243. Jeremiah, born 1812, 11, 23; died 1817, 4, 9.

244. Elisha, born 181–, 12, 14; died 1859, 2, 28. Married Rachel, daughter of Thomas and Rachel Bradway, of Nottingham, Chester county. Elisha resided at Goshen, Lancaster county. He was a farmer.

245. Jeremiah, born 1817, 2, 14. Married Margaretta (631), daughter of Jeremiah B. and Mabel Haines, of Pleasant Grove, Lancaster county. Jeremiah resides on the homestead, carries on milling, and at the present time is lessee of the extensive slate quarries at Peach Bottom, Lancaster county.

246. Rachel A., born 1822, 10, 1. Married Jos. C. Stubbs, son of Daniel and Jane Stubbs. Joseph C. resides in Fulton township, and manages a couple of farms.

247. Mary H., born 1827, 3, 17. Married Edwin L., son of James and Zillah Morgan. After their marriage, Edwin L. returned to San Francisco, California, taking his wife with him. They resided in that city for several years, and then came to Philadelphia and purchased a residence, 1608 Wallace street, where they now reside.

Edwin is engaged in the manufacture of steam engines, boilers, &c., and is one of the firm of "Morgan, Orr & Co.," Callowhill st., Philadelphia. Within the last few years he has purchased and is improving a farm in Little Britain, Lancaster county.

CHILDREN OF LEWIS KIRK (60) AND RUTH PASSMORE.

248. Alexander H., born 1820, 5, 23. Married 1870, 5, 23, to Adriana, daughter of Jacob and Anna Reynolds, of Cecil county, Md. Alexander resides in West Chester, Pa. He has a farm in Nottingham, and has been engaged in store-keeping in West Chester.

249. Rachel, L., born 1821, 10, 27. Unmarried. Resides in West Chester.

CHILDREN OF WILLIAM BROWN AND ESTHER KIRK (61).

250. Jeremiah, born 1809, 9, 28; died 1842, 11, 18. Married Mary Lloyd.

251. Susanna, born 1811, 2, 8; died 1830, 9, 15.

252. Rachel, born 1812, 12, 5; died 1813, 2, 11.

253. Abner, born 1813, 12, 3; died 1821, 10, 16.

254. Elizabeth, born 1818, 12, 14. Married James Barnett.

255. William K., born 1821, 7, 24; died 1825, —, —.

256. Timothy K., born 1824, 4, 4; died 1868, 12, 17. Married Deborah, daughter of William and Mary Moore. No children. Timothy was a farmer.

257. William P. W., born 1827, 3, 1. Married Margaret, daughter of Nathan and Rachel Brown, of Fulton, Lancaster county. They reside near Brick Meeting House, Md. No children. William is a farmer.

258. Kirk, born 1831, 3, 17; died 1832, 4, 7.

CHILDREN OF WILLIAM B. KIRK (62) AND MARY WILLIAMS.

259. Lloyd, born 1811, 12, 31; died 1822, 7, 28.

260. Sarah, born 1813, 7, 30. Married a man named Russell. No children.

261. John, born 1815, 4, 9; died 1817, 8, 7.

262. Susanna, born 1817, 9, 12; died 1820, 8, 14.

263. Imri, born 1819, 4, 19. Married 1841, 3, —, to Lucinda Christ. Imri deceased. Lucinda married a man named Maeyers. No children.

264. Gideon, born 1821, 9, 28. Never married.

265. Joseph, born 1824, 2, 14. Married 1860, 11, 1, to Margaret Ellen Colgram.

266. Joshua W., born 1825, 12, 7. Married 1848, 10, 12, to Rachel Ball.

267. George W., born 1827, 11, 30. Married 1858, 10, to Rachel E. McVey.

268. William S., born, 1829, 6, 25; died 1852, 8, 17.

269. Eli, born 1831, 1, 12. Married 1866, 5, 22, to Ruth A. Moore.

270. Mary E., born 1832, 12, 20; died 1834, 4, 16.

CHILDREN OF ROGER KIRK (64) AND ANN TRUMP.

271. Lewis T., born 1818, —, —; died 1840, 12, 8.

272. Reuben T., born 1820, 9, 25. Married 1844, 2, 25, to Eunice Ryneer. They reside near Port Clinton, Ottawa county, Ohio.

273. Theodore J., born 1823, 2, 9. Married 1846, 11, 15, to Lucinda Knight (194). They reside near Elmore, Ottawa county, Ohio.

274. Susan, born 1825, 7, 27; died 1847, 4, 5. Married 1843, 12, 25, to W. Kirk (192), son of Immer and Esther Knight. Susan died in Ottawa county.

275. John H., born 1827, 9, 28. Married 1859, 5, 19, to Mary G. Smith. He resides near Richfield, Hennepin county, Minnesota. Have no children.

276. Abraham E., born 1830, 9, 1; died 1838, 11, 1.

277. Sarah E., born 1832, 6, 7. Married 1854, 3, 16, to Thomas J. Baldwin, and now resides at Elmore, Ottawa county, Ohio.

278. Grace A., born 1835, 7, 8. Married 1854, 9, 10, to Westley Critchet. They now reside in Central City, Colorado Territory.

CHILDREN OF JOHN DONOHOO AND ELIZABETH KIRK (67).

279. Susanna, born 1823, 8, 7, died 1825, 6, 4.

280. James Eli, born 1826, 5, 2. Married Susan Thomas. He moved from Nottingham to Ohio, and from thence to Nineveh, Indiana, where he follows the occupation of a carpenter.

281. Esther, born 1830, 7, 3. Married William J. Marchbank. They resided at Penn Hill for several years, where William carried on coach-making extensively. From Penn Hill he moved to Brick Meeting House, continuing the business. He afterward purchased "The Oxford House," Oxford, and "run this hotel" for about three years. Disposed of this and purchased another, located at Oak Hill. Here he remained about two years, when he left this in the hands of a tenant, and migrated to the town of Seaford, Delaware,

where he has erected a fine hotel, for the accommodation of visitors during the warm months of the year.

282. Naomi, born 1832, 7, 11; died 1839, 10, 22.

283. Mary A., born 1837, 12, 25.

284. Hannah, born 1840, 6, 7. Married Abner (411), son of William and Elizabeth Kirk.

285. Catharine E., born 1842, 7, 25; died 1854, 12, 7.

286. Ruth A., born 1845, 7, 5; died 1854, 12, 7.

287. Sarah R., born 1848, 2, 17; died 1851, 6, 30.

CHILDREN OF JOHN KIRK (68) AND BELINDA KNIGHT (186).

288. Artabanes, born 1831, 7, 5. Married 1857, 4, 19, to Thirza Hall. They reside near Port Clinton, Ohio.

289. Hannah E. ——, born 1833, 11, 26. Married 1855, 5, 22, to David Merion. They reside in Ottawa county, Ohio. David died in the service of his country at Fort Ethan Allen, 1864, 7, 5.

290. Susanna E., born 1837, 4, 25; died 1862, 2, 10. Married 1856, 4, 2, to Henry F. Harrison. They reside in Ottawa county, Ohio.

291. Immer Lawson, born 1839, 10, 30.

292. Lucretia M., born 1843, 4, 15.

293. Eli John, born 1845, 8, 14; died 1849, 4, 7.

294. Naomi L., born 1849, 12, 31.

295. John Milton, born 1852, 9, 25; died 1853, 6, 22.

CHILDREN OF THOMAS KNIGHT AND ANN KIRK (69).

296. William, born 1812, 3, 29. Married 1841, 9, 9, to Jane, daughter of Col. Samuel Coates, of Eagle Station, Chester co., Pennsylvania.

297. Emily, born 1814, 6, 14. Married Henry Sheaff, of Lancaster city; Henry, dec'd; Emily still resides in Lancaster. No children.

298. Levi, born 18—, —, —; died 1849, —, —.

299. Lydia, A., born 18—, —, —. Married John Summers, and resides somewhere in Baltimore city.

300. Caroline, born 18—, —, —. Married John Ditlow; John dec'd. They resided in South Queen st., Lancaster.

301. Thomas, born 18—, —, —, Never married.

CHILDREN OF WILLIAM M. KIRK (70) AND ANN ENGLAND.

302. Mary E., born 1813, 9, 18; died 1814, 9, 16.

303. Levi, born 1814, 9, 12; died 1827, 9, 22.

304. Amelia, born 1817, 10, 7; died 1843, 10, 18.

305. Elisha, born 1819, 2, 28. Married 1843, 10, 17, to Rebecca A., daughter of James Hanna, Esq., of Fulton, Lancaster co., Pa. Elisha resides near Brick Meeting House, Md., and by occupation is a farmer.

306. Elizabeth, born 1820, 7, 3. Married Thomas, son of Montillion and Ann Brown. Thomas Brown was born 1816, 9, 6. They reside in Cecil county, Md.

CHILDREN OF JOSEPH HAINES (165) AND HARRIET KIRK (74).

307. Charles, born 1826, 6, 7; died 1866, 1, 23. He was engaged for several years in keeping store at Brick Meeting House, Md. He was elected clerk of the Courts of Cecil county, Md., and afterward appointed cashier of the Cecil Bank at Port Deposit, holding both positions at the time of his decease. He was interred in the cemetery at Brick Meeting House the same day with his father. He never married.

308. Cornelia, born 1828, 10, 29. Married Dr. Turner. They reside at Brick Meeting House, where the Doctor is engaged in the practice of his profession. No children.

309. Lewis K., born 1831, 8, 16; died 1835, 1, 29.

310. Mary E., born 1834, 1, 9. Married John Ireland.

John is a merchant and resides at the residence of his late father-in-law, Brick Meeting House, Md.

311. William L., born 1825, 5, 29. Married Annie, daughter of Horace Duyckinck, of Brick Meeting House, Md.

312. Reuben, born 1840, 6, 29. Not married. Reuben studied law and practices his profession in Elkton, the county town of Cecil county, Md. He has held the position of District Attorney for that county.

CHILDREN OF WASHINGTON KIRK (75) AND ELEANOR DUNGAN.

313. Amelia M., born 1836, 3. 10. Unmarried. Resides in Baltimore, Md.

314. Elizabeth D., born 1841, 4, 4.

CHILDREN OF NORRIS LEWIS AND ELIZA KIRK (76).

315. William, born 1832, 1, 1. Married ——, —, —; no children.

316. Joseph K., born 1833, 8, 28. Married ——, —, —.

317. Eliza A., born 1835, 9, 17. Married I. Day Carter, of Cecil county. He is extensively engaged in the manufacture of printing paper, and has a large mill situated on Elk creek, some six miles north of Elkton. He has supplied Philadelphia *Press* and Baltimore *Sun* associations with printing paper. His post-office address, Elkton, Md.

318. Amelia, born 1837, 1 27. Married ——, —, —, Slater B. (779), son of John and Amelia Russell. Slater after his marriage removed from Lancaster county, Pa., to Washington, D. C., where he had received an appointment as clerk in the Quartermaster's Division, War Department. He remained in Washington during Lincoln's Administration and part of Johnson's. Resigning his position, he returned to Lancaster county, and conducted his father's farm for two

years. In the spring of 1870, in partnership with Joseph Swift, Jr., he engaged in the grain and commission business at Nottingham Station, Baltimore Central railroad. Since commencing business he removed to the borough of Oxford. At present time is one of the firm of Russell & Alexander—door, sash and planing mill—Oxford, Pa.

319. Robert C., born 1840, 5, 8. Married Lida Biddle.

320. Harriet, born 1844, 1, 24. Married 1870, 12, 22, to Vincent K. Alexander, son of John and Mary Alexander. Vincent resides in Little Britain, Lancaster county, and manages a farm.

321. Mary, born 1846, 5, 10.

322. Amanda, born 1849, 2, 13.

323. Henry B., born 1853, 7, 18.

CHILD OF TIMOTHY ROGERS (80) AND ANN M. GIBBS.

324. Levi, born 1839, 8, 21. Married Mary Jane, daughter of William and Jane Miller. Levi resided for several years in Lancaster city; then removed to Drumore township, Lancaster county, where he now resides. He has been engaged in cropping the large farm of his step-mother—Jane Rogers.

CHILDREN OF ROBERT LAPPIN AND ELIZABETH KIRK (83).

325. Samuel, born ——, —, —. Resided at Eddysville, Warren county, Iowa. (Nothing further known of him.)

326. Rachel, born ——, —, —. Married William Todd, and resided at Chester Hill, Ohio.

327. Ann, born ——, —, —; died 1853, 11, 2. Married 1820, 9, 1, to John Starbuck. John died 1864, 3, 13.

328. Robinson, born 1802, 8, 12. Married 1828, 8, 11. Resides at Jeffersonville, Wayne county, Ohio.

329. Montgomery, born ——, —, —. Resides in Jeffersonville, Wayne county, Ohio. (Nothing further known of him.

CHILDREN OF ISAAC COPE AND SARAH KIRK (84).

330. Mary, born 1791, 4, 30; died 1826, 11, 18. Married 1814, 7, 7, to Thomas Price. His P. O. address is Loche, Elkhart county, Indiana.

331. Joseph, born 1793, 1, 6; died 1825, 3, 4. Married 1816, 10, 30, to Elizabeth, daughter of Isaac and Elizabeth Fisher, of Bedford county, Pa. Elizabeth died 1851, 3, 10. They reside in Fayette county, Pa.

332.. John, born 1795, 9, 8; died 1849, 9, 11. Married 1819, —, —, to Sarah, daughter of George Smith, of Washington county, Pa. They resided in Fayette county until 1846, when they removed to Washington county.

333. Judith, born 1798, 1, 15; died 1843, 7, 1. Married 1821, 1, 4, to Moses, son of William and Mary Pennock. They removed from Fayette county, Pa., to Stark county, Ohio, where Moses died 1847, 9, 12.

334. Sarah, born 1800, 8, 12. Married 1821, 5, 24, to Michael, son of John and Mary Hagaman, of Fayette county, Pa. They removed to Michigan. Address, Amboy, Hillsdale county.

335. Anna, born 1802, 12, 4; died 1828, 2, 16. Never married.

336. Isaac, born 1804, 12, 23. Married 1827, 12, 12, to Rachel, daughter of Moses and Abigail Embree. Isaac's address, Marboro, Stark county. Rachel was born 1810, 11, 2; died 1857, 10, 1. Isaac's second marriage, 1858, 7, 2, to Rachel Vancoyoc, daughter of Benjamin and Susanna Elliott.

337. Kirk, born 1807, 5, 19; died 1807, 5, 21.

338. Ruth, born 1809, 4, 30. Married 1827, 8, 22, to Aaron Vancoyoc. They removed from Washington county, Pa., in 1842, to Stark county, Ohio. In 1854 they migrated to Warren county, Iowa.

339. Jesse, born 1812, 3, 10. Married 1833, 12, 6, to Elizabeth, daughter of James and Rebecca McGrew, of North Huntingdon township, Westmoreland county, Pa. Their address, Redstone, Fayette county, Pa.

CHILDREN OF JOHN TAYLOR AND MARY KIRK (85).

340. Samuel, born 1794, 4, 17; died ——, —, —. Married —— Pile. Second wife, Rebecca Morris.

341. Abigail, born 1797, 11, 1. Married Nathan Price. Nathan deceased.

342. Joseph, born 1799, 2, 20. Married Hannah Hutton. Hannah deceased. Joseph married a second time, and resides in Salem, Columbiana county, Ohio.

343. Aaron, born 1802, 2, 15. (Nothing further ascertained.)

344. Judith, born 1804, 5, 31. Married Alexander Maxwell.

245. Amy, born 1806, 12, 12. Married Jos. Winder (350).

346. Sarah, born 1809, 12, 3; died 1854, 6, 25. Married 1834, 9, 28, to Wilkinson Elliott. Wilkinson married a second time, and resides in Hardin county, Ohio.

347. Levi K., born 1811, 11, 21. Married Rosater Yankey, and resides near Forsythe, Taney county, Missouri.

348. John, born 1814, 7, 28. Married —— Craig. John deceased. His widow married John Thompson, and resides in Madison, Ohio.

349. Abner, born 1818, 10, 29. Married 1844, 6, 18, to C. Werner. His address, New Baltimore, Ohio.

CHILDREN OF JAMES WINDER AND ANN KIRK (87).

350. Joseph, born 1805, 4, 22. Married 1828, 6, 10, to Amy (345), daughter of John and Mary Taylor.

351. James, born 1806, 6, 27. Married 1829, 10, 20, to Mary Swena. Mary was born 1813, 5, 10. James' address, Topeka, Kansas.

352. William, born 1808, 2, 2. Married Sybil Harrison. Both deceased.

353. Sarah, born 1810, 2, 7. Married 1828, 10, 28, to Charles Shreve. His address: Bloomfield, Crawford co., Pa.

354. Judith, born 1812, 4, 16. Married 1837, 9, —, to David Nash. David deceased. Judith married John Julion.

355. Eliza, born 1813, 12, 26. Married 1835, 11, 19, to Lemuel Swena. Their address, Rock Creek, Butler county, California.

356. Hannah, born 1815, 10, 5. Married 1842, 5, 26, to Alfred Green. Their address, Money Creek, Houston county, Minnesota.

357. Mary, born 1817, 6, 25. Married 1837, 1, 8, to Azzam Gillet. Their address, Pilot Grove, Cooper county, Mo.

358. Knight Kirk, born 1819, 5, 8. Married 1839, 4, 25. No children. His address, Kingsville, Ashtabula county, Ohio.

359. Susan, born 1822, 2, 4. Married Madison Alderman, 1838, 8, 24. Madison, born 1813, 8, 26. They resided at Haney's Valley, Crawford county, Wisconsin.

CHILDREN OF WILLIAM KIRK (89) AND ELIZABETH JORDAN.

360. Priscilla, born 1804, 5, 5. Married Abner Davis, 1820, 12, 31. Abner was a distinguished Baptist preacher and politician. At one time he was a candidate for Congress

in his district. He resided in the northern part of Kentucky, and was a Representative in the State Legislature.

361. Joseph, born 1805, 12, 12. Married 1827, 8, 2, to Janett Emmons. (Nothing further ascertained.)

362. Jane, born 1809, 2, 6. Married 1831, 12, 15, to Thomas B. Jones, of Popular Plains, Kentucky. Thomas is a farmer and school teacher. Has been a Justice of the Peace for twelve years.

363. Edward J., born 1812, 3, 2. Married 1834, 10, 9, to Lucinda Northcot. Edward is a minister in the Methodist Episcopal church, and is located at Valparaiso, Indiana.

364. Sarah A., born 1816, 8, 3. Married 1835, 3, 19, to John C. Hinton.

365. Eleanor M., born 1818, 10, 28. Married 1838, 2, 13, to David M. Williams. David resides in Kansas. Is a farmer.

366. Melinda D., born 1820, 8, 3. Married 1837, 10, 19, to John F. Summers. John deceased. He was by profession a physician, and at one time had a large practice.

367. Eliza, born 1821, 12, 7. Married 1841, 2, 21, to George Muse.

368. William G., born 1826, 5, 5. Married Julina Benton. He was a soldier in the Mexican war.

CHILDREN OF LEWIS BROOMFIELD AND SUSANNA KIRK (90).

369. Margaret, born 1807, 12, 12; died 1842, 12, 12. Married Caleb Winder.

370. Joseph K., born 1808, 10, 24; died 1847, 9, 19. Married Emeline Wells.

371. Eliza, born 1811, 5, 30. Married 1834, 3, 12, to Elihu Nash. P. O. address, Plymouth, Indiana.

372. Sarah A., born 1813, 6, 5. Married 1834, 10, 16, to

Thomas Maxwell. Thomas' address, Marboro, Stark county, Ohio.

373. Lewis M., born 1815, 12, 11. Married 1838, 6, 7, to Lydia Ingledue.

374. John, born 1817, 1, 15.

375. Judith, born 1819, 6, 15. Married 1837, 2, 2, to Thomas McCall. Thomas resides near Mt. Victory, Hardin county, Ohio.

376. Andrew, born 1823, 4, 25; died 1846, 4, 29.

377. Susan, born 1825, 7, 25; died 1850, 9, 7.

378. William, born 1828, 10, 6. P. O. address, Mt. Sterling, Brown county, Illinois.

CHILDREN OF DAVID WHITE AND RACHEL KIRK (92).

379. Ann, born ——, —, —; died ——, —, —. Never married.

380. Mary, born ——, —, —; died ——, —, —. Married William Plum, and moved West. (Nothing further ascertained.)

381. Absalom, born ——, —, —; died in infancy.

382. Jonathan, born ——, —, —; died in infancy.

383. Hannah, born ——, —, —; died in infancy.

384. David, born 1806, 1, 22; resides near Davisonville, Md.

385. Absalom K., born ——, —, —; died——, —, —. Had a son Absalom. (Nothing further ascertained of this branch of the family.)

386. Catharine, born ——, —, —. Married Henry Doughty.

387. Rachel, born ——, —, —. Married Isaac Nolan. Isaac died 1839.

388. Elizabeth, born ——, —, —. Married David Gilmore, and resided at Port Deposit, Md.

389. Rebecca, born ——, —, —. Died in infancy.

CHILDREN OF ELISHA ENGLAND AND MARY KIRK (93).

390. Ann, born 1791, 5, 20; died 1821, 2, 2. Married William M. Kirk (70), son of Levi and Amelia Kirk.

391. Sarah, born 1792, 12, 16; died ——, —, —. Married Jehu Brown.

392. George, born 1795, 12, 4. Married Mary Kirk (113) daughter of Jacob and Rachel Kirk.

393. Elizabeth, born 1798, 1, 23. Married Isaac Brown,

394. John, born 1800, 2, 8. Married Mary Kirk (433), 1826, 6, 22. John resides near Rising Sun. Is a farmer. He married a second wife, Sarah Gamble, 1843, 6, 15.

CHILDREN OF WILLIAM KIRK (94) AND LYDIA JOB.

395. Mary, born 1796, 3, 26 ; died 1855, 2, 8. Married 1818, 9, 17, to Nathan, son of William and Alice Griffith, of Nottingham, Md. Nathan resides at the Brick Meeting House.

396. Ann, born 1797, 9, 16. Resides with her sister, Hannah, near Brick Meeting House. They manufacture carpets.

397. Abner, born 1799, 10, 6 ; died 1806, 5 2.

398. Hannah, born 1801, 9, 24. Never married. Resides with Ann.

399. Jacob, born 1804, 1, 24; died 1857, 12, 1. Married 1842, 5, 5, to Hannah, daughter of Elisha and —— Brown. Hannah deceased.

CHILDREN OF WILLIAM KIRK (94) AND ELIZABETH HAINES (48).

400. Lewis, born 1807, 12, 20 ; died 1847, 10, 3. Married 1836, 3, 23, to Jane Hollingsworth, daughter of Joshua and Hannah Hollingsworth. Lewis moved to the West, where he died.

401. Job H., born 1809, 1, 10. Married Lydia, daughter of Samuel and Phebe Wilson. Lydia was born 1806, 10, 14. Job H. is a farmer, and resides on part of the homestead near Brick Meeting House, Md.

402. Joseph, born 1810, 3, 19; died 1864, 12, 15. Married 1836, 8, 25, to Jane S. (426), daughter of Abner and Sarah Kirk.

403. Lydia, born 1811, 6, 11; died 1832, 11, 24.

404. William A., born 1812, 12, 18. Married 1846, 5, 23. to Lydia Spenser, of Ohio. Lydia deceased. William married a second time, 1850, 4, 22, to Jane Kirk (formerly Hollingsworth), widow of his brother Lewis. William resides at Huntsville, Indiana.

405. Reuben, born 1814, 3, 20. Married 1841, 4, 22, to Hannah C., daughter of Thomas and Elizabeth Brown. Hannah, born 1821, 2, 9; and died 1868, 7, 27. Reuben is a farmer and resides east of Rising Sun, Cecil county, Md.

406. Esther E., born 1815, 7, 25. Married John (431), son of William and Elizabeth (Howell) Kirk. John is a machinist and blacksmith. He has worked at his trade for many years in Rising Sun village.

407. Infant son, born 1816, 9, 9; died in a few days after birth.

408. Mira, born 1817, 1, 19. Married 1849, 4, 19, to Alphonso C. (440), son of William and Sarah (Haines) Kirk.

409. Samuel, born 1819, 9, 16; died 1820, 2, 29.

410. Rachel, born 1821, 3, 2. Married Elwood, son of Samuel and Elizabeth Brown; Elwood dec'd. Rachel married Jacob, son of Daniel and Rachel Job. Jacob resides about two miles east of Rising Sun, Md. He has a farm and cooper shop.

411. Abner, born 1822, 9, 3. Married Mary (667), daugh-

ter of Isaac and Moriah England. Abner served as an apprentice to the tailoring business under Wm. Hutton, Esq., of Little Britain, Lancaster county. Serving his time, he returned to Maryland, and "set up" for himself. After the death of his father he took the home place, where he now resides. His wife, Mary, died 1863, 8, 2. Abner married again; second wife Hannah (284), daughter of John and Elizabeth Donohoo. Date of second marriage 1866, 4, 15.

412. Emeline, born 1825, 12, 26. Married 1863, 12, 31, to Samuel, son of Montillion and Ann Brown. Samuel, born 1821, 9, 22. P. O. address, Brick Meeting House, Md.

CHILDREN OF WILLIAM MILLER AND HANNAH KIRK (96).

413. Ann, born ——, —, —; died young.

414. Abner, born ——, —, —. Married, and resides at Mt. Pleasant, Ohio.

415. Joseph, born ——, —, —; deceased.

CHILDREN OF WILLIAM BROWN AND ELIZABETH KIRK (97).

416. Samuel, born ——, —, —; died ——, —, —. Married Eliza Leslie. Second marriage, to Susan Long. He resided in the neighborhood of Brick Meeting House, Md.

417. Mary, born ——, —, —; died young.

418. Abner, born ——, —, —. Married 1819, 7, 20, to Naomi, daughter of Israel and Jane Miller. Abner is a blacksmith, and removed to Little Britain, Lancaster county, Pa., in the year 1826. He worked at his trade for many years, at what is now known as Wakefield, Fulton township. He owns a farm, and resides near Penn Hill.

419. Mark, born ——, —, —; died ——, —, —. Married Lydia A. Brown, daughter of David and Rebecca.

420. Sarah, born ——, —, —. Married John Allen Brown.

421. Kirk, born ——, —, —. Moved to Queen Ann's county, Md. He became a virulent pro-slavery man, and during the occupation of his neighborhood by the Union soldiers, in the time of the great rebellion, he persisted in passing the lines. For his persistence he was shot.

422. Luke, born 1813, 7, 19. Married 1838, 4, 19, to Phebe, daughter of Samuel and Elizabeth Brown. She was born 1811; 7, 18. Luke is a plasterer, and resides in Rising Sun, Cecil county, Md. He now holds the office of school commissioner for that borough.

CHILDREN OF ABNER KIRK (99) AND SARAH STEVENSON.

423. Infant, born 1809, 1, 1; died ——, —, —.

424. John, born 1810, 3, 18; died ——, —, —. Was strangled by swallowing a bean.

425. Washington, born 1813, 2, 18. Married Maria Hagens. He resides in Baltimore.

CHILDREN OF ABNER KIRK (99) AND MARY M'CREA.

426. Jane S.. born 1815, 12, 19; died 1869, 8, 19. Married Joseph Kirk (402), son of William and Elizabeth.

427. William, born 1817, 9, 26. Married 1842, 2, 17, to Hannah B. England, daughter of Elisha and Elizabeth England. William resides at Brick Meeting House. He is a carpenter by trade.

CHILDREN OF WILLIAM KIRK (102) AND ELIZABETH HOWELL.

428. Ann, born 1794, 11, 14; died 1806, 3, 30.

429. Howell, born 1797, 12, 4. Married 1822, 6, 10, to Lydia, daughter of Nathan and Susan Harris. Lydia was born 1801, 1, 1, and died 1844, 10, 29.

430. Elizabeth, born 1799, 3, 17; died 1800, 8, 25.

431. John, born 1801, 1, 16. Married Esther Reynolds, daughter of Jacob and Esther Reynolds. Esther died 1840, 10, 1. John married Esther (406), daughter of William and Elizabeth Kirk. Resides at Rising Sun.

432. Nathaniel, born 1802, 12, 1. Married a Cameron.

433. Mary, born 1805, 1, 11; died 1841, 5, 8. Married 1826, 6, 22, to John (394), son of Elisha and Mary England.

434. Lydia, born 1806, 11, 2. Married William Mitchell. They reside in Wilmington, Del.

CHILDREN OF WILLIAM KIRK (102) AND SARAH HAINES.

435. Hannah, born 1809, 6, 23. Never married.

436. Jacob W., born 1810, 9, 27; died 1866, 2, 19. Married 1836, 11, 4, to Annie, daughter of Taylor and Eliza Reynolds. Jacob resided at Rising Sun.

437. Elizabeth, born 1812, 5, 5. Married 1842, 3, 10, to Job Gatchell.

438. William Haines, born 1813, 8, 12. Married 1836, 4, 20, to Sarah Brown. Sarah deceased. W. Haines married Mary E. House. At one time was engaged in the mercantile business at Nottingham. From thence removed to Philadelphia, where he commenced the commission business. He resides at 1228 Market street, and is one of the firm of Kirk and Brown, commission merchants.

439. Rufus M., born 1815, 6, 5. Married 1836, 6, 14, to Mary Brown. Mary deceased. Married 1855, 8, 9, to Mary M. Long.

440. Alphoso C., born 1818, 6, 24. Married 1849, 4, 19, to Mira Kirk, (408) daughter of William and Elizabeth.

CHILDREN OF JEHU BROWN AND LYDIA KIRK (103).

441. Absalom, born 1799, —, —; died ——, —, —. Married 1824, —, —, to Phebe Lewis. He resided in Wilmington, Delaware.

442. Sarah, born ——, —, —; died ——, —, —.

443. Ann, born 1811, 5, 3. Married 1841, 8, 12, to Amasa Churchman. He resided near North East Creek, not far from Brick Meeting House. Amasa was born 1818, 6, 30; and died ——, —, —. Ann still resides on the farm of her husband.

CHILDREN OF ELISHA KIRK (106) AND ELIZABETH WOOLISTON.

444. William, born 1808, 4, 9.

445. Jacob, born 1809, 10, 22. Married 1838, 1, 23, to Frances Whittaker. Frances died 1840, 10, 25. Jacob married a second time. Second marriage, 1844, 6, 25, to Clarissa Whittaker.

446. Ann, born 1811, 4, 4. Residing near Farmington, Maryland.

447. Abner, born 1813, 10, 14. Married 1843, 7, 31, to Mary E. Miller.

448. George, born 1815, 7, 10; died 1851, 10, 15.

449. Maria, born 1818, 2, 16.

450. Elizabeth, born 1820, 7, 30. Married 1840, 9, 3, to Augustus G., son of Benjamin and Nancy Pierson. Augustus born 1817, 8, 31.

CHILDREN OF THOMAS SLICER AND DEBORAH KIRK (108).

451. Joseph, born 1808, 1, 8; died 1828, 7, 6.

452. Elizabeth, born 1809, 10, 24. Married Samuel Harris. Post-office address, Brick Meeting House, Md.

453. Rachel, born 1811, 8, 10; died 1847, 5, 5. Married

Hugh Armor. They had one child. (Nothing further ascertained.)

454, Sarah A., born 1813, 7, 17. Married 1845, 6, 12, to Capt. William Wilson. He died 1861, 11, 30. Sarah married 1864, 10, 27, to John C. Hamer.

455. Deborah, born 1815, 10, 14. Married Allen (114), son of Elisha and Mary Kirk.

456. Harriet, born 1817, 11, 14. Married Thomas Brabson. No children.

457. Mary, born 1820, 2, 6. Married 1842, 6, 28, to Roswell Wakeman. Roswell was born 1812, 9, 14, in Chenango county, New York. He has a position on the Baltimore Central Rail Road.

458. Samuel, born 1822, 5, 14. Married Priscilla Pyle, of Cecil county, Md., daughter of Jesse and Sarah.

459. Jacob, born 1824, 5, 29. Married 1858, 2, 12, to Mary E. Nicoles, of Rising Sun, Md. Mary died 1863, 7, 28.

460. John I., born 1826, 10, 31. Married 1851, 10, 2, to Martha J. Reed. She was born 1828, 1, 8.

461. Elisha, born 1829, 3, 20; died 1860, 3, 10. Not married.

CHILD OF LEVI KIRK AND RACHEL KIRK (109). See (58).

CHILDREN OF JACOB KIRK (111) AND SOPHIA BROWN.

462. Allen, born 1812, 5, 12; died in infancy.

463. Rebecca, born 1814, 12, 17. Married 1837, 6, 29, to Joseph Miller. Joseph resided in West Nottingham, Chester county. He was murdered 1852, 1, 2, near Stemmer's Run Station, on the Philadelphia, Wilmington and Baltimore Railroad, two miles east of Baltimore. Joseph, in company with several citizens of West Nottingham, went down to Baltimore to rescue a colored woman named Parker, who had been

kidnapped from his neighborhood. He was returning home in the cars. Stepping out on the platform, he was seized by a squad of pro-slavery assassins, killed, and his body, by passing a hankerchief around the neck, suspended to a small tree. He was discovered next morning and the body taken to Baltimore. After considerable trouble his friends secured his body, and brought it to House's Meeting House, where it was interred.

464. Rachel, born 1816, 11, 13. Not married. Resides near Hilaman's inn, where she and sister keep a notion store.

465. Levi, born 1818, 12, 11; died ——, —, —. No children.

466. Jesse B., born 1820, 2, 10. Married Sabina Wright (471), daughter of David and Hannah. Jesse resides at Glen Roy, Chester county. Is a merchant and blacksmith; he is also postmaster at that place. They have no children.

467. Mary B., born 1824, 1, 23. Not married.

468. Hannah A., born 1826, 8, 26.

469. Jacob A., born 1828, 9, 28. Married, ——, —, —, to Jane Pollock. He resides near Stubb's mill, West Nottingham. Is a farmer. Has several children. (Nothing further ascertained of his family.)

470. Sophia C., born 1834, 5, 19. Married Lewis McElrath. They reside in the vicinity of Farmington.

CHILD OF DAVID WRIGHT AND HANNAH KIRK (112).

471. Sabina, born 1815, 7, 10. Married Israel Pierce. He died. Sabina married Jesse B. (466), son of Jacob and Sophia Kirk. They reside at Glen Roy, Pa.

CHILDREN OF GEORGE ENGLAND AND MARY KIRK (113).

472. Rachel, born ——, —, —. Married Charles Gamble, and resides near Port Deposit, Md.

473. Hannah, born ——, —, —; died in infancy.

474. Mary, born ——, —, —. Married Jonathan Brown.

475. Kirk, born ——, —, —. Married Maria Pierson, and resides in Iowa.

476. Haines, born ——, —, —. Not married.

477. Townsend, born ——, —, —. Married Eliza Grant.

478. Sarah, born ——, —, —. Married Taylor Janney.

CHILDREN OF ALLEN KIRK (114) AND MARTHA M'CULLOUGH.

479. Evander, born 1814, 5, 26; died 1823, 8, 27.

480. James R., born 1815, 1, 4; died 1850, 2, 3. No children.

481. Benjamin F., born 1817, 4, 8. Married Elizabeth Carothers.

482. Rebecca, born 1819, 2, 15. Married 1839, 6, 11, to James Cameron.

483. Elijah, born 1820, 8, 27; died 1850, 5, 5.

484. Jesse A., born 1822, 6, 22. Married 1856, 3, 21, to Hannah Mount. Jesse was, for a number of years, engaged in the mercantile business at Rising Sun; also, concerned in an iron foundry located in that village. He represented his district in the House of Delegates. At the present time he resides in Rising Sun, and has a hardware and tinware store.

485. Martha J., born 1824, 1, 21; died 1852, 3, 28. Not married.

486. William A., born 1826, 3, 28; died 1850, 1, 1.

487. Lemuel, born 1827, 3, 15; died 1827, 6, 22.

488. Mary A., born 1828, 3, 27; died 1837, 10, 20.

489. John, born 1829, 9, 24. Married 1853, 10, 20, to Margaret Carothers.

CHILDREN OF ALLEN KIRK (114) AND DEBORAH SLICER (455).

490. Joseph T., born 1853, 4, 29.
491. Isaac N., born 1854, 5, 21; died 1863, 3, 22.
492. Nathan, born 1856, 3, 11; died 1861, 4, 24.
493. Delia, born 1859, 7, 29.

CHILDREN OF JONATHAN KIRK (115) AND MARY THOMPSON.

494. William T., born 1815, 11, 13. Married Louisa Riddle. Louisa, born 1821, 5, 17. They reside in Rockford, Ill.

495. Jonathan H., born 1817, 8, 31. Married Marcella Dennis. She was born 1819, 3, 18. They reside in the town of Rockford, Ill.

496. Elisha A., born 1819, 3, 19. Married Rachel Dennis. Rachel, born 1824, 1, 28. They reside in Rockford, Illinois.

CHILDREN OF WM. KIRK (116) AND CATHARINE SELHEIMER.

497. Isabella, born 1823, 6, 24. Not married.

498. Columbus, born 1825, 1, 22; died 1866, 9, 25, in New York.

CHILDREN OF WILLIAM KIRK (116) AND RACHEL PIERSON.

499. William A., born 1835, 10, 30; died 1839, 3, 3.
500. Henry Broughton, born 1838, 1, 29.
501. Elisha A., born 1840, 4, 3; died 1845, 8, 8.
502. Mary R., born 1841, 11, 29; died 1845, 7, 20.
503. William T., born 1843, 9, 10; died 1843, 9, 24.
504. Ann, born 1844, 9, 24; died 1844, 9, 24.
505. Mary E., born 1845, 10, 5.
506. William, born 1849, 7, 8; died 1850, 6, 15.

CHILDREN OF JOSEPH KIRK (117) AND ELIZA SCOTT.

507. Mary E., born 1820, 5, 30. Married Samuel, son of Ephraim and Barbara Blackburn. Samuel deceased. Mary

resides at the residence of her late husband near, Glen Roy, Chester county, Pa.

508. James Scott, born 1822, 12, 20. Married 1868, 5, 11, to Martha J., daughter of Samuel and Eliza M. Neeper, of Fulton, Lancaster county, Pa. James has been engaged for a number of years in buying and selling cattle. He owns a farm near Lewisville, but resides in the borough of Oxford, Chester county, Pa.

509. Amanda, born 1825, 9, 9. Married Ephraim, son of Samuel and Barbara Blackburn. Ephraim resides on a farm near Glen Roy, West Nottingham, Pa.

510. William T., born 1828, 3, 7. Married 1871, 1, 19, to —— Brown, daughter of Jacob and Jane Brown. He resides with his father at Kirk's Bridge, Chester county, Pa.

Margaret A., born 1830, 8, 10. Unmarried. Resides at her father's, near Kirk's Bridge.

511. Rachel T., born 1833, 9, 4. Married John T., son of John and Rachel Kimble. John is a farmer by occupation, and resides on a farm near Nottingham Station, Chester county.

Joseph, born 1836, 5, 4; died in infancy.

Elisha, born 1839, 7, 5. Unmarried. Resides at Kirk's Bridge, West Nottingham, Chester county. By occupation he is a farmer.

512. Hannah A., born 1842, 10, 13. Married William T., son of Jefferson and Nancy Fulton, of East Nottingham, Chester county, Pa.

William T. was born in West Nottingham, on the 27th of February, 1835. He received a common school education, and then attended an academy, conducted by Evan Pugh. In the spring of 1852 he commenced learning the trade of a blacksmith, and worked at the business about four years, when he resolved to desert the hammer and anvil, and enter one of "the learned professions." With this object in view, in the fall of 1856, he entered the office of Hon. Thaddeus Stevens, at Lancaster, and remained there eighteen months. During this time he was an assiduous student; but his limited circumstances prevented him from completing his studies in the usual period allotted to the study of the law.

Leaving Mr. Stevens' office, he taught school and pursued his studies at intervals. On the 13th of May, 1861, he was admitted to the bar of Chester county. Soon afterward he opened an office at Oxford, in that county. The rebellion breaking out, and clients being scarce, young Fulton threw down his law-tomes, and entered the service. He assisted in raising a company, and on the 1st of September, 1861, was mustered into the service of the U. S. as Captain of Co. E., Purnell Legion, Md. Vol. He remained in the army until the last of January, 1863, when he was honorably discharged on "account of disability." While in the army, he took part in many engagements in the Shenandoah valley and Eastern Virginia. At the battle of Antietam he held the third position in his regiment. The colonel and lieutenant-colonel being absent, the command of the regiment devolved upon Major Fulton (he having been promoted previous to this battle). It was ordered into action at sunrise of that day, and remained under fire until one o'clock P. M., During this battle many of those in the regiment were killed, and wounded, but Major Fulton came out of the action unscathed. Since the war he has resided in the borough of Oxford, where he practices his profession.

CHILDREN OF NATHAN KIRK (118) AND CATHARINE WHITE.

513. Edwin R., born 1834, 3, 17. Married Mary Sawyer, and removed from the vicinity of Port Clinton, Ohio, to Sioux City, Iowa. He is extensively engaged in the lumber trade.

514. Charles, born 1836, 5, 13; died 1863, 11, 23. Not married.

515. E. Granville, born 1839, 2, 7. Married Alice A. Kirk (942), daughter of Theodore J. Kirk and Lucinda, of Elmore, Ottawa county, Ohio. E. Granville resides in Sioux City, Iowa, where he is extensively engaged in the mercantile business.

516. Cornelia, born 1841, 4, 20. Married James Thomas. They reside at Elmore, Ohio.

517. John M., born 1843, 10, 23; died 1845, 6, 21.

518. Ellis, born 1846, 5, 25.

519. Mary, born 1847, 9, 27; died ——, —, —.

520. Nathan Allen, born 1849, 10, 20.

521. William Webster, born 1852, 11, 24.

522. Eveline, born 1856, 3, 16.

523. Eunice, born 1858, 7, —.

CHILD OF ELISHA HAINES AND HANNAH KIRK (120).

☞ See 50.

CHILDREN OF ABEL CAMPBELL AND SUSANNA DIXON (122).

524. Elizabeth, born 1792, 1, 17; died 1855, 10, 16. Married 1810, 5, —, to Samuel Mitchell, of Uniontown, Fayette county, Pa. Samuel is a blacksmith.

525. Joseph, born 1794, 1, 5; died 1794, 1, 9.

526. Lewis, born 1794, 12, 27. Married 1823, 4, 10, to Deborah, daughter of Caleb and Martha Antrim, of Fayette county, Pa. She was born 1801, 1, 18. Post Office address, New Salem, Fayette county, Pa.

527. William, born 1797, 4, 18; died 1863, 9, 24. Married 1824, 3, 7, to Mary Nixon, daughter of William and Frances, of Fayette county. Mary, born 1805, 7, 7. They removed to Van Buren county, Iowa, in 1844.

528. James, born 1799, 10, 22. Married 1829, 1, 22, to Rebecca Hanshaw, daughter of William and Ann, of Fayette county. She was born 1808, 3, 15. They removed to Van Buren county, Iowa, in 1855. Address, Sheriden.

529. Mary, born 1802, 3, 1. Married 1826, 3, 2, to William Price, son of William and Hannah, of Fayette county. William, born 1796, 10, 21. Address, Redstone, Fayette county.

530. Susanna, born ——, —, —. Is married, but her residence is unknown.

531. Abel, born ——, —, —. Married Eliza Woodward, and resides at Ottawa, Illinois.

532. Ellis, born ——, —, —. Married Lydia Stone. Their address, Carmichaeltown, Green county, Pa.

CHILDREN OF WILLIAM DIXON (125) AND JESSE MADISON.

533. Sarah, born ——, —, —. Married Jessie Johnson, of Fayette county.

534. Thomas, born ——, —, —.

535. Samuel, born ——, —, —.

536. William, born ——, —, —. Married —— Ramage.

537. Hannah, born ——, —, —. Married —— Aikens.

538. Susan, born ——, —, —.

539. Joseph, born ——, —, —.

All these, except Sarah, went to Ohio with their parents.

CHILDREN OF NATHAN SHARPLESS AND LYDIA PAINTER (127).

540. Joseph, born 1799, 3, 19; died 1833, 12, 27. Never married.

541. Edith, born 1797, 2, 2; died 1867, 8, 20. Married 1824, 3, 3, at Concord Meeting to George Martin, of Upper Chichester, son of George and Elizabeth. George was born

1787, 2, 28; died 1847, 7, 26. She married again, 1864, 5, 4, at Concord, to John Bennington, of Thornbury, Delaware county, Pa.

542. Elizabeth, born 1801, 8, 17; died 1844, 8, 19. Married 1824, 5, 8, at Concord, to Ferree Brinton, of Strasburg, Lancaster county, son of William and Lydia. Ferree was born 1800, 10, 9. He was elected Associate Judge of the several Courts of Lancaster county, and held this position until failing health admonished him to retire from the bench. He lives on a fine farm named Belmont.

CHILDREN OF ELI HARVEY AND MARY PAINTER (128).

543. Hannah, born 1802, 6, 4. Married 1821, 1, 23, to Robert Pierce, son of Thomas and Margaret, of Thornbury. Robert, born 1797, 4, 11. They joined the Mormons, settling at Nauvoo, and from thence removing to Salt Lake.

544. Joseph P., born 1803, 10, 16; died 1863, 4, 15. Married 1827, to Lydia, daughter of Thomas and Mary Hoopes. She died 1863, 10, 6. Residence, Birmingham, Delaware county, Pa.

545. Amos, born ——, —, —; died 1861. Unmarried.

546. Eli, born 1811, 4, 6; died in infancy 1812, 1, 17.

CHILDREN OF JOSEPH PAINTER (130) AND LYDIA MARSHALL.

547. Mary Ann, born 1806, 7, 11; died 1809, 11, 11.

548. Rachel M., born 1808, 4, 17; died 1865, 11, 15. Unmarried.

549. Samuel M., born 1809, 9, 16. Married 1833, 10, 17, at Uwchlan Meeting, to Ann Vickers, of Uwchlan, daughter of John and Abigail. Abigail, born 1810, 2, 26. They reside in West Chester, Pa.

550. Elizabeth P., born 1813, 5, 31; died 1863, 9, 8. Mar-

ried Joseph Vickers, son of John and Abigail. Joseph, born 1811, 10, 1; died 1864, 2, 4.

551. Lydia S., 1815, 8, 3; died 1832, , 11,24, at Westtown boarding school. Interred at West Chester, Pa.

552. Sarah, born 1816, 12, 8; died 1817, 6, 30; buried at Birmingham.

553. Joseph H., born 1818, 10, 5. Married 1840, 2, 19, at Bradford Meeting, to Esther Kersey, daughter of Joseph and Charity, and granddaughter of Jesse Kersey. They have resided at various places. At the present time, in Richmond, Va.

554. Mary H., born 1820, 9, 30. Married 1840, 12, 30, to Chalkley M. Valentine, son of John and Asenath. Chalkley born 1819, 2, 13. He is a dentist, and resides in Maryland.

555. James G., born 1823, 5, 12. Married Mary H. Pierce, and resides in Maryland.

556. Cyrus P., born 1825, 11, 20. Married Abigail A. Allison, daughter of Oliver, of Uwchlan, where they reside.

557. Thomas, born 1830, 7, 7, in West Chester, where he now resides.

CHILDREN OF ISAAC PIERCE AND ELIZABETH PAINTER (131).

558. Sarah Elizabeth, born 1811, 1, 11. Married James Michener, of Ohio, son of William and Ann, of Bucks county and Chester county, Pa. James was born 1802, 3, 18. He was a widower, with eight children: by occupation a farmer. They removed in the spring of 1869 from Akron, Ohio, to Stevensburg, Culpepper county, Virginia. They have no children.

559 Alfred B., born 1812, 9, 12. Married Hannah Fisher. Second wife, Margaret Elizabeth Borden, daughter of Isaac and Elizabeth, of Salem, Ohio. She was born 1827,

7, 26, in Conhocton, Steuben county, N. Y. Married 1845, 2, 21, at Enon Valley, by Isaac Newton, Esq. Their present address, Massillon, Ohio.

560. Joseph, born 1814, 6, 17, died 1815, 5, 25.

CHILDREN OF BENJ. SWAYNE AND SUSANNA WOODWARD(132).

561. William, born 1802, 11, 4; died 1838, 8, 7, in East Marlborough. Married 1126, 10, 18, at London Grove, to Mary Ann Marshall, of East Marlborough, daughter of Jacob and Elizabeth. They reside in Pennsbury twp. Mary Ann deceased.

562. Joel, born 1804, 5, 22; died 1840, 5, 9. Married 1827, 10, 11, at West Grove Meeting, to Lydia Ann Jackson, daughter of Israel and Sarah, of London Grove. Lydia Ann was born 1810, 2, 2; died 1846, 10, 5. They resided in East Marlborough, where Joel died. He was a member of the State Legislature, and an estimable citizen. He left no children. His widow married 1844, 3, 14, to John Barnard, of West Marlborough.

563. Susanna, born 1806, 2, 25; died 1836, 9, 11. Married 1827, 10, 11, at London Grove, to Jacob Hayes, of Brandywine Hundred, Del., son of Mordecai and Mary. Jacob married a second time; second wife, Caroline Phillips, daughter of —— and —— Phillips. Jacob resides in Newlin twp., where he superintends and owns two farms. He is the sole manufacturer of the celebrated "Brandywine Whetstones." The quarry is situated on his "upper place."

CHILDREN OF SAMUEL WOODWARD (134) AND ANN SWAYNE.

564. Margaret, born 1801, 2, 5. Married 1821, 4, 11, at Centre Meeting, to John Kinsey, of Christiana Hundred, Del., son of John and Margaret. Margaret resides at No. 449, North Fifth street, Philadelphia.

565. Joel, born 1803, 4, 7; died 1804, 5, 22. Interred at London Grove.

566. Sarah, born 1804, 11, 16. Married 1827, 2, 15, at Centre Meeting, to William E. Bailey, of West Marlborough, son of William and Tacey. William born 1804, 1, 2; died 1855, 10, 21. They settled in West Marlborough, near London Grove Meeting House, in 1842, where Sarah now resides.

567. Mary Ann, born 1808, 11, 22; died 1825, 9, 27. Unmarried. Buried at Centre.

568. Susanna, born 1811, 3, 29. Married 1836, 12, 29, to Richard B. Smedley, son of John and Mary. They reside in Willistown twp., Chester county.

569. Rachel, born 1814, 4, 5; died 1868, 5, 22. Married 1832, 12, 13, at Centre Meeting, to Thomas Chandler, of Christiana Hundred, son of Jesse and Rebecca. He was born 1811, 9, 22. They removed to Wilmington, Delaware, in 1859, where Thomas now resides.

CHILDREN OF JOHN FELL AND SARAH WOODWARD (135).

570. Joel, born in New London twp., Chester county, 1801, 11, 30; died 1806, 4, 23. Interred at West Grove.

571. Rachel, born 1804, 3, 9; died 1826, 9, 8. Buried at West Nottingham. Married 1821, 11, 15, at West Grove Meeting, to Isaac Chambers, of London Grove, son of Joshua and Rebecca. He was born 1797, 5, 7; died 1862, 11, 2. Buried at New Garden. Isaac was a wheelwright and resided in Maryland at the time of Rachel's decease. Afterward he returned to Chester county. He married a second wife—Susanna Bell—in 1829.

572. Samuel, born 1807, 8, 24; died 1851, 3, 6. Buried at West Grove. Married 1829, 6, 11, at West Grove Meeting, to Patience Chambers, daughter of Joshua and Rebecca,

of London Grove. She was born in 1807, 12, 26. They resided for some time in New London township. Patience now lives in London Grove township. Address, West Grove Post-office.

CHILDREN OF WILLIAM WOODWARD (136) AND SARAH BOLTON.

573. John J., born 1812, 11, 23. Married 1838, 11, 7, at Concord Meeting, to Hannah Mattson, of Concord, daughter of Levi and Rebecca. She was born 1816, 8, 7. He is a farmer, and resides in Kennett, twp., Chester county, Pa.

574. Washington B., born 1814, 5, 29; died 1844, 12, 14. Married Edith B., daughter of Jacob Lamborn. She resides in Philadelphia.

275. Isaac, born 1817, 12, 21. Married Hannah, daughter of John Sharpless. He removed to Ohio about 1850, but has since migrated further West. His present residence not ascertained.

CHILDREN (F THOMAS WOODWARD (137) AND MARY BARNEY

576. Eliza, born 1810, 9, 15. Married 1830, 3, 11, at Kennett Square, to Gibbons Kendall of East Marlborough, son of John and Mary. She was born 1801, 12, 23, in Lancaster county, and died 1864, 5, 8, in Mill Creek Hundred, Delaware, and interred at Hokessin.

577. Phebe A., born 1812, 3, 6. Lives in Kennett Square. Unmarried.

578. Jackson, born 1814, 12, 27. Married 1838, 3, 8, at Birmingham Meeting, to Sybilla T. Entriken, of East Bradford, daughter of Emmor and Ann. She was born 1815, 11, 14. He is a farmer living near Russellville, Chester co.

579. Mabel, born 1820, 3, 31. Married Emmor S. Entriken, son of Emmor and Ann of East Bradford. Emmor

was born 1818, 3, 15. He is a saddle and harness maker in West Chester.

580. Lewis B., born 1827, 5, 10. Married 1849, 4, 26, to Elizabeth S. Witsil of Wilmington, Delaware. They reside at Harrisburg, Pa.

CHILDREN OF LEVI WOODWARD (138) AND PHEBE HUTTON.

581. Sarah H., born 1817, 2, 16. Married 1847, 12, 23, to Edward McGee, who was born in Philadelphia, 1810, 4, 11. In 1823 he was bound to Smith Sharpless, of East Goshen, to learn farming; went to York county, 1846, and lived for a time with George M. Hickman. He now resides on a farm of 53 acres, situated near McCall's Ferry on the Susquehanna.

582. Isaac J., born 1818, 8, 10; dec'd. Unmarried.

583. Sybilla, born 1820, 4, 1. Married 1845, 6, 11, to Matthew Sample. He was born 1817, 10, 29, in Lancaster co., and moved to York county, in 1844, and is now settled on a farm. He is a mason by occupation.

584. Samuel, born 1821, 12, 16. Married 1861, 8, 29, to Margaret Dickey. He is a farmer and lives at the homestead.

585. Joseph, born 1823, 5, 7; dec'd. Never married.

586. Cassandra, born 1825, 7, 1; dec'd. Never married.

587. Hadassah, born 1827, 9, 16; dec'd. Never married.

588. Ann Eliza, born 1832, 6, 16; died 1865, 1, 31. Married 1864, 1, 18, to Robt. B. Ailes, of Lancaster county. He was a farmer. Died 1865, 10, 15. No children.

CHILDREN OF LEVI WICKERSHAM AND RACHEL WOODWARD, (139.)

589. Thomas, born 1811, 7, 3. Married 1835, 10, 15, at West Grove Meeting House, to Priscilla, daughter of Joseph and Elizabeth Jones, of New Garden. Post-office address, West Grove Chester county.

590. Sarah, born 1815, 8, 15. Married 1838, 4, 11, at Sadsbury Meeting, to Andrew Moore, of Sadsbury, Lancaster county; son of Andrew and Anna. He was born 1805, 11, 10. Is a farmer by occupation, and resides near Christiana, Lancaster county.

591. John, born 1818, 12, 6; died 1839, 8, 18. Unmarried.

592. Preston, born 1820, 12, 3. Married 1849, 5, 31, to Rebecca Chambers, daughter of Isaac and Rachel. They resided in Sadsbury township, Chester county, for some time, but removed to West Marlborough township, in 1869.

593. Levi, born 1828, 1, 22. Married in Detroit, Michigan, to Angeline P. Russell. They now reside in Philadelphia, Pa., at No. 459 North Eighth street.

CHILDREN OF LEWIS WOODWARD (141) AND SARAH SHIPLEY.

594. Samuel S., born 1822, 8, 10; died 1842, 11, 17. Unmarried. He was a school teacher by vocation.

595. Louisa, born 1824, 8, 12; died 1845, 6, 26, in Londonderry township. Married in 1844, 1, 18, to Harvey S. Stackhouse, of New Garden, son of Silas and Mary. He was born 1821, 12, 27; is a farmer, and resides in New Garden township; is married a second time.

CHILD OF ELISHA SPEAKMAN AND HANNAH WOODWARD (142.)

596. Anna Mary, born 1844, 5, 24. Not married. Her vocation is teaching, and she is now engaged in this profession at West Chester, Pa.

CHILDREN OF STEPHEN PUSEY AND ELIZABETH WOODWARD (143).

597. Philena, born 1825, 6, 17, in East Marlborough; died 1864, 10, 13. Married 1853, to Enoch Hannum, of Londonderry. No children.

598. David, born 1827, 5, 31, in East Marlborough. Married 1856, 12, 3, to Edith G. Hoopes, daughter of Garrett and Hannah, of East Bradford. She was born 1835, 3, 9; died 1869, 8, 5. David has lived on rented farms in various parts of Chester county. At present in Willistown twp.

599. Lewis, born 1829, 11, 11, in East Marlborough; died 1835, 3, 28.

600. Phebe A., born 1837, 4, 3, in West Fallowfield. Married 1868, 3, 12, to Edwin S. Walton, son of Isaac and Martha, of London Grove. He was born 1840, 5, 1.

601. Samuel W., born 1839, 6, 13, in West Fallowfield. Married 1864, 12, 8, to Sarah, daughter of Garrett and Hannah Hoopes, of East Bradford. She was born 1837, 11, 23; died 1865, 11, 26, in West Chester. Samuel married a second time, 1869, 3, 4, to Sarah R. Sill of Edgemont, Delaware county. She was born in 1852, —, —. He now resides in Thornbury twp., Delaware county.

CHILDREN OF ELI SWAYNE AND DEBORAH WOODWARD (147).

602. Hannah, born 1808, 7, 5; died 1808, 7, 22.

603. Joel W., born 1810, 5, 29. Married 1839, to Susan Cunningham. They reside in Philadelphia.

604. Thomas P., born 1812, 7, 3; died 1813, 9, 21.

605. Deborah A., born 1813, 12, 22; died 1814, 10, 26.

CHILDREN OF JOSEPH HAWLEY AND ELIZABETH WOODWARD (148.)

606. George W., born 1817, 2, 26. Lives in West Chester. Unmarried. May be termed an amateur machinist.

607. Thomas P., born 1818, 6, 1. Married, 1855, 11, 28, to Anna M. Palmer, daughter of John and Sarah, of West Bradford. She was born 1824, 9, 17. They reside in West Chester. Thomas owns a grist and saw mill near the borough.

608. Lydia, born 1820, 8, 18. Resides with her brother George. Unmarried.

609. Joseph, born 1824, 2, 15. Died in infancy.

CHILDREN OF ELLIS WOODWARD (149) AND RACHEL WOODWARD.

610. Pusey, born 1823, 9, 4; died 1826, 7, 16.

611. Sarah, born 1826, 11, 25. Married 1847, 10, 20, to John Byerly, son of David and Rachel, of Wallace twp., Chester county. On account of ill treatment from her husband, Sarah obtained a divorce, and was afterward married, 1857, 3, 12, to Aaron Commons, son of John and Lydia. They live in East Marlborough. Aaron is a farmer by occupation.

612. Mary, born 1828, 5, 8.

613. Lea P., born 1832, 5, 6. Married 1852, 11, 10, to Clara Everson. He is a clerk, and resides in Philadelphia.

614. Lydia, born 1836, 6, 3. Married 1859, 12, 31, to Robert Bruce, shoemaker, son of Ebenezer and Ann, of East Fallowfield. He is foreman in a rolling mill near Coatesville, Pa.

615. Ellis, born 1839, 8, 8.

CHILD OF JOSHUA WOODWARD (152) AND REBECCA NUTT.

616. Mary, born 1822, 12, 8. Married 1855, 1, 9, in Philadelphia, to Caleb Wood. Caleb is a grocer and successful merchant, No. 524 South Second street, Philadelphia. No children.

CHILDREN OF JOSHUA WOODWARD (152) and REBECCA LEWIS.

617. Owen Lewis, born 1829, 8, 12. Married 1855, 10, 2, to Sarah Ralston, daughter of George and Hannah. She was born 1831, 2, 13. Their address, Chester Springs, Chester-co

618. Sarah Ann, born 1831, 10, 26. Married 1858, 12, 30, to Nathan G. Buckwalter, son of Christopher and Mary Nathan, born 1826, 6, 12. They live on French Creek, about four miles from Phœnixville, Chester county.

619. Joshua P., born 1833, 5, 27.

CHILDREN OF WILLIAM KENT AND ANN WOODWARD (153).

620. Esther H., born 1819, 8, 26; died 1843, 5, 19. Buried at Penn's Grove.

621. Thomas W., born 1821, 5, 19; died 1847, 4, 20. Buried at Penn's Grove, Chester county.

622. Mary Ann, born 1823, 6, 20. Married 1851, 3, 12, at her father's, in Upper Oxford, to Charles Plumley, of Upper Oxford, son of Robt. and Ann, of Penn's Grove. He was born 1823, 1, 4. They now reside in London Grove village, Chester county, Pa.

623. Elizabeth, born 1826, 1, 20; died 1863, 3, 2. Buried at Penn's Grove. Unmarried.

624. Daniel, born 1828, 7, 29. Married 1853, 12, 8, to Margaret Broomer. They reside in Nottingham township, Chester county.

625. William, born 1832, 9, 24. Married 1863, 11, 27, to Mary F. Kinsey, daughter of John R. and Elizabeth L. They reside in East Nottingham.

626. Lewis P., born 1836, 9, 13; died 1843, 9, 4. Interred at Penn's Grove.

CHILDREN OF JOHN W. SMITH (155) AND ALICE WILKINSON.

627. Elizabeth, born 1814, 9, 24. Married 1837, 9, 7, to Charles W. McGeath. They reside in Henry county, Ind.

628. Mary, born 1817, 8, 28. Married 1834, 10, 29, to Thorban W. Smith. Post-office address, Dublin, Wayne county, Ind.

629. Sarah Anne, born 1821, 8, 4. Married 1838, 7, 5, to Mahlon W. Pickering. Residence, Wayne county, Ind.

630. Thomas Wilkinson, born 1823, 10, 11. Married 1844, 6, 6, to Rachel Lewis. She died 1860, 4, 13. Thomas married Louisa Pratt. Residence in Henry county, Ind.

☞ Three other members of this family died in infancy.

SIXTH GENERATION.

CHILDREN OF JEREMIAH B. HAINES (156) AND MABEL HUTTON.

631. Margaretta, born 1820, 8, 16. Married Jeremiah (245), son of Slater and Mary (Kirk) Brown.

632. Sarah, born 1822, 11, 19. Married Andrew Lewis. They resided east of Peach Bottom, Lancaster county. Andrew has been engaged in mercantile business for many years. He owns a store, and is, at the present time, engaged in the manufacture of slate at Peach Bottom, being one of the firm of Lewis & Dorsey.

633. Esther, born 1824, 12, 21; died in infancy.

634. William P., born 1825, 12, 25. Married Mary (217) daughter of Jacob and Hannah Kirk, of Kirk's Mills, Lancaster county. William has been engaged in store keeping, at Kirk's Mills at intervals, amounting to some five years. From this place he moved to a farm in Little Britain. Disposing of this he has returned to Pleasant Grove, where he is now engaged in keeping store.

635. Milton, born 1828, 6, 7; died 1855, 10, 21. Milton studied medicine under direction of Jeremiah B. Stubbs, M. D.; attended one course of medical lectures at the University of Maryland in Baltimore, and another at the medical department of the University of New York. He graduated at

the latter named institution, in the spring of 1852. Soon after graduating he took a voyage to California and Oregon. Returning home he located and commenced the practice of his profession at Battle Swamp, Cecil county, Md. About four months after locating at this place, he was admonished that phthisis, inherited from his maternal ancestors, was making inroads upon his constitution. He returned home to his father's, at Pleasant Grove, where he died.

636. Albert, born 1830, 5, 17. Married Hannah, daughter of Morris and Eleanor Jackson, of Fulton, Lancaster county. He is a farmer and resides on one of his father-in-law's farms.

637. Merrit S., born 1832, 11, 23. Not married. For several years Merrit has resided at Clear Springs, Washington county, Md., where he is engaged in keeping store and managing an interest in an iron furnace.

638. Mabel, born 1835, 7, 11; died 1857, 9, 21. Unmarried.

CHILDREN OF JEREMIAH B. HAINES (156) AND SARAH (ROMAN) THOMAS.

639. Rebecca, born 1842, 5, 25; died 1848, 5, 30.

640. Louisa, born 1844, 6, 7; died 1858, 9, 20.

641. Joseph, born 1847, 10, 20; resides near Clear Spring, Md. Is engaged in keeping store.

642. Rebecca, born 1851, 7, 19; died 1860, 6, 10.

CHILDREN OF EDWIN HAINES (158) AND MARGARET HUTTON.

643. Job, born 1823, 7, 8. Married Elizabeth, daughter of John and Sarah Dunn. Job commenced business, at store keeping; afterward entered into partnership with Jesse A. Kirk, and his brother-in-law, S. B. Stubbs, M. D., as merchants and proprietors of the Rising Sun Foundry, under the firm

of Haines, Kirk & Stubbs. Job received an appointment at Annapolis, in the office of State Controller of Md. He held this position for several years. After resigning he returned to Rising Sun, where he now resides.

644. Joseph H., born 1825, 3, 27. Died 1867, 11, 2, at the town of Danville, New York, whence he had repaired for his health. He was married 1846, 8, 13, to Rebecca Frances, daughter of John and Francina Lincoln. She was born 1828, 1, 5. Joseph was a miller by occupation, and resided near Rising Sun village.

645. Elmira, born 1827, 1, 5. Married Marshall, son of —— and Rebecca Hunt. He resides near Rising Sun, on a part of the original tract settled by Jos. Haines, one of the first settlers of that neighborhood. Marshall is a machinist and inventor. He has machine shops at Rising Sun.

646. Sarah B., born 1853, 5, 21. Married Slater B. Stubbs, son of Isaac and Hannah. They resided in Rising Sun. Slater was born 1821, 3, 10, and died 1867, 7, 3. He was a physician. Read medicine under direction of his brother, Jeremiah B. Stubbs, M. D., of Fulton, Lancaster county; attended two courses of lectures at the Jefferson Medical College, Philadelphia, where he graduated in the class of March 10, 1842, being rated among the first of the class of that year. Soon after graduating he located, for a short time, in the village of Abbottstown, York county, but left and returned to Rising Sun, where he permanently located and practiced his profession until a few years before his decease.

During his residence in Cecil county, Md., he was twice elected to represent his district in the House of Delegates, and afterward was elected one of the School Commissioners of Cecil county. From the time of the organization of the company until his decease, he held the position of director of the Philadelphia and Baltimore Central R. R. Wherever known professionally, he was universally conceded to be a skillful and "good physician."

CHILDREN OF LEWIS HAINES (159) AND SARAH HUTTON.

647. Isaac H., born 1831, 12, 1. Unmarried. Isaac has been engaged in the mercantile business—first at Pleasant Grove, and Goshen, Lancaster county, of late years at Rising Sun, Md.—being one of the firm of "Haines Brothers." On account of ill-health, he disposed of his interest at the latter place and removed to Pleasant Grove.

648. Mary, born 1833, 2, 24. Resides with her father.

649. Levi, born 1836, 1, 19; died 1838, 4, 4.

650. Sarah H., born 1840, 6, 3. Married 1870, 10, 5, to George, son of Evan and Joanna Brown, of New Garden, Chester county. They reside on a farm near West Grove Station, Baltimore Central Railroad, Chester county, Pa. George is a farmer by occupation.

CHILDREN OF LEWIS HAINES (159) AND SARAH KIRK.

651. Hannah K., born 1843, 9, 11. Unmarried. Resides at Kirk's Mills, Lancaster county.

652. Hanson H., born 1844, 11, 25. Unmarried. For the last four years has been engaged in the mercantile business, in partnership with his brother Isaac, at Rising Sun, Md.

CHILDREN OF MARK HAINES (160) AND MERCY COOK.

653. William, born 1837, 1, 21. Married 1862, 2, 12, to Frances M. Bailey, daughter of Jeremiah and Miriam, of Delavan, Ill. She was born 1841, 3, 22. William removed from Fulton township, Lancaster county, and purchased a farm near the village of Delavan, Tazewell county, Ill, where he now resides.

654. Levi, born 1838, 9, 14; died in Lancaster, "*en route* home from the West," 1867, 11, 7. He married Priscilla, daughter of James and Sarah McConkey, of Peach Bottom, Lancaster county, Pa. Priscilla died. Left no children.

655. Howard, born 1840, 7, 10; died in the service of his country, 1863, 3, 31. Interred somewhere in the vicinity of Fredericksburg, Va.

656. Mary Susan, born 1842, 1, 16. Married 1868, 11, 11, to Joel J., son of Henry and Mary Ann Carter, of New Texas, Lancaster county. Joel was born 1843, 6, 16. During the rebellion he entered the United States service, and remained for nine months, or until the regiment was discharged. He was present and took part in the battle of Chancellorsville. Is now engaged in farming, and resides south of new Texas, Lancaster county. May be termed an amateur botanist.

657. Sarah A., born 1843, 5, 25; died, 1844, 2, 18.

658. Emeline, born 1845, 2, 27. Married 1869, 6, 9, to Kirk Brown (869), son of Kirk and Susanna, of Nottingham, Md., formerly of Fulton, Lancaster county, Pa. Kirk resides two miles east of Peach Bottom.

659. Priscilla, born 1846, 12, 30. Married 1867, 10, 24, to Joseph, son of Jeremiah and Miriam Bailey. Joseph was born 1838, 12, 31. He resides on a farm near Delavan, Ill.

660. James Leander, born 1852, 1, 27. Resides with his brother, near Delavan, Ill.

CHILDREN OF TIMOTHY HAINES (164) AND RACHEL E. KIRK (214).

661. Sarah B., born 1842, 4, 15. Married 1868, 9, 10, to Charles H. (805), son of Jeremiah B. and Rachel H. Stubbs, of Fulton, Lancaster, county, Pa.

662. Jacob, born 1845, 9, 1; died 1850, 9, 21.

663. Theodore, born 1847, 11, 9; died 1863, 1, 6.

CHILDREN OF JOSEPH HAINES (165) AND HARRIET KIRK.

☞ See No. 74.

CHILDREN OF ISAAC ENGLAND AND MORIAH HAINES (167).

664. Hannah P., born 1820, 9, 25. Not married.

665. Joseph T., born 1821, 8, 11. Married 1850, 1, 31, to Mary Alexander, daughter of Joseph Alexander.

666. Reuben H., born 1823, 3, 3. Married Margaret Fields, and resides in Columbus, Georgia. Margaret dec'd.

667. Mary Elizabeth, born 1829, 8, 9; died 1863, 8, 2. Married Abner Kirk (411), son of William and Elizabeth.

668. Deborah A., born 1831, 4, 12. Married William, son of Thomas and Rachel Clayton, of Rising Sun, Md.

CHILDREN OF SAMUEL ENGLAND AND ESTHER HAINES (168).

669. John, born 1822, 10, 3. Married 1847, 8, —, to Mary S., daughter of Peter and Sophia Young.

670. Robert Haines, born 1824, 2, 16. Married 1846, 11, 5, to Sarah A., daughter of Aaron B. and Zeepha Newton.

671. George, born 1826, 1, 25; died 1850, 8, 34. Married 1847, 2, 11, to Mary, daughter of Nathan and Rachel Brown of Fulton, Lancaster co., Pa. Mary married a second time; present husband, John Gregg of Fairfield, Drumore township.

672. Sarah A., born 1828, 6, 18. Married 1848, 5, —, to Stephen J., son of Elisha and Nancy Brown. Stephen deceased. Sarah married a second husband, named Charles Parker.

673. Seth, born 1831, 3, 18. Married Elizabeth Larrison.

674. Job, born 1832, 11, 26. Married Mary Bowers.

675. Lewis, born 1836, 2, 9. Not married.

676. Hannah E., born 1841, 10, 15. Married William, son of Joseph and Mary Hambleton.

677. Samuel G., born 1843, 10, 30. Married Annie, daughter of Cloud and Rebecca Pierson.

678. Joseph H., born 1847, 10, 6. Married 1868, 8, 1, to Ella, daughter of Christian and Margaret Reeder.

CHILDREN OF ISAAC STUBBS AND EILZABETH HAINES (169).

679. Reuben H., born 1825, 1, 21. Married Hannah daughter of Enoch and —— Swayne. Reuben is a farmer and resided for a time in York county, Pa. He disposed of his farm in York county, and moved to London Grove, where he purchased a farm, upon which he now resides. Have no children.

680. Vincent G., born 1826, 2, 28. Married 1853, 4, 28, to Elizabeth Pierson, daughter of Edward, of New Garden, Chester county. Elizabeth was born 1827, 5, 11. Vincent resides in the village of Delta, Peach Bottom twp., York county. He has been engaged for a number of years in the mercantile business at this place. Is, also an agent in the sale of roofing slate.

681. Mary E., born 1828, 12, 27; died 1851, 4, 5.

682. Sarah H.. born 1830, 10, 13. Married 1857, 1, 22, to Jacob, son of Enoch and —— Swayne of London Grove, Chester county. Jacob learned the trade of a cabinet maker under C. C. Cauffman, and then moved to Delta, York county, where he carried on the trade for a number of years. He has abandoned the business, and now resides in the house of his father-in-law. Failure of sight caused him to relinquish his trade.

683. Emeline, born 1832, 1, 21. Married Samuel W. Pass-

more, son of Andrew M. and Judith, of East Nottingham. Samuel resides on a farm and is engaged in the dairy business.

684. Albert, born 1833, 9, 19. Married 1859, 1, 13, to Phebe A., daughter of George and Hannah Hickman, of York county. Phebe was born 1836, 5, 17. Albert is a farmer, and resides on the farm of his late father-in-law, which he has purchased.

685. Priscilla C., born 1835, 8, 14; died 1846, 3, 5.

686. Joseph H., born 1837, 10, 14. Unmarried. Joseph H. taught school several terms in York, Lancaster and Chester counties. He then read medicine, under direction of Jeremiah B. Stubbs, M. D., of Fulton, Lancaster county; attended two full courses of lectures at the Jefferson Medical College, Philadelphia, and graduated in the class of March, 1862. Soon after receiving his degree, he located at the village of London Grove, Chester county, where he still resides and practices his profession.

687. Daniel, born 1839, 4, 23; died, 1839, 10, 14.

688. Daniel, born 1840, 11, 24. Resides in York county. Unmarried. Is a farmer by occupation.

689. Thomas, born 1843, 7, 19. Resides with his father, in York county. Is a farmer.

690. Henry J., born 1847, 3, 9. Henry read medicine, under direction of his brother, Joseph H., at London Grove; attended two courses of lectures at Jefferson Medical College, and graduated in the class of March, 1869. He has located in Kennett Square, Chester county.

CHILDREN OF BENJ. J. PASSMORE AND SARAH HAINES (172).

691. Reuben H., born 1833, 8, 22. Reuben at one time was a clerk in the Recorder's office, West Chester. Leaving

this position he engaged in the coal and lumber business, under the firm of "Lackey & Passmore." He removed to the farm of his father, where of late years he has been engaged in agricultural pursuits. He has recently opened a lumber and coal yard in the borough of Oxford—firm, "B. J. Passmore & Son."

CHILDREN OF SAMUEL HAINES (173) AND MARY E. REYNOLDS.

692. Franklin, born 1833, 9, 19. Died 1864, 9, 14. Not married.

693. Jonathan R., born 1835, 8, 2. Died 1851, 7, 6. Not married.

694. Eli Henry, born 1836, 11, 13. Married Esther, daughter of Oliver and Ann Furnace, of Little Britain. Henry is a surveyor, and for several years resided on a farm in west Nottingham. Disposing of this he purchased another from Timothy Haines, near Peach Bottom, upon which he now resides.

695. Jefferson, born 1839, 2, 24. Married ——, —, —. No children.

CHILDREN OF ISAAC REYNOLDS AND MYRA HAINES (176).

696. Ashton, born 1827, 2, 22.

697. Jonathan, born 1829, 3, 29. Married Elizabeth, daughter of John and Francina Lincoln.

CHILDREN OF ABSALOM ROMAN AND ELIZA REYNOLDS (177).

698. Eli H., born 1833, 7, 5. Died 1852, 4, —.

699. Sarah E., born 1835, 10, 5. Married Gilbert, son of Robert Maxwell.

700. Joseph A., born 1837, 8, 26. Married Alice Ann, daughter of Nathan and Hannah Milner. Alice born 1842,

2, —. They reside in the eighth district, Cecil county, Md., not far from Bald Friar Ferry, where Joseph is engaged in farming.

Joseph entered the Union army, August 16, 1861, for a term of three years; was discharged, December 20, 1862, to accept promotion in Co, G., Sixth Md. Vols. He was promoted to the rank of Captain, and was in many engagements during the war. In one of these battles he received a wound in the face. At the storming of Fort Fisher, he led his company in the land assault. He continued in the service until the suspension of hostilities.

701. Samuel T., born 1839, 9, 26. Married 1867, 12, 25, to Harriet M., daughter of Samuel C. and Hannah Wood. Harriet born 1838, 1, 3.

CHILDREN OF ELI HAINES (178) AND MARY MARSHALL.

702. Mary E., born 1837, 6, 30; died 1851, 12, 14.

703. Elmira R., born 1840, 2, 22; died 1847, 11, 11.

704. Rachel A., born 1844, 5, 3.

705. Lewis Marshall, born 1846, 12, 10. Not married. Lewis was engaged for some time in teaching school. He read law, and is now engaged in the practice of his profession, at Elkton, Cecil co., Maryland. Office with W. J. Jones, Esq.

706. Samuel, born 1849, 11, 20.

CHILDREN OF THOMAS HUIE AND SARAH HAINES (179).

707. John, born 1835, 10, 26. Married 1861, 7, 4, to Elizabeth Groundry.

708. Prudence, born 1837, 11, 2. Unmarried.

709. George, born 1840, 7, 18. Married 1866, 3, 15, to Jennie Kinney.

710. Sarah, born 1842, 2, 22. Married 1866, 2, 22, to Samuel M. Blair.

CHILDREN OF JOHN C. POWLEY AND ESTHER HAINES (180).

711. Helen Maria, born 1833, 1, 5. Married 1855, 12, 25, to John H. McKissick. They reside in Oxford, Chester co. John practices dentistry. No children.

712. Mary Emma, born 1834, 10, 31. Not married.

713. George C., born 1837, 2, 3; died 1855, 8, 3.

714. Lucy Matilda, born 1839, 1, 20; died 1843, 2, 23.

715. Ann Elizabeth, born 1842, 11, 25.

716. Henry S., born 1845, 1, 28.

717. Eri Haines, born 1847, 1, 21.

718. Ella Cresswell, born 1850, 1, 12; died 1852, 7, 23.

CHILDREN OF WILLIAMSON M'CULLOUGH AND LUCY HAINES (181).

719. Hester, born ——, —, —. Married —— Bond. Have a family of children. Names not ascertained.

720. John H., born ——, —, —. Married ——, —, — Studied medicine, and practiced for a time south of Rising Sun, Md.

721. Lucy, born ——, —, —.

CHILDREN OF BASIL HAINES (182) AND LYDIA A. TAYLOR.

722. Thomas Job, born 1837, 7, 20; died 1838, 2, 28.

723. George W., born 1840, 6, 23. Married 1862, 12, 30, to Sarah Elizabeth Cooper, daughter of Samuel Cooper.

724. Anna Maria, born 1842, 6, 20. Married John Bowden. John is a blacksmith and machinist. He carries on the foundry at Rising Sun.

725. James Eri, born 1844, 3, 7.

726. Indiana V., born 1846. Married Amos Cooper, son of Samuel and —— Cooper. Have several children. Names not ascertained.

CHILDREN OF ERI WASHINGTON HAINES (184) AND SARAH E. M'KOWN.

727. Eva Eriella, born 1853, 12, 1; died 1857, 1, 20.
728. A son, born 1859, 11, 25.

CHILDREN OF ANDREW GAMBLE AND NAOMI KNIGHT (185).

729. Esther, born 1839, 4, 20. Married 1859, 8, 18, to George W. Allyn.
730. John Lawson, born 1841, 11, 1. Married 1868, 12, 1, to Mary E. Hall.
731. Jane Elizabeth, born 1845, 2, 10.
732. Belinda Ann, born 1849, 6, 24.

CHILDREN OF JOHN KIRK AND BELINDA KNIGHT (186).

☞See under (68.)

CHILDREN OF ABRAHAM AND HANNAH BELL KNIGHT (188).

733. James K., born 1846, 4, 21.
734. Nathan H., born 1847, 12, 4,
735. William E., born 1849, 9, 27; died 1866, 11, 16.
736. Immer F., born 1852, 9, 1.

CHILDREN OF IMMER KNIGHT (189) AND ELIZA MERION.

737. Philena R., born 1843, 10, 22.
738. Evelyn S., born 1845, 4, 4.
739. Mary E., born 1846, 6, 19.
740. Nathan H., born 1849, 10, 7; died 1863, 2, 12.
741. D. Eugene, born 1853, 6, 9; died 1864, 3, 6.
742. Immer A., born 1858. 11, 1,
743. Harley V., born 1861, 5, 6.

CHILDREN OE JAMES KINGHAM AND LYDIA A. KNIGHT (190).

744. Thirza, born 1838, 5, 28; died 1857, 1, 24.

745. Joseph, born 1839, 12, 5. Married 1868, 9, 27, to Mary A. Parlow.

746. Clarissa, born 1842, 2, 4.

747. William, born 1847, 5, 12; died 1857, 3, 26.

CHILDREN OF CYRUS MOORE AND ESTHER H. KNIGHT (191).

748. Eleanor E., born 1838, 8, 29. Married 1864, 10, 2, to Isaiah Gibbons.

749. Immer C., born 1841, 8, 21.

750. Celina S., born 1844, 8, 4.

751. Lucina, born 1846, 9, 6.

752. Abigail E., born 1848, 8, 25.

753. Robert B., born 1850, 9, 26.

754. Mary A., born 1857 10, 30.

CHILDREN OF WILLIAM K. KNIGHT (192) AND SUSAN J. KIRK (274).

755. Naomi J., born 1844, 9, 15; died 1862, 10, 31. She was returning from a relative's, waylaid and murdered by a German, formerly in the employ of her uncle, Theodore J. Kirk.

756. Nathan Lewis, born 1846, 3, 13; died in infancy.

757. Wallace, born 1849, 11, 21. Married Lucinda Rosenberger.

CHILDREN OF WILLIAM K. KNIGHT (192) AND ANNA L. KLEINHAUS.

758. Quintus, born 186-. —, 10.

CHILDREN OF PHILIP HAINES (196) AND MARY MILES.

759. James M., born 1837, 11, 20.

760. Harriet R., born 1839, 11, 1; died 1840, 5, 12.

761. Eliza I., born 1842, 5, 3.

CHILDREN OF REUBEN HAINES (198) AND MIRIAM ROBINSON.

762. Mary K., born 1851, 11, 1.

763. Howard R., born 1859, 6, 26; died 1862, 8, 1.

CHILDREN OF THOMAS BOWKER AND MARGARETTA HAINES. (202).

764. Miriam H., born 1854, 11, 18.

765. James F., born 1858, 4, 4.

CHILDREN OF GEORGE W. KIRK (204) AND MARIA THOMPSON.

766. William T., born 1823, 12, 19. Married 1850, 2, 26, to Deborah Smedley. William resides in Philadelphia, at No. 1509 Poplar st.; is a merchant and until lately was of the firm of "Boggs and Kirk," wholesale grocers.

767. Abby A., born 1826, 2, 15. Married 1846, 9, 17, to William J. Harlan. They have resided in Jersey city and in Brooklyn, N. Y. William is a coal merchant.

768. Amelia M., born 1828, 6, 25; died in infancy.

769. Elisha H., born 1831, 1, 12; died in infancy.

770. George H., born 1834, 7, 1. Married 1859, 4, 12, to Harriet H. Craig, of Northampton county, Pa. She died 1834, 3, 25. George's second marriage 1866, 4, 24, to Annie N., daughter of John N. and Amelia Russell of Drumore, Lancaster county, Pa. George H. Kirk commenced business as a clerk in a country mercantile establishment in Delaware county, Pa. He remained in this situation two years, then returned to Philadelphia, and was engaged in the weighing business "with profit and satisfaction," until 1857. In that year he migrated to Freemansburg, Pa., as bookkeeper for a coal company. He returned to the city and weighing in 1859. In 1862 he entered the service of a cotton house, the interests of the business requiring his presence in the vicinity of Mem-

phis, Tenn. The war progressing in that year and section invested his enterprise with considerable danger. He again returned to Philadelphia, where in 1863 he engaged satisfactorily with A. Whitney & Sons, " Car Wheel Manufacturers, Callowhill and Sixteenth streets, and is still connected with them. His residence is No. 1528 Brown street.

771. Theodore M., born 1837, 8, 12 ; died in infancy.

772. Charles H., born 1839, 10, 9 ; died in infancy.

CHILDREN OF WILLIAM HUTTON AND RACHEL KIRK (205).

773. Elisha, born 1823, 12, 16 ; died 1824, 6, 29.

774. Sarah A., born 1825, 4, 5 ; died 1838, 10, —.

775. Mary Amelia, born 1836, 2, 15 ; died 1868, 10, 21. Married 1857, 9, 17, to Walter F., son of Thomas and Margaret Neal, of Drumore, Lancaster county, Pa. They resided at the residence of her mother, where both died. Walter died 1870, 7, 20. He was U. S. Mail Agent between Philadelphia and Harrisburg.

CHILDREN OF HUGHES KIRK (206) AND RUTHANNA ROBINSON.

776. George Hughes, born ——, —, —. Has a position on the Baltimore & Ohio R. R. His address, O'Konoka, Hampshire county, West Virginia.

777. Savanna, born ——, —, —.

CHILDREN OF JOHN N. RUSSEL AND AMELIA KIRK (207).

778. William H., born 1832, 1, 27 ; died 1834, 6, 4.

779. Slater B., born 1834, 6, 18. Married 1861, 10, 23, to Amelia (318) daughter of Norris and Eliza Levis, of Rock, Cecil county, Maryland. (See further under No. 318.)

780. Annie N., born 1837, 7, 24. Married 1866, 4, 24, to George H. (770), son of George W. and Maria Kirk.

781. Mary B., born 1840, 2, 9. Married 1863, 3, 25, to

Jacob T., son of Moses Whitson, of Sadsbury, Lancaster co. They reside near Christiana, Lancaster co. Jacob is a farmer and resides on a large tract of land.

782. Rachel H., born 1842, 9, 16. Married 1865, 10, 5, to William Mortimer, son of Jacob and Carolien Hayes, of Newlin, Chester county. William was born 1840, 5, 13. Studied law under J. Smith Futhey, Esq., of West Chester, Pa.; attended two courses of lectures in the Law Department of the University of Michigan, where he graduated in the spring of 1864. Returning East, he located for a short time in Oil City, Venango county, Pa. From thence, removed to West Chester and was admitted to the bar, November 30, 1864. He resides in this place and practices his profession. At the present time is one of the solicitors of the Wilmington & Birdsboro R. R. Company.

783. George Hughes, born 1845, 4, 19. Unmarried. Resides with his father in Drumore twp., Lancaster county.

784. Hannah, born 1847, 6, 7. Married 1868, 11, 11, to Elwood, son of Joel and Martha Smedley, of Fulton House, Lancaster county. Elwood resides on a farm, and is, by occupation, a farmer.

CHILDREN OF JAMES MORRISON AND ANN M. KIRK (208).

785. John, born 1839, 12, 13. Unmarried. John learned the trade of a carpenter. At one time was engaged in storekeeping at Centreville, being one of the firm of "Pusey & Morrison."

786. Rachel, born 1844, —, —. Died 1853, 9, —.

CHILDREN OF JOHN KIRK (209) AND ELLEN BENDER.

787. Jacob, born 1850, 10, 12.

788. Slater R., born 1852, 4, 10.

789. Sarah E., born 1855, 8, 29.

CHILDREN OF ISAAC PIERCE AND HANNAH KIRK (212).

790. Sarah, born 1829, 3, 14. Married Amos Coates.

791. Henry, born 1831, 2, 26. Died 1846, 3, 8.

792. Jane, born 1834, 9, 24. Married Charles Lewis.

793. Elizabeth, born 1838, 3, 1. Married Eliab Axtell Vaughn.

794. Jacob K., born 1842, 9, 28. Died 1871, 6, 24.

795. John H., born 1848, 2, 6. Died 1858, 4, 16,

CHILDREN OF LEWIS HAINES AND SARAH KIRK (213).

(See No. 159.)

CHILDREN OF TIMOTHY HAINES AND RACHEL E. KIRK. (214)

(See No. 164.)

CHILDREN OF WILLIAM P. HAINES AND MARY KIRK (217).

796. Eugene, born 1849, 9, 14. Has been engaged in keeping store.

797. Jeremiah, born 1851, 7, 27.

798. Mabel, born 1857, 11, 7.

799. William P., born 1862, 2, 13.

CHILDREN OF LEWIS J. KIRK (218) AND ADALINE CALDWELL.

800. Robert C., born 1866, 7, 10.

801. Mary A., born 1870, 5, 16.

CHILDREN OF JACOB R. KIRK (219) AND HANNAH B. STUBBS.

802. Lewis R., born 1832, 10, 3. Married 1869, 9, 23, to Mary C., daughter of Henry and Mary Richardson, of Charlestown, Cecil county, Md. Lewis read medicine under direction of his uncle, Jeremiah B. Stubbs, M. D., of Fulton, Lancaster county, attended two courses of lectures at the Jefferson Medical College, Philadelphia, and graduated in the class of March 9, 1853.

He located at the village of Charlestown, Cecil county, Md., and practiced his profession nine years. Relinquishing the practice and moving to Nottingham, Chester county, he engaged in the mercantile business two years. Not long after the commencement of the rebellion, he sold out his interest in the store and entered the service of the United States, August 22, 1862, as Assistant Surgeon of the 131st Regt. of Pa. Vols.; was with this regiment at the battles of Antietam, first Fredericksburg and Chancellorsville. After expiration of regiment's term, was commissioned Assistant Surgeon of the 112th Regt. Pa. Vols. (2d Pa. Heavy Artillery); the regiment at that time was garrisoning the forts north of Washington, D. C. On the 16th of October, 1863, he was commissioned Surgeon of the 26th Regt. Pa. Vols., in the 5th Corps, "Army of the Potomac." With it was engaged in battles of Kelley's Ford —where he was wounded—Mine Run, Wilderness and Spottsylvania Court House. Mustered out at expiration of regiment's term of service, and appointed Post Surgeon, U. S. A., in which capacity had charge of Hospitals at Fort Lyons and Fort Williams, Virginia; Fort Fisher, Fort Johnson, Raleigh and Fayettsville, North Carolina. Resigned and left the service January 1, 1868. At the present time resides in the village of Rising Sun, Cecil county, Maryland, where he is engaged in the drug business.

803. Isaac S., born 1834, 8, 14. Married Fannie, daughter of John and Francina Lincoln, of Rising Sun, Maryland. Isaac commenced as a clerk in the mercantile business. Purchased a store near House's Meeting House, also a farm. Is a merchant, and carries on farming and a store.

804. Jacob R., born 1838, 10, 26; died 1842, 5, 30.

CHILDREN OF JEREMIAH B. STUBBS AND RACHEL H. KIRK (220).

805. Charles H., born 1839, 12, 30. Married 1868, 9, 10, to Sarah B. (661), daughter of Timothy and Rachel E. Haines. In 1861 he commenced the study of medicine, reading in his father's office, and in 1862, while a student, received from Surgeon General Hammond the appointment of Medical Cadet. He joined the medical staff of Brigade Surgeon David McRuer, commanding the floating hospital Louisiana, which was engaged in removing the wounded from McClellan's army to Washington. After attending two courses of lectures at the Jefferson Medical College, he graduated in the class of March 10, 1863. In July of that year, he was appointed Assistant Surgeon 40th Reg't., P. V., and remained with the regiment until it was mustered out of service. In 1864, he served on the staff of Surgeon Joseph Hopkinson Mower, U. S. A. Hospital, Chesnut Hill, Philadelphia. Since then he has resided at the homestead in Fulton township, Lancaster county, where he practices his profession.

806. Cassius E., born 1844, 3, 22. Unmarried. Resides in Shepherdstown, Jefferson county, West Virginia. He read law under A. Herr Smith, Esq., of Lancaster, Pa.; attended two courses of lectures at the law department of the University of Michigan, at Ann Arbor, where he graduated in the spring of 1865. He has held the position of State's Attorney in Jefferson county, for two terms, and was recently elected to the State Legislature, as a member of the House of Delegates.

CHILDREN OF MONTGOMERY R. GRYDER AND ANN M. KIRK (222).

807. Mary Virginia, born 1841, 12, 21.

808. Hannah M., born 1843, 7, 7; died 1845, 6, 2.

809. John M., born 1846, 7, 29; died 1864, 10, 19.
810. Florence A., born 1849, 8, 28.
811. Walter E., born 1851, 8, 28.
812. Lewis Wilmer, born 1858, 5, 24.

CHILDREN OF SAMUEL WEBSTER AND DEBORAH KIRK (225).

813. Walter F., born 1830, 7, 26. Died 1849, 11, 3.

814. Sarah B., born 1832, 4, 26. Married 1852, 7, 30, to Charles Beaumont. He was a saddler by occupation, and resided in Monmouth, Illinois, where he died. Sarah still resides in that place.

815. John Randolph, born 1835, 6, 8. Married Susan Nye. He is a physician, and practices his profession in Monmouth, Illinois.

816. Mary E., born 1842, 12, 8. Married 1862, 6, 18, to Henry Ewing. He is a merchant, and resides in the town of Monmouth, Illinois.

CHILDREN OF JEREMIAH KIRK (227) AND ELIZA HATTON.

817. Hannah, born 1841, 3, 20. Unmarried.
818. Sarah Ann, born 1843, 12, 7. Unmarried.
819. Deborah B., born 1848, 1, 21. Married 1871, 1, 24, to Marshall Carr, of Huntsville, Alabama.
820. Anna Rebecca, born 1851, 1, 26.

CHILDREN OF WILLIAM C. IRVINE AND RACHEL KIRK (228).

821. John, born 1839, 2, 9; died 1858, 2, 7. John committed suicide by shooting himself with a pistol.

822. Mary D., born 1844, 2, 16. Married Samuel Bailey of Philadelphia. At the present time they reside in Huntsville, Alabama, where Samuel is engaged at his trade, a jeweler.

CHILDREN OF ALEXANDER JOHNSON AND MERCY KIRK (229).

823. Julia V. born 1844, 1, 9. Married 1866, 10, 11, to William Whitall. They reside at No. 137, North 15th st., Philadelphia. William is a Fire Insurance agent and conveyancer.

824. Helen J., born 1845, 10, 24. Married 1866 ,4, 24, to Samuel J. Hogdson of Chester county. They resided for several years, near Penningtonville, Chester county, but have removed to the vicinity of Richmond, Va., where they conduct a "truck farm."

825. Robert J., born 1847, 9, 27; died 1848, 6, 14.

826. Mary E., born 1849, 3, 31; died 1852, 8, 6.

827. Henry C., born 1852, 4, 14; died 1855, 6, 28.

828. Mary E., born 1854, 3, 13; died 1861, 7, 18.

829. Alexander, born 1856, 9, 26.

830. Ellis I., born 1863, 4, 28.

CHILDREN OF ELLIS P. KIRK (232) AND SARAH A. HILAMAN.

831. Martha E., born 1836, 10, 1. Unmarried.

832. Mary Amanda, born 1838, 12, 29. Married 1870, 11, 23, to Franklin Pusey.

833. Charles Franklin, born 1840, 6, 22. Married Sarah Kirk (886), daughter of Jacob L. and Jane Kirk, of Glen Roy. Charles is engaged in milling, and is a Life Insurance Agent.

834. Jacob H,, born 1842, 8, 20. Married Elmira, daughter of Clarkson and Eliza Cook, of Fulton, Lancaster county, Pa. Jacob resides at Pleasant Grove, and is engaged in the commission business, farming, etc.

835. Josiah P., born 1844, 10, 22. Married Annie, daughter of Haines Reynolds, of Rising Sun, Md.

836. Mellissa P., born 1846, 7, 20. Married 1870, 10, 27, to Charles B., son of Amos Pugh, of Nottingham, Chester county, Pa.

837. Lewis Henry, born 1848, 11, 16.

838. Ellis Hughes, born 1850, 9, 6.

CHILDREN OF ROGER H. KIRK (233) AND DEBORAH BROWN.

839. Levi B., born 1848, 12, 9. Unmarried. Resides near Pleasant Grove.

840. Lewis H., born 1651, 2, 26. Engaged in farming.

841. Mercy A., born 1853, 2, 27.

842. Harriet Rachel Hughes, born 1858, 6, 24.

CHILDREN OF JOSIAH FRANKLIN KIRK (234) AND SARAH A. BILES.

843. William B., born 1841, 12, 9. Married ——, —, —. Resides on a farm near Blue Ball, Chester county, Pa.

844. Washington H. born 1842, 12, 22. Died in infancy.

845. Leroy Passmore, born 1846, 12, 30.

846. Samuel W., born 1848, 8, 31.

CHILDREN OF DANIEL STUBBS AND RACHEL A. KIRK. (235)

847. Theodore K., born 1847, 6, 8. Unmarried. Has chosen the profession of law and is studying under J. Smith Futhey, Esq., of West Chester. Attended one course of lectures in the law department of the University of Michigan, Ann Arbor. Resides at Nottingham Station, Baltimore Central R. R.

848. Isaac F., born 1848, 12. 29. Resides at Nottingham Station, where he is engaged in the grain business. Is one of the firm of "D. Stubbs & Sons."

849. Phebe M., born 1850, 7, 1. Resides at Nottingham. Might be termed an amateur artist.

850. Daniel A., born 1852, 6, 29.

851. Ida Ella, born 1853, 10, 23.

CHILDREN OF SAMUEL C. WOOD AND HANNAH BROWN (236).

852. Hannah C., born 1846, 1, 15; died 1850, 7, 31.

853. Ann E., born 1844, 8, 6. Unmarried. Resides at Goshen, Lancaster county, Pa.

854. Samuel D., born 1850, 6, 10. Unmarried. Has been clerking in the store at Goshen.

CHILDREN OF ALLEN COOK AND RACHEL K. BROWN (237).

855. Edward, born 1831, 9, 25; died 1854, 12, 16. Edward was a farmer, and managed his mother's farm for a number of years. He discontinued this and migrated to California, where he was engaged in erecting houses. He died in that State.

856. Jeremiah B., born 1834, 6, 22. Jeremiah removed to Delavan, Illinois, and was residing there at the breaking out of the rebellion. He entered the United States service, and soon arose to the rank of Captain in the cavalry. For bravery he was recommended in a special request for promotion, by General E. R. S. Canby, and was advanced to the rank of Lieutenant-Colonel. He continued in the service until the close of the war. He returned to his farm in Illinois. Has held the position of Whisky Inspector in the United States Revenue Service, and was a candidate in his district for the State Legislature.

857. Anna Mary, born 1836, 4, 29. Married 1858, 12, 29, to Joseph Slaughter, son of John and Sarah. They reside near Delavan, Illinois.

858. William, born 1837, 12, 15. Removed to Illinois, and from thence migrated to Texas, where, it is said, he is the

owner of a great number of cattle. He served some time in the U. S. service.

859. Charles A., born 1840, 9, 7. Married 1862, 1, 26, to Evelyn, daughter of Joseph and Susan Lownes. She was born 1844, 7, 20. Charles resides on a farm in some part of Illinois.

860. Henry, 1843, 4, 22. Single. Resides in Illinois.

861. Julia A., born 1846, 4, 22; died 1855, 4, 23.

CHILDREN OF KIRK BROWN (238) AND SUSANNA HAMBLETON.

862. Sarah A., born 1833, 4, 5. Unmarried. Has been residing along with her mother.

863. William R., born 1834, 8, 27. Married 1856, 2, 27, to Nancy A. Owens. William resides in Clearfield county, and carries on the manufacture of wagons, etc.

864. Jeremiah, born 1836, 3, 29; died 1842, 12, 29.

865. Lewis F., born 1837, 10, 28; died 1843, 1, 2.

866. Emma, born 1839. Married 1864, 11, 24, to George W. Gifford. George is a farmer, and resides in the vicinity of Rising Sun, Md.

867. Joseph H., born 1841, 12, 9; died 1850, 10, 25.

868. Hannah W., born 1843, 12, 3.

869. Kirk, born 1845, 7, 22. Married 1869, 6, 8, to Emeline (658), daughter of Mark and Mercy Haines, of Fulton, Lancaster county, Pa.

Kirk entered the military service of the United States soon after the breaking out of the rebellion. He enlisted as a member of Co. G., 90th Reg't Penn'a Vols., Col. Lyle, on the 29th of November, 1861, and was present and engaged with his company at the battle of Cedar Mountain, August 8th and 9th, 1862; Rappahannock Station, August 26th and 27th, 1862; Thoroughfare Gap, and Bull Run—the latter fought August 29th, 1862. In this battle he was severely wounded in the ankle and shoulder; was placed in a U. S. A. hospital, and remained there until Dec. 10, 1862, when he returned to his regiment in time to participate in the battle of Fredericksburg, which was fought Dec. 12 and 13, 1862. In this engagement he had the gun shot out of his hands, but sustained no injury. After this battle, he was placed on detached duty at army head-quarters. He was honorably discharged on the 29th of November, 1864.

Since the war Kirk has been engaged in farming. He now resides on the farm of his late father-in-law.

870. Mary Amelia, born 1847, 12, 1.

871. Elizabeth, born 1849, 10, 19. Died 1850, 11, 2.

872. Lewis H., born 1851, 10, 13.

873. Eugene M., born 1854, 1, 19. Died 854, 17, 31.

874. Josephine C., born 1854, 1, 19.

CHILDREN OF LEVI K. BROWN (239) AND HANNAH MOORE.

875. William H., born 1836, 2, 29. Married Sarah Remell. William has been engaged as a civil engineer since 1858, principally upon the location, constructing and operating of railroads. At the present time he is chief engineer of the Sunbury & Lewistown R. R.; also principal assistant engineer of the Eastern Division Penna. Central. He resides at Harrisburg, Pa.

876. Mercy A., born 1837, 12, 16; died 1842, 9, 8.

877. Joseph M., born 1840, 10, 4; died 1840, 10, 20.

878. Jacob K., born 1842, 9, 5. Unmarried. Resides at Goshen. Is a farmer by occupation.

879. Charles E., born 1843, 12, 23. Married 1870, 1, 8, to Mrs. Mary E. Hall.

880. Theodore F., born 1845, 8, 29. Married 1869, 6, 18,

to Anna M. Loomis. Theodore resides in Corry, Venango county, Pa. Has a position connected with the railroad at that place.

881. Levi K., born 1846, 12, 29; died 1864, 4, 28. He was killed by being kicked by a horse.

882. Mary L., born 1856, 4, 29.

883. Anna. born 1857, 10, 9.

CHILDREN OF LEWIS BROWN (240) AND ELIZABETH BRADWAY.

884. Rachel A., born 1842, 4, 21; died 1851, 10, 9.

885. Edwin L., born 1845, 8, 7. Married 1869, 4, 8, to Matilda Freed. He resides at No. 1819 North Eleventh St., Philadelphia. Has a position in a dry goods store.

CHILDREN OF JACOB L. KIRK (241) AND JANE MILNER.

886. Sarah, born 1837, 9, 6. Married Chas. F. (833), son of Ellis and Sarah Kirk, of Nottingham.

887. Ruth Ada, born 1839, 3, 5. Died 1867, 2, 23. Married 1863, 4, 23, to Benjamin F., son of Joseph C. and Jane Taylor, of Little Britain. Franklin is engaged in the mercantile business at Ashville, Lancaster county, Pa. He married a second wife—Elizabeth Y. Harkness, daughter of Adam and Margaret, of Little Britain, and by this wife has one child, named Joseph Craig Taylor, born 1870, 6, 28.

888. Levi, born 1840, 10, 17. Married ——, —, —.

889. Rachel, born 1840, 10, 17. Married Levi K. (1554), son of Joseph and Rebecca Miller.

890. Cyrus, born 1844, 6, 1. Married 1869, 8, to Henrietta S. (1553), daughter of Joseph and Rebecca Miller.

891. Thaddeus S., born 1846, 3, 17.

892. Jacob Franklin, born 1848, 3, 22. Resides somewhere in the West. Has been engaged in store keeping.

CHILDREN OF JACOB L. KIRK (241) AND ELIZABETH P. KEECH.

893. Lewis, born 1856, 4, 29.

894. Harry, born 1859, 2, 7; died 1863, 5, 6.

895. Frederick, born 1861, 9, 2; died 1863, 5, 25.

CHILDREN OF ELISHA BROWN (244) AND RACHEL BRADWAY.

896. Slater F., born 1841, 3, 28. Unmarried. Resides on the homestead at Goshen, Lancaster county. Is a farmer by occupation.

897. Mary E., born 1842, 8, 31. Married William, son of Abner and Rebecca Pugh. They reside on a large farm south of the borough of Oxford. William conducts a dairy in connection with the farm.

898. Thomas B., born 1844, 8, 19. Unmarried. During the rebellion he served for a short time as Assistant Paymaster's clerk, and made a voyage to the Florida coast, remaining at Key West. Within the last few years he has been engaged in learning the banking business, and is one of the firm of "Pyle & Brown," bankers and brokers, West Chester, Pa.

899. Charles H., born 1847, 5, 28. Resides in Philadelphia, where he has been engaged in the produce business. At the present time he is one of the the firm of "Kirk & Brown," 1228 Market street, Produce and Commission merchants. Unmarried.

900. Worthington, born 1851, 7, 13; died 1856, 11, 26.

901. Walter, born 1857, 12, 10.

CHILDREN OF JEREMIAH BROWN (245) AND MARGARETTA HAINES.

902. Jacob K., born 1842, 1, 22. Unmarried. Resides at Goshen, Lancaster county, and manages the flour mill.

903. Sarah Ann, born 1845, 8, 7. Married 1869, 4, 28,

to Neal Hambleton, formerly of Ohio, but now of Philadelphia. He resides at 1528 Swayne street. He is an inspector of steam boilers.

904. Mabel E., born 1848, 4, 29.
905. Mary A., born 1848, 4, 29.
906. Hannah E., born 1853, 1, 13; died 1854, 8, 21.
907. Emma L., born 1855, 2, 16; died 1864, 12, 27.
908. Ruthanna H., born 1859, 8, 22.

CHILDREN OF JOSEPH C. STUBBS AND RACHEL A. BROWN (246)

909. Mary A., born 1855, 8, 6; died 1855, 9, 20.
910. Jane, born 1857, 5, 13.
911. Mary B., born 1858, 8, 21.
912. Hannah, born 1860, 1, 31.
913. Ruthanna, born 1861, 10, 26.

CHILDREN OF EDWIN L. MORGAN AND MARY H. BROWN (247).

914. Mary Zillah, born ——, —, —; died ——, —, —.
915. Slater B., born 1856, 5, 12.
916. Hannah I., born 1858, 6, 15.
917. Joshua P., born 1860, 2, 11; died 1865, 8, 27.
918. Edwin L., born 1863, 7, 5; died 1864, 4, 17.
919. Mary Lincoln, born 1865, 6. 24.

CHILDREN OF JEREMIAH BROWN (250) AND MARY LLOYDE.

920. Benjamin F., born ——, —, —. Not married.
921. Sarah A., born ——, —, —. Married H. Shepherd.
922. William H., born ——, —, —. Not married. Resides in the city of Indianapolis, Indiana.
923. Darlington, born ——, —, —. Married ——, ——.

CHILDREN OF JOSEPH KIRK (265) AND MARGARET E. COLEGRAN

924. Mary E., born 1862, 1, 5.

925. Sarah Salina, born 1863, 11, 25; died 1864, 5, 24.
926. Clara Adelaide, born 1865, 1, 29.
927. Edwin Ellsworth, born 1865, 1, 29.

CHILDREN OF JOSHUA W. KIRK (266) AND RACHEL BALL.

928. Mary Jane, born 1849, 11, 17.
929. Sarah Ann, born 1852, 1, 10.
930. William W., born 1854, 11, 2.
931. Eli M., born 1858, 4, 28.
932. Gideon W., born 1860, 4, 3.
933. Emma F., born 1865, 10, 23.

CHILDREN OF REUBEN T. KIRK (272) AND EUNICE RYNEER.

934. Lewis S., born 1845, 1, 19,
935. Thomas W., born 1847, 10, 19. Died 1848, 9, 24.
936. Susan E., born 1851, 8, 17.
937. Roger, born 1856, 4, 6.
938. William H., born 1858, 3, 2. Died 1858, 3, 10.
939. Theodore I., born 1860, 3, 10.
940. Elmer, born 1862, 10, 12.
941. Alma, born 1867, 2, 14.

CHILDREN OF THEODORE J. KIRK (273) AND LUCINDA KNIGHT.

942. Alice A. born 1847, 10, 27. Married 1868, 1, 29, to E. Granville (515), son of Nathan and Catharine Kirk, of Elmore, Ohio.

Granville Kirk resides in Sioux city, Iowa, and is engaged in the dry goods business.

943. Amy Esther, born 1850, 9, 2. Died 1862, 10, 31. It will be noticed that this little girl died on the same day as her cousin, Naomi I. Knight (755). They were murdered by a German, formerly in the employ of Theo. J. Kirk.

944. Edgar R., born 1852, 8, 30.

945. Clara Edna, born 1856, 2, 23; died 1858, 7, 26.
946. Emmett Haines, born 1858, 3, 12.
947. Clara Elmira, born 1860, 2, 25.
948. Ella May, born 1864, 3, 16.
949. Reuben John, born 1867, 12, 4.

CHILDREN OF WILLIAM KIRK KNIGHT AND SUSAN J. KIRK (274).

(See 192.)

CHILDREN OF THOMAS J. BALDWIN AND SARAH E. KIRK (277).

950. William E., born 1855, 4, 19.
951. Thirza N., born 1855, 4, 19.
952. Mary A , born 1858, 9, 23.
953. Arthur M., born 1860, 1, 11; died 1865, 11, 13.
954. Myra K., born 1867, 2, 12.

CHILDREN OF WESTLEY CRITCHET AND GRACE A. KIRK (278).

955. Mary Ellen, born 1855, 6, 23; died 1856, 2, 18.
956. Martha Elva, born 1855, 6, 23; died 1855, 9, 16.
957. Sarah E., born 1857, 8, 17; died 1859, 9, 6.
958. Theo. K., born 1859, 9, 26; died 1863, 7, 16.
959. Earnest C., born 1862, 2, 14; died 1863, 7, 15.
960. Harriet E., born 1863, 11, 30.
961. Westley V., born 1866, 6, 30.

CHILDREN OF JAMES ELI DONOHOO (280) AND SUSAN THOMAS.

962. Ida E., born 18—, —, —.
963. John, born 18—, —, —.
964. William, born 18—, —, —.
965. Caroline, born 18—, —, —.

CHILDREN OF WILLIAM J. MARSHBANK AND ESTHER DONOHOO (281).

966. Rachel A , born 1849, 11, 18.
967. Francina E., born 1853, 1, 19.
968. Elizabeth, born 1855, 6, 3.
969. Mary Alice, born 1857, 6, 31.
970. Susan A., born 1859, 12. 18.
971. Lilly May, born 1866, 6, 4.

CHILDREN OF ABNER KIRK AND HANNAH DONOHOO (284.)

☞ See No. (411).

CHILDREN OF ARTABANES KIRK (288) AND THIRZA HALL.

972. Belinda, born 1859, 2, 11.
973. Eveline E., born 1861, 1, 27.
974. Emma Lavinia, born 1863, 11, 15.
975. Martha Lucretia, born 1857, 3, 1.

CHILDREN OF DAVID MERION AND HANNAH E. KIRK (289).

976. John K., born 1856, 7, 31.
977. Wilber Francis, born 1858, 12, 26.
978. Mary Etta, born 1864, 3, 8.

CHILDREN OF HENRY F. HARRISON AND SUSANNA E. KIRK (290).

979. John W., born 1857, 3, 17 ; died 1857, 6, 9.
980. Mary E., born 1858, 8, 19.

CHILDREN OF WILLIAM KNIGHT (296) AND JANE COATES.

981. Margaret A., born 1842, 6, 11.
982. Thomas, born 1844, 3, 11 ; died 1850, 8, 11.
983. Emily J., born 1846, 8, 8.
984. Samuel, born 1849, 4, 12.
985. William T., born 1851, 8, 9.

986. Mary Bertha, born 1854, 3, 25; died 1857, 4, 6.
987. Gertrude, born 1856, 12, 13.
988. Grace Irene, born 1859, 3, 13.
989. Blanche Eva, born 1861, 9, 12.
990. Paul Gardiner, born 1865, 1, 31.

CHILD OF JOHN DITLOW AND CAROLINE KNIGHT (300).

991. Emily J., born 1851, 2, 1. Unmarried. Resides in Lancaster city, along with her aunt, Emily Sheaff.

CHILDREN OF ELISHA KIRK (305) AND REBECCA A. HANNA.

992. William M., born 1844, 7, 21. Married 1868, 8, 6, to Margaret Gilbert. Resides in the vicinty of Brick Meeting House, Md.
993. Ettie A., born 1845, 10, 3.
994. Norris Levis, born 1848, 12, 3.
995. James H., born 1851, 1, 6.
996. Emily E., born 1852, 12, 14.
997. Charles H., born 1855, 12, 14.
998. Martha R., born 1857, 6, 9.
999. Elisha E., born 1859, 4, 22.
1000. Turner E., born 1861, 3, 11.
1001. Harry Ellsworth, 1863, 12, 30.
1002. Walter, born 1869, 2, 21.

CHILDREN OF THOMAS BROWN AND ELIZABETH KIRK (305).

1003. Lewis K., born 1843, 10, 16. Thomas entered the U. S. service, and was wounded in the leg to such an extent that amputation had to be resorted to. He now holds a clerkship in the 4th Auditor's office, Treasury Department, Washington.
1004. Montillion, born 1845, 7, 28.

1005. Amelia, born 1848, 1, 26. Died 1851, 3, 1.
1006. Mary, born 1850, 5, 9.
1007. Emma, born 1853, 8, 27.
1008. William, born 1855, 10, 13.
1009. Theodore, born 1857, 12, 8.

CHILDREN OF JOHN IRELAND AND MARY E. HAINES (310).

1010. Joseph, born 1860, 7, 1. Died 1861, 5, —.
1011. Cordelia, born 1862, 5, —.
1012. Selma M., born 1865, 2, —.

CHILDREN OF WILLIAM L. HAINES (311) AND ANNIE DUYCHINK.

1013. Joseph, born 1863, 1, —.
1014. Emily, born 1866, 8, —.

CHILDREN OF JOSEPH K. LEVIS (316) AND ——— — ———.

1015. Walter K., born 1864, 10, 24; died 1866, 10, 12.
1016. Norris L, born 1866, 7, 31.

CHILDREN OF I. DAY CARTER AND ELIZA A. LEVIS (317).

1017. Harry L., born 1855, 10, 3.
1018. Mary E., born 1857, 6, 17.
1019. Annie C., born 1859, 1, 17.
1020. Robert D., born 1865, 1, 22.
1021. Emily, born 1867, 4, 23.

CHILDREN OF SLATER B. RUSSELL AND AMELIA LEVIS (318).

1022. Annie L., born 1863, 7, 26.
1023. Mary, born 187–, —, —.

CHILD OF LEVI ROGERS (324) AND MARY JANE MILLER.

1024. Timothy, born 1867, 7, 17.

CHILDREN OF JOHN STARBUCK AND ANN LAPPIN (327).

1025. George, born 1821, 7, 8 ; died 1840, 10, 20.
1026. Samuel, born 1823, 5, 12.
1027. Hezekiah, born 1825, 8, 19 ; died 1836, 1, 7.
1028. John, born 1827, 4, 11.
1029. Robert, born 1829, 5, 3 ; died 1841, 6, 22.
1030. William, born 1831, 2, 8.
1031. Elizabeth, born 1833, 4, 14; died 1853, 10, 13.
1032. Daniel, born 1835, 9, 25.
1033. Ruth A., born 1837, 12, 23.
1034. Elisha, born 1839, 5, 24 ; died 1840, 3, 23.
1035. Thomas, born 1843, 3, 8 ; died 1864, 4, 29.

CHILDREN OF ROBINSON LAPPIN (328) AND —— ——.

1036. Elizabeth, born 1829, 6, 11. Married 1855, 6, 3.
1037. Robert, born 1830, 8, 7. Married 1854, 3, 10.
1038. Sarah, born 1832, 1, 13. Married 1854, 4, 16.
1039. Mary, born 1834, 6, 10. Married 1854, 3, 2.
1040. William, K., born 1836, 3, 8. Married 1858, 5, —.
1041. Ann, born 1838, 4, 11. Married 1857, 5, 17.
1042. Rachel, born 1840, 3, 11.
1043. Alice, born 1842, 1, 11 ; died 1867, 10, 25. Married 1867, 2, 27.
1044. John Westley, born 1844, 3, 5.
1045. George F., born 1846, 5. 5 ; died 1863, 3, 3.
1046. Eliza Jane, born 1849, 11, 13.
1047. Sylvester, born 1851, 11, 6 ; died 1852, 12, 27.
1048. Phebe, born 1855, 1, 5 ; died 1857, 8, 8.

CHILDREN OF THOMAS PRICE AND MARY COPE (330).

1049. Ezekiel, born 1815, 6, 1. Married Lydia Stambaugh, and resides near Mansfield, Ohio. (No account of children.)

1050. Jesse, born 1818, 1, 20; died 1857, 10, —. Married Isabella Ray.

1051, Isaac, born 1819, 11, 28. Married Jane Ray. Jane dec'd. Isaac married a second wife, named Asentha P. Hurlbut. They reside at Beverly, Washington county, Ohio.

1052. Sarah, born 1822, 1, 21. Married Jeheil Con. He is deceased. Sarah married a second husband, named James Kelley.

1053. John, born 1824, 1, 10.

1054, Thomas, born 1826, 10, 29. Married Elizabeth Williamson.

CHILDREN OF JOSEPH COPE (331) AND ELIZABETH FISHER.

1055. Ruth, born 1817, 8, 18. Married 1840, 6, 16, to Stephen, son of Moses and Abigail Embree, of Columbiana county, Ohio. Stephen was born 1805, 8, 28. Resides at Westfield, Hamilton county, Ind.

1056. Elihu, born 1819, 1, 21. Married Catharine ———. (Nothing further ascertained.)

1057. Uriah, born 1821, 1, 31. Died 1841, 5, 5.

1058. Anna, born 1822, 12, 7. Married 1847, 3, 14, to Justis L. Blarney.

1059. Sarah R., born 1824, 9, 1. Married 1841, 8, 27, to John, son of John and Martha Naylor, of Belmont county, Ohio.

CHILDREN OF JOHN COPE (332) AND SARAH SMITH.

1060. George, born 1820, 6, 11. Married 1843, 7, 6, to Almira Hewitt, of Perry township, Fayette county. She was born 1818, 8, 1. No children.

1061. Oliver, born 1822, 2, 28. Married 1847, 4, 29, to Mary H. Enloes, and resides in Stark county, Ohio.

1062. Isaac P., born 1824, 1, 22. Married 1848, 3, 3, to Ann Cummings, of Little Corly, England. She was born 1827, 10, 8. They reside near Olney, Richland county, Ill.

1063. Hannah, born 1826. 4, 14. Married 1844, 8, 2, to Cyrus Benedict. He was born 1823, 5, 5. Resides in Omro, Wisconsin.

1064. John S., born 1827, 11, 27; died 1832, 8, 25.

1065. Sarah A., born 1829, 10, 8; died 1830, 5, 30.

1066. Mary Ann, born 1831, 7, 22. Married 1850, 8, 25, to Thompson McCutcheon. They reside in Omoro, Winnebago county, Wisconsin.

1067. Dawsey, born 1833, 4, 20. Married 1858, 10, 31, to Adeline Riggs, of Ottawa county, Ill. She was born 1842,9, 9.

1068. Ruth Ann, born 1835, 6, 29. Married Jonathan Knight. Ruth dec'd. No children.

1069. Sarah Jane, born 1839, 12, 28. Married 1857, 4, 25, to John E. Lopez. He was born 1830, 3, 2.

1070. Henry, born 1837, 8, 10. Married 1857, 7, 1, to Sarah Gray. She was born 1841, 4, 25. No children.

1071. John C., born 1842, 3, 5.

1072. Charles B., born ——, —, —.

CHILDREN OF MOSES PENNOCK AND JUDITH COPE (333).

1073. Isaac C., born 1822, 3, 16; died 1849, 6. Married 1845, 6, to Rebecca Encloes.

1074. Mary, born 1823, 12, 18; died 1848, 3, —.

1075. Sarah C., born 1826, 4, 22; died 1847, 9, 23.

1076. Hannah, born 1828, 5, 3; died 1848, 9, 18.

1077. William, born 1830, 6, 14; died 1855, 12, 30. Married 1851, —, —, to Eliza N. Paxson.

1078. John C., born 1832, 7, 24; died 1859, 4, 3.

1079. Esther, born 1834, 8, 22; died 1852, 9, 18.

1080. Elizabeth, born 1837, 4, 29. Married 1856, to William C. Garrettson. No children.

1081. Anna, born 1840, 1, 13.

CHILDREN OF MICHAEL HAGAMAN AND SARAH COPE (334).

1082. Ruth, born 1822, 6, 10; died 1857, 3, 26. Married 1844, 12, 23, to John Reeder. They reside near Amboy, Hillsdale county, Michigan.

1083. Maria, born 1824, 3, 22. Married 1845, 4, 3, to William Elliott.

1084. Isaac C., born 1826, 5. 12. Married 1846, 4, 9, to Margaret Elliott.

1085. Anna, born 1828, 8, 25. Married 1852, 5, 22, to Mayhew Elliott. No children.

1086. John, born 1831, 3, 9. Married 1851, 4, 14, to Annie Briton. No children.

1087. Joseph, born 1833, 7, 19. Married 1851, 4, 11, to Eliza Cook. No children.

1088. Sarah, born 1836, 9, 13. Married 1854, 3, 18, to Zackary Brown. They reside in Williams county, Ohio.

1089. Martha, born 1840, 9, 8.

1090. Rachel, born 1843, 3, 4.

CHILDREN OF ISAAC COPE (336) AND RACHEL EMBREE.

1091. John A., born 1829, 7, 12. Married 1859, 6, 1, to Ada Winder, daughter of Joseph and Epphana. He resides in Stark county, Ohio.

1092. Abiah, born 1830, 10, 9; died 1853, 6, 25.

1093. Ellis W., born 1832, 7, 8. Married 1853, 10, 1, to Deborah Fowler. Resides at Amboy, Hillsdale county, Michigan. Deborah deceased. Ellis, second wife, Mary E. Blackford.

1094. Hiram, born 1834, 5, 5; died 1849, 9, 8.

1095. Mellissa A., born 1836, 1, 8; died 1853, 5, 10.

1096. Cyrus, born 1838, 2, 3.

1097. Lucinda, born 1841, 8, 10. Married 1863, 11, 12, to Dawsey Armstrong. Dawsey was born 1830, 8, 20. Their post-office address, Fairfield, Columbiana county, Ohio.

1098. Sarah Annette, born 1843, 9, 13. Married 1864, 9, 29, to Porter Rice.

1099. Emeline, born 1846, 2, 14. Married 1867, 9, 25, to Samuel Armstrong. Samuel born 1843, 11, 7.

1100. Oliver, born 1848, 8, 23; died 1849, 4, 25.

CHILDREN OF AARON VANSYOC AND RUTH COPE (338).

1101. Isaac, born 1828, 7, 15.

1102. Enos P., born 1830, 1, 19. Married 1852, 9, 2, to Phebe Crew. They reside near Salem, Columbiana county, Ohio.

1103. John, born 1831, 11, 10; died 1842, 5, 5.

1104. Jesse, born 1833, 3, 14. Married 1857, 4, 20, to Rachael Morrison. They reside in Warren county, Iowa.

1105. Abraham E., born 1834, 12, 6, Married 1858, 12, 5, to Mary Jane Cook. They reside in Warren county, Iowa.

1106. Sarah Jane, born 1836, 11, 28. Married 1855, 5, —, to Enoch Berrier.

1107. Amos, born 1838, 4, 18.

1108. Harrison, born 1840, 1, 18.

1109. Simeon, born 1842, 10, 26.

1110. Oliver T., born 1846, 7, 18.

1111. Lydia, born 1848, 2, 28.

1112. Aaron E., born 1850, 3, 21.

CHILDREN OF JESSE COPE (339) AND ELIZABETH M'GREW.

1113. Rebecca M., born 1834, 11, 3.

1114. Sarah Ann, born 1835, 11, 20. Married 1856, 5, 3, to William Bundy, and resides in Jefferson county, Ohio.

1115. Caroline, born 1837, 4, 30.

1116. Emily, born 1838, 12, 29.

1117. Mary, born 1840, 11, 25.

1118. James A., born 1842, 10, 14.

1119. Mercy, born 1844, 11, 3.

1120. Albert, born 1846, 10, 26.

1121. Allen, born 1848, 11, 30.

1122. Lydia, born 1850, 12, 27.

1123. Almira, born 1853, 10, 12.

CHILD OF SAMUEL TAYLOR (340) AND —— PILE.

1124. Levi P., born ——, —, —. Resides in Keokuk, Iowa.

CHILDREN OF SAMUEL TAYLOR (340) AND REBECCA MORRIS.

1125. Mary, born ——, —, —.

1126. Oliver, born ——, —, —.

1127. Morris, born ——, —, —.

1128. Abner, born ——, —, —.

1129. Elizabeth, ——, —, —.

1130. Emily, born ——, —, —.

CHILDREN OF NATHAN PRICE AND ABIGAIL TAYLOR (341).

1131. John, born ——, —, —.

1132. Joseph, born ——, —, —.

1133. Levi, born ——, —, —.

1134. Elias, born ——, —, —.

CHILDREN OF JOSEPH TAYLOR (342) AND HANNAH HUTTON.

1130. ———, }
1131. ———, } Names not ascertained.
1132. ———, }
1133. Eliza Jane, born 18—, —, —.

CHILDREN OF ALEXANDER MAXWELL AND JUDITH TAYLOR (344)

1135. Milton, born ——, —, —.
1136. John, born ——, —, —.
1137. Lucinda, born ——, —, —.
1138. Mary, born ——, —, —.
1139. Hannah, born——, —, —.
1140. Hesther, born ——, —, —.

CHILDREN OF JOSEPH WINDER AND AMY TAYLOR (345).

1141. Mary Ann, born 1829, 7, 9. Married 1850, 10, 5, to Henry Stauffer. He was born 1826, 6, 10.

1142. Sarah Amelia, born 1831, 6, 16. Married 1849, 10, 14, to Joseph Miner. Joseph was born 1826, 4, 1; died 1863, 4, 5, at Murfreesboro, Tenn., in the service of the U. States.

1143. Abigail, born 1833, 10, 15. Married 1854, 10, 29, to John Stauffer. He was born in Ohio, 1828, 12, 15.

1144. James Newton, born 1836, 6, 24; died 1839, 5, 29.

1145. Hannah Louisa, born 1839, 1, 8. Married 1866, 4, 5, to C. W. Swartz. He was born 1837, 7, 1.

1146. John Taylor, born 1841, 10, 26; died 1842, 3, 8.

1147. Nancy L., born 1843, 6, 15. Married 1861, 8, 15, to Lyman Wooster. Lyman born 1834, 2, 13.

1148. Amy Sophia, born 1846, 4, 18. Married 1869, 3, 20, to Ancil B. Miller. He was born 1846, 3, 23.

1149. Samuel J., born 1848, 12, 17. Not married.

1150. Joseph A. K., born 1851, 7, 30. Died 1853, 11, 25.

CHILDREN OF WILKINSON ELLIOT AND SARAH TAYLOR (346).

1151. Abner K., born 1835, 6, 24. Married 857, 11, 12, to Harriet A. Rochelle. They reside in Hardin county, Ohio.

1152. Angeline E., born 1837, 4, 2; died ——, —, —, in Hayti, while on a visit to the West Indies.

1153. Susanna E., born 1838, 8, 16; died 1841, 1, 17.

1154. Judith C., born 1841, 11, 17. Married 1857, 10, 26, to Henry Mitchell. They reside in Missouri.

1155. Rachel A., born 1844, 5, 30.

1156. Mary A., born 1849, 1, 26

1157. Benjamin M. O., born 1851, 10, 3.

1158. Elby E., born 1854, 5, 18; died 1854, 10, —.

CHILDREN OF LEVI K. TAYLOR (347) AND ROSATER YANKEY.

1159. Prentice, born ——, —, —.

1160. William, born ——, —, —.

1161. Louisa, born ——, —, —.

1162. Mary, born ——, —, —.

1163. Erastus, born ——, —, —.

1164. Joseph, born ——, —, —.

1165. Elma, born ——, —, —.

CHILDREN OF JOHN TAYLOR (348) AND ——— CRAIG.

1166. John C., born ——, —, —. Married, and resides in Elkhart, Ohio.

1167. Mary, born ——, —, —.

CHILDREN OF ABNER TAYLOR (349) AND C. WERNER.

1168. Joseph H., born 1845, 6, 3.

1169. Eliza J., born 1846, 10, 25; died 1849, 6, 26

1170. Mary I., born 1848, 8, 1.

1171. John W., born 1850, 6, 12.
1172. Wilson T., born 1852, 6, 1.
1173. Leora J., born 1854, 4, 19.

CHILDREN OF JOSEPH WINDER (350) AND AMY TAYLOR.

☞ See No. 345.

CHILDREN OF JAMES WINDER (351) AND MARY SWENA.

1174. Amanda, born 1834, 10, 20.

1175. Mary A., born 1836, 9, 5. Married 1859, 8, 11, to Alexander McQuiston.

1176. Joseph K., born 1838, 11, 15; died 1864, 8, 16. He was killed in the United States army.

1177. Benjamin S., born 1840, 9, 20.

1178. Lorenzo Dow, born 1842, 11, 3. Married 1869, 4, 27, to Annie H. Wallace.

1179. Francina A., born 1846, 9, 9.

1180. Eliza H., born 1849, 9, 8.

1181. James Alonzo, born 1851, 12, 12.

1182. Alice A., born 1856, 6, 22.

CHILDREN OF WILLIAM WINDER (352) AND SYBIL HARRISON.

1183. Thomas H., born ——, —, —. Married and moved to Salt Lake City, Utah. He has three children.

1184. Anna, born ——, —, —. Married Elmer Connor, who lives at Americus, Lyons county, Kansas.

CHILDREN OF CHARLES SHREVE (353) AND SARAH WINDER.

1185. Seth, born 1831, 9, 21. Married 1856, 9, 10, to Alma Birds. They have six children. (Nothing further known of them.)

1186. Lydia, born 1833, 6, 4; died 1860, 3, 25. Married

——, 7, 3, to Andrew J. Westfield. They have two children, names not learned

1187. Hannah, born 1835, 2, 25; died at Great Salt Lake City. Married 1856, 5, 1, to Thomas Winder, and has three children.

1188. Charlotte, born 1837, 6, 23. Married 1854, 9, —, to John P. Bacon. They have three children.

1189. James, born 1839, 6, 6. Married 1860, 12, —, to Sarah M. Churchill. They have two children.

1190. Charles Henry, born 1842, 4, 9. Married 1864, 9, 9, to Cordelia E. Berger. No children.

1191. Levi, born 1844, 11, 8; died 1864, 6, 1, from wounds received while in the United States Army.

1192. Joseph L., born 1847, 7, 12.

1193. Amy, born 1849, 7, 24.

CHILDREN OF DAVID NASH AND JUDITH WINDER (354).

1194. Mary Ann, born ——, —, —. Married Henry Fields. Her address, Geneva, Michigan. She has one son.

1195. James W., born ——, —, —. Married. Has one son and a daughter.

CHILDREN OF JOHN JULION AND JUDITH WINDER (354).

1196. Joseph K., born 1847, 5, 20.

1197. Maria Lavinia, born 1850, 1, 1. She married James Moody.

CHILDREN OF LEMUEL SWENA AND ELIZA WINDER (355).

1198. Anson, born 1836, 10, 10.

1199. Eliza, born 1839, 4, 28. Married 1865, 6, 10, to Frances Wookey. They have two children.

1200. Emeline A., born 1841, 4, 2. Married 1860, 4, 3, to Reuben W. Kratz, and have two children.

1201. Lemuel, born 1833, 1, 28; died 1845, 9, 27.

1202. Caroline, born 1844, 11, 27; died 1844, 11, 30.

1203. Orlando, born 1846, 4, 18.

1204. Maria S., born 1849, 12, 18. Married 1865, 1, 26, to Harris C. Overton, and have two children.

1205. Amelia, born 1852, 5, 28.

1206. Lemuel B., born 1854, 12, 24; died 1869, 6, 7.

CHILDREN OF ALFRED GREEN AND HANNAH WINDER (356).

1207. Levi N., born, 1843, 6, 1. Married 1859, 7, 29, to Hannah L Thompson. They have two children.

1208. Phebe, born 1844, 6, 14.

1209. Joseph, born 1846, 4, 20.

1210. Eliza A., born 1847, 8, 10. Married 1867, 11, 16, to Lewis Obert.

1211. Olive, born 1849, 12,9.
1212. Mary, born 1851, 7 13.
1213. Harriet, born 1853, 2, 3.
1214. James W., born 1855, 3, 9.
1215. Emily C., born 1857, 3, 8.
} Not married.

CHILDREN OF AZZAM GILLETT AND MARY WINDER (357).

1216. Valentine, born 1838, 7, 29; died ——, —, —.

1217. Ruth Ann, born 1840, 5, 21. Married James Wing.

1218. Hannah, born 1841, 9, 11; died ——, —, —. Married —— Freeman, and had one son.

1219. James H., born 1843, 3, 28.

1220. Elizabeth, born 1845, 9, 17; died ——, —, —.

1221. Nancy, born 1847, 9, 30.

1222. Joseph, born 1849, 10, 11.

1223. Azzam, born 1852, 1, 26.

1224. Betsey Miranda, born 1854, 5, 19.
1225. Westly, born 1856, 1, 27.
1226. Joanna, born 1858, 5, 7.
1227. Mary Jane, born, 1860, 7, 1.

CHILDREN OF MADISON ALDERMAN AND SUSAN WINDER (359).

1228. Laura Ann, born 1840, 3, 14; died 1843, 6, 31.

1229. Zelpha L., born 1843, 10, 18. Married 1861, 3, 1, to John R. Shaw.

1230. James B., born 1847, 10, 18.
1231. Angeline, born 1849, 12, 29.
1232. Clinton B., born 1853, 7, 27.
1233. William A., born 1858, 12, 1.
1234. George M., 1863, born 9, 26.

CHILDREN OF ABNER DAVIS AND PRISCILLA KIRK (360).

1235. Henry S., born 1827, 1, 21; died 1863, 1, 12, at Camp Nelson.

1236. Elizabeth J., born 18—, 8, 31; died 1843, 8, 15.

1237. John A., born 1833, 4, 1. Married 1856, 1, 22, to Sarah A. Hinton.

1238. Lydia A., born 1835, 7, 1. Married Anthony Johnson.

CHILDREN OF THOMAS B. JONES AND JANE KIRK (362).

1239. Priscilla D., born 1832, 10, 29. Married 1851, 5, 1, to Samuel Hiner.

1240. William K., born 1834, 10, 3. Married 1859, 12, 13, to Matilda Jones.

1241. Joseph A., born 1837, 4, 8; died 1865, 1, 11 Married Bridget A. Lewis.

1242. Matilda, born 1840, 12, 18. Married 1861, 4, 11, to James M. Hurst.

1243. Thomas A. born 1843, 6, 3. Married 1865, 10, 30, to Louisa F. Gardner.

1244. John A., born 1846, 8, 10.

1245. Sarah J., born 1849, 3, 7.

1246. Julina, born 1851, 1, 14.

CHILDREN OF EDWARD J. KIRK (363) AND LUCINDA NORTHCOTT.

1247. William C., born 1836, 11, 30. Married 1864, 6, 8.

1248. Lucinda P., born 1850, 2, 5.

1249. Joseph H., born 1851, 12, 28; died 1856, 2, 8.

1250. James W., born 1853, 9, 1.

1251. Sarah E., born 1856, 8, 7; died 1862, 5, 5.

1252. Martha P., born 1858, 2, 29.

1253. Eliza Jane, born 1860, 4, 19.

1254. Edward J., born 1862, 3, 3.

1255. Julianna B., born 1864, 9, 20.

1256. Vicola M., born 1867, 10, 28.

CHILDREN OF DAVID M. WILLIAMS AND ELEANOR KIRK (365).

1257. Elizabeth S., born 1840, —, —. Married 1864, —, —, to Minear T. Graham.

1258. Eliza Jane, born 1842, —, —. Married 1865, —, —, to George H. Williams.

1258. Harriet M., born 1848, —, —. Married 1869, to Hiram Hawkins.

1259. Almaranda, born 1851, —, —.

1260. David P., born 1858, —, —.

CHILDREN OF JOHN F. SUMMERS AND MELINDA KIRK (366).

1261. Priscilla, born 1838, 12, 12; died 1843, 8, 29.
1262. William K., born 1841, 3, 15; died 1869, 9, 20.
1263. John B., born 1843, 1, 1; died 1843, 1, 29.
1264. Elizabeth A., born 1844, 6, 17.
1265. Mason, born 1851, 9, 1.
1266. James, born 1853, 3, 24; died 1855, 2, 2.
1267. Franklin, born 1855, 1, 24; died 1857, 7, 15.
1268. Sarah, born 1862, 3, 16.

CHILDREN OF GEORGE MUSE AND ELIZA KIRK (367).

1269. Elizabeth S., born 1842, 11, 19; died 1868, 6, 1. Married 1864, 9, 17. to John Reed.

1270. James W., born 1847, 10, 25. Married 1869, 3, 4, to Margaret Kelley.

1271. Margaret, born 1849, 9, 15. Married 1852, 4, 8, to H. C. Morrison.

1272. Robert H., born 1852, 5, 4.

CHILDREN OF WILLIAM G. KIRK (368) AND JULIA BENTON.

1273. John W., born, 1849, 10, 28; died 1850, 1, 18.
1274. Thomas J., born 1851, 3, 23.
1275. Mary E., born 1852, 10, 23.
1276. Sarah E., born 1854, 9, 5.
1277. John M., born 1856, 9, 4.
1278. Coleman B., born 1858, 9, 28.
1279. Jane I., born 1860, 5, 24; died 1862, 9, 5.
1280. Joseph G., born 1862, 4, 6.
1281. Mary F., born 1864, 4, 10.
1282. Jesse B., born 1866, 4, 14.
1283. Edward I., born 1868, 5, 8.

CHILDREN OF ELIHU NASH AND ELIZA BROOMFIELD (371).

1284 Marinda. born 1835, 6, 18; died 1835, 6, 19.

1285. Emeline, born 1837, 4, 18; died 1849, 1, 14.

1286. Asahel F., born 1840, 3, 12; died 1862, 11, 3.

1287. Andrew F., born 1844, 5, 20; died 1845, 3, 14.

1288. William L., born 1846, 3, 20. Married 1867, 12, 25, ·o Harriet Brown.

1289. Albert McB., born 1848, 1, 20.

1290. Sarah A., born 1849, 12, 6.

1291. James F., born 1851, 8, 15; died 1853, 2, 13.

1292. Mary E., born 1854, 5, 9.

1293 Henry I., born 1857, 12, 14.

CHILDREN OF THOMAS MAXWELL AND SARAH A BLOOMFIELD (372).

1294. Cyrus M., born 1836, 3, 25. Married 1858, 1, 3, to Sarah A. Crocket.

1295. Emily M., born 1838, 10, 28. Married 1865, 11, 25, to Henry Kendel.

1296. Lewis B., born 1841, 2, 13. Married 1867, 4, 11, to Sylvester Hatcher.

1297. William I., born 1843, 11, 28. Married 1865, 12, 20, to Amanda Underwood.

1298. Louisa S., born 1847, 7, 25. Married 1866, 9, 28, to Joseph A. Putt.

1299. Erastus, born 1850, 4, 4.

1300. Susan A., born 1854, 8, 4.

CHILDREN OF LEWIS M. BROOMFIELD (373) AND LYDIA INGLEDUE.

1301. Alpheus S., born 1839, 3, 18. Married 1866, 4, 11, to Elmira Dixon.

1302. Celestine H., born 1842, 1, 1. Married 1865, 11, 23, to Madison Walker.

1303. Thomas M., born 1844, 9, 26. Married 1868, 9, 29, to Samantha Chane.

1304. Susan G., born 1846, 5, 4. Married 1869, 2, 23, to Joseph Marshall.

1305. Ascenath, born 1850, 12, 20.

CHILDREN OF THOMAS M'CALL AND JUDITH BLOOMFIELD (375).

1306. Mary E., born 1837, 12, 26; died 1856, 2, 26.

1307. Henry, born 1838, 12, 4; died 1863, 12, 3.

1308. Almira, born 1841, 11, 2; died 1858, 4, 13.

1309. Melissa, born 1843, 3, 31. Married 1860, 11, 25, to Evan James.

1310. Samantha, born 1845, 2, 15; died 1865, 6, 29.

1311. Oliver, born 1846, 7, 25.

1312. Lucinda, born 1847, 5, 23.

1313. Susan, born 1849, 7, 22.

1314. Lewis B., born 1851, 9, 6.

1315. William, born 1854, 2, 4.

1316. Thomas M., born 1856, 2, 26.

1317. Sarah M., born 1858, 4, 18.

1318. Matilda I., born 1860, 9, 19.

1319. Salmon P. C., born 1863, 1, 29.

CHILDREN OF WILLIAM BROOMFIELD (378) AND HESTER A. BURNS.

1320. Alice L., born 1850, 3, 21; died 1868, 8, 14.

1321. Robert A., born 1853, 9, 2.

1322. Florence F., born 1857, 11, 5.

1323. Morris L., born 1860, 6, 9.

1324. Vienna E., born 1864, 11, 6; died 1865, 11, 13

1325. William C., born 1867, 2, 9.

CHILDREN OF DAVID WHITE (384) AND MELISSA CAZIER.

1326. Edwin C., born 1835, 12, 6.
1327. David G., born 1837, 10, 30.
1328. Cornelia F., born 1840, 2, 6.
1329. Willier F., born 1843, 1, 6.
1330. Mary H., born 1845, 6, 15; died 1866, —, —.
1331. William C., born 1849, 12, 23.
1332. Samuel R., born 1853, 3, 31.

CHILD OF ABSALOM K. WHITE (385) AND —— ——.

1333. Absalom, born ——, —, —.

CHILDREN OF HENRY DOUGHTY AND CATHARINE WHITE (386).

1334. Susan, born ——, —, —; died ——, —, —.
1335. Joseph, born ——, —, —.
1336. Rachel, born ——, —, —.

CHILDREN OF ISAAC NOLAN AND RACHEL WHITE (387).

1337. Mary E., born ——, —, —; died in infancy.
1338. Mellissa, born ——, —, —; died in infancy.

CHILDREN OF DAVID GILMORE AND ELIZABETH WHITE (388).

1339. David, born ——, —, —.
1340. John G., born ——, —, —.
1341. Clarissa, born ——, —, —.
1342. Columbus, born ——, —, —.
1343. Charles, born ——, —, —.
1344. Isabella, born ——, —, —.

CHILDREN OF WILLIAM M. KIRK AND ANN ENGLAND (390).

See (70).

CHILDREN OF JOHN BROWN AND SARAH ENGLAND (391).

1345. Elisha, born ——, —, —.

1346. Ann Eliza, born ——, —, —. Married Job Watson and had one child. (Nothing further known of the family.)

1347. Mary, born ——, —, —; died ——, —, —. No children.

1348. Sarah, born ——, —, —. Married Levi Hill.

1349. Henry, born ——, —, —.

1350. William, born ——, —, —; died young. No children.

1351. Albina, born ——, —, —.

CHILDREN OF GEORGE ENGLAND (392) AND MARY KIRK.

See (113).

CHILDREN OF ISAAC BROWN AND ELIZABETH ENGLAND (393).

1352. Mary Ann, born 1823, 9, 26. Married 1843, 3, 28, to John White. John deceased. Second marriage, 1859, 1, 27, to John R. Abrahams.

1353. Ruth A., born 1825, 3, 14; died 1831, 8, 31.

1354. Samuel J., born 1826, 10, 21. Married 1854, 10, 2, to Mary L. Cameron. She was born 1837, 11, 4.

1355. Allen K., born 1829, 10, 1; died 1833, 11, 2.

1356. Narcissa A., born 1832, 6, 16. Married 1857, 8, 12, to Isaiah D. Passmore.

1357. Hannah E., born 1836, 1, 9.

CHILDREN OF JOHN ENGLAND (394) AND MARY KIRK.

1358. William, born 1829, 6, 26. Married Julia Pierson. No children.

1359. Mary E., born 1831, 3, 17. Married Henry, son of John and Sarah Brown. He resides in Wilmington, Delaware.

1360. Eli Elisha, born 1834, 1, 14. Married Catharine Clawson.

1361. Granville Hughes, born 1836, 10, 22.

CHILDREN OF JOHN ENGLAND (394) AND SARAH GAMBLE.

1362. Joanna, born 1844, 3, 16.

1363. Francis, born 1846, 3, 28.

1364. Henrietta, born 1848, 2, 27.

1365. John C., born 1850, 3, 16; died 1858, 3, 29.

1366. James T., born 1854, 9, 19; died 1860, 5, 5.

1367. George L., born 1860, 4, 29.

CHILDREN OF NATHAN GRIFFITH AND MARY KIRK (395).

1368. Lydia A. born 1818, 6, 17. Married 1844, 2, 21, to Clemson Brown.

1369. Sarah, born 1822, 4, 13; died 1824, 8, 14.

1370. William K., born 1825, 6, 4. Married 1847, 11, 4, to Jane C. Cameron.

1371. Job M., born 1927, 7, 25. Married 1863, 12, 31, to Mary E. Brown.

1372. Hannah A., born 1829, 12, 28. Not married.

CHILDREN OF JACOB KIRK (399) AND HANNAH BROWN.

1373. Selinda, born 1843, 3, 10; died 1851, 8, 24.

1374. Mary Ann, born 1845, 1, 5; died 1855, 6, 25.

1375. Hannah A., born 1846. 9, 16; died 1855, 6, 1.

1376. Lydia Emeline, born 1848, 10, 18. Resides in Ohio, and follows the profession of teaching.

1377. Slater B. born 1850, 11, 11; died 1859, 1, 28.

1378. Samuel Job, born 1852, 11, 2.

1379. Archibald A., born 1854, 8, 1.

1380. Slater L., born 1857, 3, 7.

CHILDREN OF LEWIS KIRK (400) AND JANE HOLLINGSWORTH.

1381. Joshua, born 1836, 12, 22. Married 1859, 10, 18, to Clarrissa, daughter of Francis and Deborah Smith, of Cecil county, Md. No children,

1382. Hannah E., born 1840, 2, 16; died 1860, 9, 6.

1383. William H., born 1842, 6, 5; died 1864, 4, 26.

1384. Mary Emeline, born 1844, 8, 27. Moved West, and married Theodore Hilaman.

1385. Rachel L., born 1846, 11, 18. Married 1867, 11, 18, to George Swayne. They migrated West.

CHILDREN OF JOB H. KIRK (401) AND LYDIA WILSON.

1386. William L., born 1834. Married 1866, 2, 6, to Laura Gamble. Laura, born 1841, 9, 10.

1387. Samuel W., born 1837, 7, 15. Married 1861, 9, 19, to Annie Boston. Annie, born 1838, 1, 22. No children.

1388. Job H., born 1840, 2, 17. Married 1868, 1, 1, to Elizabeth, daughter of Hiram and Sarah Brown. Elizabeth, born 1841, 7, 4.

CHILDREN OF JOSEPH KIRK (402) AND JANE S. KIRK.

1389. Luther M., born 1838, 9, 11. Married 1862, 12, 4, to Margaret Quimby.

1390. Ann Elizabeth, born 1840, 2, 2.

1391. William, born 1841, 11, 24; died 1857, 6, 17.
1392. Abner, born 1844 2, 10.
1393. Joseph A., born 1846, 2, 2.
1394. Allen, born 1848, 1, 4.
1395. Lewis, born 1850, 3, 25.
1396. Mary Jane, born 1852, 4, 6.
1397. Priscilla E., born 1854, 6, 8; died 1869, 6, 13.

CHILD OF WILLIAM KIRK (404) AND LYDIA SPENCER.

1398. Eunice E, born 1847, 4, 13. Married 1866, 9, 6, to John Hardin. Had one son, William.

CHILDREN OF WILLIAM KIRK (404) AND JANE (HOLLINGSWORTH) KIRK.

1399. Jane A., born 1852, 8, 2.
1400. Lester A., born 1854, 10, 2.
1401. Esther Ilena, born 1857; died 1867, 12, 30.

CHILDREN OF REUBEN KIRK (405) AND HANNAH C. BROWN.

1402. George H., born 1841, 3, 10.
1403. Charles H., born 1843, 11, 6.
1404. Ellis B., born 1845, 9, 21.
1405. Emily J., born 1847, 8, 23.
1406. Mira E., born 1850, 7, 17.
1407. Rachel A., born 1853, 1, 24.
1408. Reuben E., born 1858, 6, 23; died 1860, 7, 19.

CHILDREN OF JOHN KIRK AND ESTHER E. KIRK (406.)

☞ See No. 431.

CHILDREN OF ALPHONSO C. KIRK AND MIRA KIRK (408).

☞ See No. 440.

CHILDREN OF ELWOOD BROWN AND RACHEL KIRK (410).

1409. Elizabeth R., born 1846, 7, 21; died 1848, 3, 21.
1410. Infant, born 1847, —, —; died 1847, —, —.

CHILD OF JACOB JOB AND RACHEL (KIRK) BROWN (410).

1411. Haines, born 1865, 6, 1.

CHILDREN OF ABNER KIRK (411) AND MARY ENGLAND.

1412. Emma E., born 1851, 12, 27; died 1863, 8, 12.
1413. Marcella, born 1854, 3, 12; died 1854, 7, 23.
1414. Leora, born 1858, 2, 28; died 1861, 4, 28.
1415. Rachel, born 1860, 7, 1.
1416. Louisia, born 1862, 11, 6.

CHILDREN OF ABNER KIRK (411) AND HANNAH DONOHOO.

1417. Caroline E., born 1867, 1, 27.
1418. William, born 1868, 8, 4.

CHILDREN OF SAMUEL BROWN AND EMELINE KIRK (412).

1419. Infant, born 1864, 12, 4; died 1864, 12, 5.
1420. Ann Elizabeth, born 1866, 4, 28.
1421. William, born 1868, 5, 30; died 1868, 8, 1.

CHILD OF SAMUEL BROWN (416) AND ELIZA LESLIE.

1422. Helen, born ——, —, —. Married Nathaniel Touchstone. After his decease she married Franklin Terry. Franklin born 1832, 7, 7, and died 1871, 4, 2. He resided near Rising Sun, Cecil county, Md. Date of Helen's last marriage, 1863, 4, 10.

CHILD OF SAMUEL BROWN (416) AND SUSAN LONG.

1423. Maria, born ——, —, —. Married William Kirk. No children.

CHILDREN OF ABNER BROWN (418) AND NAOMI MILLER.

1424. Elizabeth, born 1825, 1, 1. Married William J., son of Jonas and Abbie Hess. William resides on a farm near Quarryville, Lancaster county, Pa., and is engaged in burning and selling lime.

1425. Franklin, born 1827, 11, 20, Married Ellen Woodland. Ellen died. Franklin married Elizabeth, daughter of Elcana and Susan Koomes. Franklin now resides on a farm near Wakefield, Lancaster county, Pa.

1426. Sophia J., born 1830, 4, 25. Married 1847, 1, 21, to William A. son of Thomas and Elizabeth Towson, of Fairfield, Lancaster county, Pa. William, born 1824, 2, 30. Died 1861, 1, 15. He resided at New Mexico, Cecil county. Md.

1427. William K., born 1832, 5, 24. Married Mary, daughter of Benjamin and Elizabeth Harlan. Mary deceased, William married Eliza Pierson. They reside near New Texas, Lancaster county, Pa. William is a carpenter.

1428. Samuel Miller, born 1835, 2, 22. Died 1861, 3, 25. Never married.

1429. Lucy, born 1837, 8, 22. Married Robert, son of Joseph and Ellen Jamison, of Little Britain. Robert resides near Elim, Lancaster county, Pa., and is a farmer by occupation.

1430. Emily, born 1840, 1, 26. Married Theodore, son of Washington Whittaker. Theodore resides on the Susquehanna, at a place known as Barnes' Mill. He is a river pilot, and is engaged in the coal and lumber business—being one of the firm of "Cain & Whittaker."

1431. Harlan, born 1842, 10, 3; died 1847, 7, 3.

CHILDREN OF MARK BROWN (419) AND LYDIA A. BROWN.

1432. William Westley, born ——, —, —. Resides at Port Deposit, Cecil county, Md.

1433. Cornelius, born ——, —, —.

1434. Granville, born ——, —, —.

1435. Mark, born ——, —, —.

1436. Rebecca, born ——, —, —.

There are two more children, names unknown.

CHILDREN OF LUKE BROWN (422) AND PHEBE W. BROWN.

1437. William, born 1839, 3, 29. Married 1863, 12, 24, to Lydia A. Re der.

1438. Warren P., born 1842, 1, 11. Married 1869, 1, 15, to Hassie Carman.

1439. Basil H., born 1846, 4, 5. Married ——, —, —, to Annie (1861), daughter of Joseph and Rebecca Haines. Basil resides in Philadelphia, and is a clerk in Keen's hat store, 62 North Second street.

1440. Elwood K., born 1853, 12, 24.

CHILDREN OF WILLIAM KIRK (427) AND HANNAH B. ENGLAND.

1441. Mary E., born 1843, 2, 2. Married 1864, 4, —, to Anthony Goodnow.

1442. Cornelia J., born 1844, 12, 31.
1443. Carrie S., born 1846, 9, 16.
1444. Margaret E., born 1849, 1, 5.
1445. Eldora, born 1851, 7, 15.
} Not married.

1446. Theodore A., born 1854, 12, 29.

1447. William C., born 1859, 9, 12.

CHILDREN OF HOWELL KIRK (429) AND LYDIA HARRIS.

1448. Mary Eliza, born 1823, 4, 23. Married 1851, 5, 1, to Robert, son of Robert and ——— Cathers. Robert died 1868, 2, 10.

1449. Jane Eleanor, born 1824, 7, 20; died 1857, 4, 5. Never married.

1450. Theodore, born 1826, 1, 31. Married 1851, 10, 23, to ——, ———.

1451. Caroline, born 1827, 9, 16. Married 1858, 4, 13, to Thomas M. Krauss.

1452. Elam, born 1830, 5, 6. Resides at Rising Sun. Unmarried. Has some reputation as a local preacher in the Methodist Episcopal Church. During the war he acted as Chaplain of —— Regt. Pa. Vols. He resides at Rising Sun village, Cecil county, Md.

1453. Maria, born 1835, 4, 17. Married 1855, 3, 1, to William A. Lockard. They reside at Conshohocken, Montgomery county, Pa.

CHILDREN OF JOHN KIRK (431) AND ESTHER REYNOLDS.

1454. Esther, born 1830, 1. 4; died in infancy.

1455. William, born 1831, 1, 9; died in infancy.

1456. Sarah E., born 1831, 12, 12. Married 1853, 1, 27, to Jonathan McCardell. Jonathan is a cabinet maker, and resides at Rising Sun, Md.

1457. Ann Eliza, born 1835, 4, 1. Married Haines, son of Jonathan and Elizabeth Reynolds. Haines deceased. Ann E. resides in the Rising Sun.

1458. Mary Jane, born 1836, 8, 28. Married John Thompson, son of William and Margaret, of Nottingham, Chester county, Pa. John is a farmer and resides in Nottingham.

1459. Esther I., born 1838, 10, 15. Married 1862, 5, 22, to Thomas Foster. They reside west of Rising Sun.

1460. Margaret R., born 1840, 10, 27. Married 1858, 10, 28, to Augustus Broomfield. They reside on a farm near Rising Sun.

CHILDREN OF JOHN KIRK (431) AND ESTHER E. KIRK.

1461. William Penn, born 1847, 12, 22. Married 1869, 1, 14, to Catharine Hannam.

1462. Eri, born 1849, 1, 14; died 1849, 6, 8.

1463. Clarinda E., born 1850, 2, 17.

1464. John, born 1855, 1, 15; died 1858, 12, 31.

CHILDREN OF JOHN ENGLAND AND MARY KIRK (433).

☞See (394).

CHILDREN OF JACOB W. KIRK (436) AND ANNIE REYNOLDS.

1465. William T., born 1838, 2, 28; died 1863, 10, 22.

1466. Adaline H., born 1840, 8, 13. Married 1866, 2, 27, to Thomas I. Wilson.

1467. Taylor R., born 1842, 10, 5; died 1865, 12, 27.

1468. Claude I., born 1846, 6, 30; died 1866, 5, 14.

1469. Charles R., born 1848, 5, 15. Married 1871, 6, 8, to Jane Stearns. Charles is engaged in keeping a confectionery at Rising Sun, Md.

1470. Cornelia A., born 1852, 7, 57. Single. Resides with her mother.

1471. Sarah E, born 1854, 10, 28.

1472. Jacob E., born 1858, 12, 6.

CHILDREN OF JOB GATCHELL AND ELIZABETH KIRK (437).

1473. William, born 1843, 3, 14; died 1843, 10, 20.

1474. Nathaniel K. born 1845, 3, 16.

1475. Job Haines, born 1849, 4, 9.

1476. David E. born 1852, 3, 31.

CHILDREN OF WILLIAM H. KIRK (438) AND SARAH BROWN.

1477. David E., born 1837, 4, 12. Married 1865, 7, 4, to Rachel A. House.

1478. Mary H., born 1838, 12, 10. Married 1860, 4, 15, to Hanson Kimble.

1479. George, born 1841, 10, 1; died 1867, 10, 2.

1480. Rufus, born 1844, 4, 16. Married ——, 11, 2, to Sarah House.

CHILDREN OF WILLIAM H. KIRK (438) AND MARY E. HOUSE.

1481. William H., born 1850, 2, 20.

1482. Annie V., born 1855, 6, 20.

CHILDREN OF RUFUS MARSHALL KIRK (439) AND MARY BROWN.

1483. Henry C., born 1840, 2, 14.

1484. William, born 1841, 12, 2. Married 1869, 2, 24, to Mary Brown.

1485. Sarah B., born 1844, 3, 18.

1486. Caroline, born 1846, 10, 10.

1487. Indiana, born 1849, 1, 5.

1488. Mary E., born 1851, 6, 4.

CHILDREN OF RUFUS MARSHALL KIRK (439) AND MARY M. LONG.

1489. Isaac N., born 1855, 12, 1.

1490. Frederick M., born 1858, 4. 6.

1491. Edwin M., born 1862, 4, 9.

CHILDREN OF ALPHONSO C. KIRK (440) AND MIRA KIRK.

1492. Sarah Elizabeth, born 1850, 6, 5.

1493. Lydia Emma, born, 1852, 2, 27.

CHILDREN OF ABSOLOM BROWN (441) AND PHEBE LEWIS.

1494. Edward L., born 1825, —, —. Married 1860, 3, 8, to Hannah Hart.

1495. Lydia, born 1827, —, —. Married 1844, 4, 11, to J. C. Rumford.

1496. Samuel S., born 1829, —, —.

1497. William K., born 1832, —, —.

1498. Albert, born 1835, —, —.

1499. Sarah E., born 1838, —, —. Married 1863, 10, 18, to James Rossiter.

1500. Park L., born 1842, —, —.

1501. Hester, born 1842, —, —.

1502. Joseph, born 1845, —, —.

CHILDREN OF AMASA CHURCHMAN AND ANN BROWN (888).

1503. John Thomas, born 1843, 2, 5. Married Annie M. Strickland.

1504. Sarah E., born 1845, 6, 17. Married Thomas Brown, son of Edward Hicks Brown.

1505. Lydia A., born 1846, 9, 10.

1506. Jehu B., born 1847, 12, 24.

1507. Amasa, born 1852, 5, 6.

1508. Charles, born 1854, 12, 1.

CHILD OF JACOB KIRK (445) AND FRANCES WHITTAKER.

1509. Elisha Allen, born 1839, 1, 31. Married 1869, 1, 21, to Mary Agnes Aiken.

CHILDREN OF JACOB KIRK (445) AND CLARISSA WHITTAKER.

1510. Frances M. W., born 1846, 4, 9. Married 1867, 12, 5, to Gilpin O. Hutton.

1511. Mary Elizabeth, born 1848, 11, 16.

1512. Maria Lucretia, born 1850, 6, 13.

1513. Jacob Hall, born 1857, 11, 23.

CHILD OF ——— ——— AND ANN KIRK (446).

1514. Alfred, born 1838, 5, 14. Married 1864, 1, 28, to Anna Thompson. Alfred is farmer by occupation, and resides near College Green, Cecil county, Maryland, on the homestead of Jacob Kirk.

CHILDREN OF ABNER KIRK (447) AND MARY E. MILLER.

1515. Sarah E., born 1844, 12, 1; died 1847, 10, 31.

1516. Jacob, born 1846, 11, 22; died 1864, 4, 26.

1517. James M., born 1848, 2, 6.

1518. Lewis C., born 1851, 7, 29.

1519. Elisha A., born 1853, 7, 25.

1520. William P., born 1855, 10, 15; died 1866, 2, 9.

1521. Abner O., born 1858, 6, 3.

1522. Charles C., born 1860, 1, 27; died 1864 3, 2.

CHILDREN OF AUGUSTUS G. PIERSON AND ELIZABETH KIRK (450).

1523. Maria J., born 1841, 12, 26.

1524. Elisha K., born 1843, 10, 30.

1525. Augustus T., born 1846, 5, 17.

1526. Ann E., born 1848, 10, 13.

1527. Benjamin F., born 1850, 10, 21.

1528. Jacob Allen, born 1852, 11, 1.

1529. William Dawson, born 1855, 1, 8; died 1855, 1, 25.
1530. Clarissa C., born 1856, 3, 30.
1531. John A., born 1858, 5, 1.
1532. Jessie Sabina, born 1860, 12. 19.
1533. Infant, twin of the above, 1860, 12, 19.

CHILDREN OF JOHN C. HAMER AND SARAH A. WILSON (SLICER) (454).

1534. Mary Virginia, born 1849, 2, 13.
1535. Fanny Deborah, born 1854, 11, 15.

CHILDREN OF ALLEN KIRK AND DEBORAH SLICER (455).

☞ See (114).

CHILDREN OF ROSWELL WAKEMAN AND MARY SLICER (457).

1536. Ella Jane, born 1844, 8, 28.
1537. Sarah L., born 1847, 12, 7.
1538. Henry T., born 1849, 9, 28,
1539. Charles R., born 1865, 2, 18.

CHILDREN OF SAMUEL SLICER (458) AND PRISCILLA PYLE.

1540. Sarah E., born 1850, 11, 22; died 1852, 12, 29.
1541. Elisha K., born 1852, 11, 24.
1542. Jesse T., born 1855, 11, 4.
1543. Clara, born 1858, 2, 14.
1544. Roswell, born 1861, 6, 4.

CHILDREN OF JACOB SLICER (459) AND MARY E. NICHOLAS.

1545. William Thomas, born 1860, 4, 22.
1546. Annie Jane, born 1862, 6. 18.

CHILDREN OF JOHN T. SLICER (460) AND MARTHA J. REED.

1547. Thomas W., born 1853, 1, 16.
1548. Sabina C., born 1855, 1, 6.
1549. John B., born 1858, 6, 10.
1550. Anna M., born 1861, 5, 12.
1551. Hannah A., born 1869, 9, 12.

CHILDREN OF JOSEPH MILLER AND REBECCA KIRK (463).

1552. Sophia J., born 1838, 4, 11; died 1849, 1, 9.

1553. Henrietta S., born 1842, 3, 19. Married 1869, 8, —, to Cyrus M. (890), son of Jacob L. and Jane Kirk.

1554. Levi K., born 1845, 3, 23. Married Rachel (889), daughter of Jacob L., and Jane Kirk. Levi is a blacksmith and resides at Drumore Centre, Lancaster co., Pa.

1555. Rachel E., born 1840, 3, 11.

1556. Jacob Allen, born 1847, 2, 2.

CHILDREN OF BENJAMIN F. KIRK (481) AND ELIZABETH CAROTHERS.

1557, Rachel, born ——, —, —.
1558. Cassius F.
1559. James A., born ——, —, —; died ——, —, —.
1560. James C., born ——, —, —.
1561. Leonidas, born ——, —, —; dec'd.
1562. George E.
1563. Martha.
1564. Margaret.

CHILDREN OF JAMES CAMERON AND REBECCA KIRK (482).

1565. Martha J., born ——, —, —.
1566. James R., born ——, —, —; died ——, —, —.

1567. Rachel L. born ——, —, —; died ——, —. —.
1568. Margaret R.
1569. Philena B.
1570. Mary E.
1571. Catharine L.
1572. Hannah R.

CHILD OF JESSE A. KIRK (484) AND HANNAH MOUNT.

1573. Mount Emmans, born 1857, 1, 10.

CHILDREN OF JOHN KIRK (489) AND MARGARET CAROTHERS.

1574. Indiana V., born ——, —, —.
1575. Rachel, born ——, —, —.
1576. Francina B., born ——, —, —.
1577. Ella M., ——, —, —.

CHILDREN OF WILLIAM T. KIRK (494) AND LOUISA RIDDLE.

1578. Mary E., born 1843, 3, 24.
1579. Elisha, born 1845, 2, 3.
1580. Susan E., born 1848, 8, 13.
1581. George Washington, born 1850, 5, —.
1582. Jamas R., born 1852, 12, —.
1583. Nancy C., born 1857, 10, 5.
1584. Martha A., born 1858, 3, 8.
1585. John H. born 1860, 2, 25.
1586. Louisa, born 1862, 9, 4.

CHILDREN OF JONATHAN H. KIRK (495) AND MARCELLA DENNIS.

1587. Mary Eliza, born 1845, 5, 14.
1588. Ellen M., born 1847, 12, 16.
1589. Henry Franklin, born 1849, 9, 28.

1590. William Hale, born 1853, 3, 24.
1591. Emma Marcella, born 1854, 11, 16.

CHILDREN OF ELISHA ALLEN KIRK (496) AND RACHEL DENNIS.

1592. Josephine, born 1845, 12, 15.
1593. Emeline, born 1847, 6, 8.
1594. Henrietta, born 1854, 1, 18.

CHILDREN OF SAMUEL BLACKBURN AND MARY E. KIRK (507).

1595. Amanda, born 1842, 11, 20.
1596. Ephraim, born 1844, 8, 28.
1597. Elizabeth, born 1846, 1, 10.
1598. Emeline, born 1847, 11, 23.
1599. Mary Amelia, born 1849, 8, 18.
1600. Martha Jane, born 1851, 12, 20; died 1852, 8, 12.
1601. Joseph K. born 1853, 4, 14.
1602. Rachel A., born 1855, 8 27.
1603. Cornelia J., born 1859, 2, 17.
1604. Laura, born 1862, 11, 21.

CHILDREN OF EPHRAIM BLACKBURN AND AMANDA KIRK (509).

1605. Adeline, born 18—, —, —.
1606. William, born 18—, —, —.
1607. Ephraim, born 18—, —, —.

CHILDREN OF JOHN T. KIMBLE AND RACHEL L. KIRK (511).

1608. Rachel E., born 1865, 3, 20.
1609. Joseph W., born 1868, 5, 1.

CHILD OF WILLIAM T. FULTON AND HANNAH A. KIRK (512).

1610. Kirk, born 1866, 8, 25.

CHILDREN OF SAMUEL MITCHELL AND ELIZABETH CAMPBELL (524).

1611. Elena, born 1812, 4, 7. Married 1832, 2, 7, to Nathaniel Broomfield, son of Thomas and Elizabeth of Fayette county, Pa. Thomas was born 1810, 10, 28. His P. O., address is Uniontown.

1612. William C., born 1815, 9, 12; died 1842, 9, 24. Married 1841, to Mary A. Goodrich. He was a cabinet maker, and died at North Bend, Ohio.

CHILDREN OF LEWIS CAMPBELL (226) AND DEBORAH ANTRIM.

1613. Martha, born 1824, 5, 4. Married 1845, 3, 25, to Jesse Coldren, son of John and Mary, of Fayette county. Jesse was born 1823, 1, 30.

1614. Susan, born 1826, 1, 22. Married 1848, 7, 28, to Nathaniel C. Gray, son of Jonathan and Hannah, of Fayette county. Nathaniel was born 1823, 10, 1. His address, New Salem.

1615. James B., born 1831, 5, 3. Unmarried.

1616. Elizabeth, born 1828, 9, 7; died 1834, 8, 16.

1617. Milton, born 1833, 6, 22; died 1834, 8, 14.

1618. Mary Ann, born 1837, 12, 5. Married 1856, 11, 6, to Elliott Hibbs, son of John and Jane, of Fayette county. Elliott was born 1832, 3, 12. Their address, New Salem.

1619. Joseph M., born 1841, 4, 11.

CHILDREN OF WILLIAM CAMPBELL (527) AND MARY NIXON.

1620. Frances, born 1825, 5, 7. Married 1844, 7, 4, to William, son of Squire and Ruth Eyres, of Fayette county. He was born 1823, 10, 23. Is a farmer, and resides in Utica, Van-Buren county, Iowa.

1621. James, born 1826, 12, 3; died 1833, 11, 24.

1622. Jane, born 1829, 1, 1. Married 1849, 10, 20, to S. N. Woodworth, son of Joel and Rhoda, of Iowa. He was born 1830, 3, 30. Is a machinist, and resides at Iowa Falls.

1623. William N., born 1832, 8, 31. Married 1857, 4, 4, to Irene S. Edmundson, daughter of Alfred and Catharine of Iowa. She was born 1840, 8, 28. William is a farmer. His address, Sheridan, Van Buren county, Iowa.

1624. Susanna, born 1834, 4, 17. Married 1859, 2, 15, to James Still, son of Ira and Deborah, of Hector, Schuyler county, New York. James is a farmer. His address, Sheridan, Van Buren county, Iowa.

1625. Sarah H., born 1839, 11, 3. Married 1865, 10, 10, to Alfred F., son of Henry and Margaret Wilson, of Iowa. He was born 1839, 8, 25. Is a farmer, and resides near Utica, Van Buren county, Iowa.

1626. Milton B., born 1849, 3, 10. Married 1866, 10, 4, to Harriet Jackson, daughter of Harvey and Mary. She was born 1845, 8, 2. Milton is a farmer, and resides near Utica, Van Buren county, Iowa.

CHILDREN OF JAMES CAMPBELL (528) AND REBECCA HANSHAW.

1627. Ann E., born 1830, 1, 10. Married 1857, 12, 2, to Jacob J. Tender, son of Gab iel and Sarah, of Iowa. He was born 1833, 3, 18. His address, Sheridan.

1628. Ellis B., born 1832, 3 17. Married 1857, 3, 18, to Sarah Nixon, daughter of Isaac and Sarah, of Van Buren county. She was born 1837, 5, 2. Ellis is a farmer. Post-office address, Hillsborough, Henry county, Iowa.

1629. Lewis, born 1834, 1, 2. Married 1859, 11, 22, to Minerva McDow, daughter of Robert and Mary P. McDow, of Van Buren county. He is a farmer. Post-office address, Hillsboro', Iowa.

1630. John P., born 1843, 10, 3. Married 1867, 7, 25, to Naomi Jordan, daughter of Roger and Sarah, of Van Buren county. She was born 1848, 12, 9. John is a farmer. His address, Sheridan, Iowa.

CHILDREN OF WILLIAM PRICE AND MARY CAMPBELL (529).

1631. Abel C., born 1828, 11, 4. Married 1852, 6, 3, to Margaret Jameson. He is a Methodist preacher, and now located at Gardner, Illinois.

1632. Emlen, born 1830, 6, 21. Married 1864, 10, 6, to Martha Shepherd. Address, Redstone, Fayette county, Pa.

1633. Hannah, born 1832, 4, 9. Married 1854, 10, 12, to Nathaniel Stephen. He was born 1825, 7, 22. Address, Redstone, Fayette county, Pa.

1634. Edith, born 1836, 10, 24; died 1841, 12, 4.

1635. Esther, born 1836, 10, 24. Living with her parents. Unmarried.

1636. Joel, born 1841, 2, 28; died 1849, 9, 28.

1637. William W., born 1843, 2, 27.

CHILDREN OF ABEL CAMPBELL (531) AND ELIZA WOODWARD.

1638. Walker, born ——, —, —.
1639. Caleb, " ——, —, —.
1640. William, " ——, —, —.
1641. Hamilton, " ——, —, —.
1642. Mary, " ——, —, —.
1643. John, " ——, —, —.
1644. Jane, " ——, —, —.
1645. Albert, " ——, —, —.

1646. Morgan, born ——, —, —.
1647. Alice, " ——, —, —.
1648. Newton, " ——, —, —.
Others died young.

CHILDREN OF ELKIS CAMPBELL (532) AND LYDIA STONE.

1649. James, born ——, —, —; died in infancy.
1650. John, born ——, —, —; died in infancy.

CHILDREN OF JESSE JOHNSON AND SARAH NIXON (533).

1651. Rebecca, born
1652. William, born
1653. Daniel, born
1654. Elwood, born

CHILDREN OF GEORGE MARTIN AND EDITH SHARPLESS (541).

1655. George, born 1827, 4, 29. Married 1850, 2, 6, at Concord Meeting, to Ann Trimble, daughter of Samuel and Rebecca, of Delaware county. He is a retired physician, now residing in West Chester, Pa.

1656. Nathan S., born 1829, 1, 11; died 1859, 5, 18. Married Susan Eves. They settled in Philadelphia, where Susan died 1869, 2, —.

1657. John, born 1831, 1, 8; died 1834, 9, 9.

CHILDREN OF FERREE BRINTON AND ELIZABETH SHARPLESS.

1658. Lydia, born 1825, 6, 5. Married 1863, 10, 28, to Rev. D. O. Timlow. They reside in Amity, New York.

1659. John F., born 1827, 7, 29. Married Annie Biney. He studied law and practiced his profession for several years in Philadelphia. Of late years he has resided in Europe.

1660. Nathan S., born 1829, 11, 10. Married Mary D. Buckley. They reside in Philadelphia.

1661. William P., born 1832, 5, 15. Married Maria Rogers. William resides in Philadelphia.

1662. Susan F., born 1834, 7, —; died in infancy.

1663. Joseph P., born 1835, 7, 22. Resides in Philadelphia. He is not married.

1664. Edith Ann, born 1837, 9, 11. Married William W. Wiltbank, of Philadelphia.

1665. Henry D., born 1840, 8, —; died in infancy.

1666. Robert M., born 1843, 6, 25. Married 1867, at Portland, Maine, to Octavia Eliza Fosdick. They reside in Philadelphia.

CHILDREN OF ROBERT PIERCE AND HANNAH HARVEY (543).

1667. Mary H., born 1821, 11, 29; died 1847, 3, 16. Unmarried.

1668. Margaret, born 1823, 4, 19. Married 1844, 7, 3, to Morris Whiteside, who died 1845, 1, 19. Married a second husband, Brigham Young, now of Utah, and leader of the Mormons at Salt Lake City.

1669. Ann Eliza, born 1825, 1, 27; died 1827, 3, 4.

1670. Eli Harvey, born 1827, 7, 29; died 1858, 8, 12. Married Susanna Neff. Reside in Salt Lake City, Utah.

1671. Thomas, born 1829, 8, 18; died 1864, 4, 1. Married Harriet A. Green. Residence, Salt Lake City.

1672. Joseph, born ——, —, —; died ——, —, —, in infancy.

1673. William, born 1833, 4, 2. Married Jerusha Smith, Salt Lake City.

1674. Edith Evaline, born 1836, 11, 18. Married 1857, 2, 12, to James Fisher, of Salt Lake City.

1675. Elizabeth, born 1839, 8, 18; died 1844, 7, 11.

CHILDREN OF JOSEPH P. HARVEY (544) AND LYDIA HOOPES.

1676. Edwin H., born 1829, 3, 21; died 1867, —, —. Married Josepha Youle.

1677. Anna M., born 1834, 1, 1. Married Gideon Speakman. Resides in Chester, Delaware county, Pa.

1678. Thomas Elwood, born 1845, 3, 29,. Married 1868, to Ella Booth, and resides in Philadelphia.

CHILDREN OF SAMUEL M. PAINTER (549) AND ANN VICKERS.

1679. John V., born 1835, 7, 20. Married first, Frances Barton, and second, Lydia Farmer. John V. is a banker, and resides in Cleveland, Ohio.

1680. Uriah H., born 1837, 3, 5. Married Belinda Avery. He resides in Washington, D. C., and is the Washington correspondent of the Philadelphia *Inquirer*.

1681. William T., born 1838, 12, 25. Married Sarah Brown. He is a banker, resides in Philadelphia, and is one of the firm of "W. T. Painter & Co," 38 South 3d street.

1682. Francis J., born 1840, 11, 1.

1683. Joseph Elwood, born 1842, 2, 11. He is a surgeon on a steamer plying between San Francisco, Calafornia, and China.

1684. Albert, born 1844, 10, 27. Married —— Taylor, of Chicago, Illinois.

1685. Henry, born 1847, 5, 31. Is a clerk in Internal Revenue office, West Chester, Pa.

1686. Howard, born 1851, 1, 29. Attending College at Frieburg, Germany.

1687. Clarence, born 1854, 5, 29.

CHILDREN OF JOSEPH VICKERS AND ELIZABETH PAINTER. (550)

1688. Jonathan, born 1840, 3, 8. Married 1864, 12, 15. to Catharine S. King, of West Chester. He is an express messenger, and resides at Buffalo, N. Y.

1689. Joseph, born 1840, 3, 8. Is a physician. Was in the U. S. Army as surgeon. Now resides in New York city.

1690. Eugene, born 1841, 12, 9. Married 1865, 5, 22, to Mary Elizabeth Davis, of Downingtown, Pa. Eugene resides in Philadelphia. Is a fireman on Pennsylvania Central R.R.

1691. Lydia Ann, born 1845, 6, 30. Resides in West Chester. Unmarried.

CHILDREN OF JOSEPH H. PAINTER (553) AND ESTHER KERSEY.

1692. Jesse K., born 1841, 3, 8, in Chester county. Married 1859, 8, 15, in Philadelphia, to Sarah Early, of Bristol, Pa. Jesse is Division Superintendent of Freight and Telegraph, Union Pacific railroad, Larimie City.

1693. Liecester M., born 1845, 6, 15. Married 1868, 9, 22, to Mary E. White, of Brooklyn, New York. He is a local agent and telegraph operator, Corinne, Utah.

CHILDREN OF CHALKLEY M. VALENTINE AND MARY H. PAINTER (554).

1694. Lydia P., born 1841, 2, 3.
1695. Joseph E., born 1844, 10, 20.
1696. Marshall J., born 1848, 10, 26.
1697. Mary Irene, born 1856, 10, 18.

CHILD OF JAMES G. PAINTER (555) AND MARY H. PIERCE.

1698. Myers, born 1849, 10, 20; died 1352, 6, 9.

CHILDREN OF CYRUS P. PAINTER (556) AND ABIGAIL A. ALLISON.

1699. Sylvester, born 1851, 7, 4; died 1857, 8, 9. Interred t West Chester, Pa.

Lydia, born 1854, 2, 14; died 1857, 8, 10 buried at West Chester, Pa.

CHILDREN OF ALFRED B. PIERCE (559) AND MARGARET E. BORDEN.

1700. Charles L., born 1847, 5, 18, at Lexington, Starke county, Ohio.

1701. Sarah E., born 1849, 9, 15, at Rochester, Starke county, Ohio.

1702. Frank B., born 1852, 7, 20, at Pierces' Mills.

1703. Mary Velma, born 1854, 8, 14, at Lima Starke county.

1704. Eugene Edwin, born 1856, 1, 5, at Lima; died 1856, 12, 9, at Minerva, Starke county.

1705. Virginia Alfaretta, born 1859, 11, 10, at Massillon, Ohio.

CHILDREN OF WILLIAM SWAYNE (561) AND MARY ANN MARSHALL.

1706. Benjamin W., born 1827, 7, 14. Married 1850, 10, 22, to Margaret Bancroft, daughter of John and Susan, of Philadelphia. Margaret died 1852, 5, 8. Benjamin married 1854, 9, 14, to Jane T. Pennock, of West Marlborough, daughter of James and Amy. She was born 1833, 1, 30. They reside in London Grove township, Chester county.

1707. William Marshall, born 1828, 12, 1. Married 1850, 11, 14, at her father's, to Mary, daughter of Richard M. and Hannah Barnard, of Newlin township. She was born 1828, 8, 9. They resided in East Marlborough for several years, but now reside in West Chester, Pennsylvania. Wm. Marshall has attained considerable celebrity as a sculptor. He has held the position of Collector of Internal Revenue for Chester county.

1708. Jacob, born 1830, 10, 21. Married Sarah J. B. Noblit, of Wilmington, Delaware. They reside on a farm in Pennsburg, Chester county.

1709. Elizabeth M., born 1833, 9, 8. Married 1852, 11, 11, to Charles, son of Richard M. and Hannah Barnard, of Newlin township. He was born 1829, 9, 12. Is a farmer.

1710. Joel J., born 1837, —, —; died 1862, 6, —, from wounds received while in the "service of his country."

CHILD OF JACOB HAYES AND SUSANNA SWAYNE (563).

1711. Benjamin, born 1828, 10, 8. At an early age he went to sea, and was killed by falling from the rigging of a vessel.

CHILDREN OF JOHN KINSEY AMD MARGARET WOODWARD (564).

1712. Samuel, born 1822, 2, 24. Married 1844, 3, 14, to Martha F. Custer, and settled in Quakertown, Bucks county. She died 1860, 12, 5, and he married 1866, 3, 8, Jane G. Carey.

1713. Caleb Pusey, born 1823, 1, 10; died 1824, 7, 2.

1714. Elizabeth, born 1824, 9, 6; died 1825, 9, 14.

1715. Elizabeth, born 1826, 6. 15. Married 1847, 3, 4, to Maris Garrett.

1716. John W., born 1828, 10, 25; died 1851, 11, 14.

1717. Margaret A., born 1830, 9, 10. Married 1863, 10, 8, to Barton G. Roberts.

1718. Philena, born 1832, 11, 23. Married 1860, 11, 7, to Heliacal A. Salter. They reside in Philadelphia.

1719. Sarah, born 1834, 7, 26.

1720. William Baker, born 1836, 5, 11. Married 1868, 1, 29, to Ada L. Wentzell.

1721. Mary, born 1838, 2, 20; died 1842, 4, 5.

1722. Anna, born 1840, 2, 27; died 1842, 4, 16.

1723. Edward W., born 1842, 1, 17. Married 1868, 4, 2, to Sarah Jane Riley.

1724. Emma, born 1844, 1, 7.

CHILDREN OF WILLIAM E. BAILEY AND SARAH WOODWARD. (566).

1725. Samuel, born 1828, 1, 17; died 1843, 7, 23.

1726. Ann, born 1830, 3, 1. Married 1866, 1, 18, to David W., son of Joseph and Tacy Branson, of Hopewell, Va. His address, Stephenson's Station, Frederick co., West Virginia.

1727. Rebecca, born 1832, 8, 8; died 1860, 5, 26. Married 1856, 4, 17, to Bennett S. Walton, of West Marlborough, son of David and Elizabeth. He was born 1829, 12, 26.

1728. Elizabeth, born 1834, 11, 14.

1729. William, born 1836, 11, 23; died 1864, 6, 29. Unmarried.

1730. Tacy, born 1839, 1, 26.

1731. Joel S., born 1841, 7, 26. Married 1864, 4, 5, to Sallie S. Welsh. They reside in Danville, Pa.

1732. Samuel, born 1844, 1, 29. Married 1864, 6, 25, to Mary Bell Radford. Address, Thorndale, Chester co., Pa.

1733. Edward S., born 1847, 4, 25; died 1859, 2, 3.

1734. Joseph, born 1581, 4, 19.

CHILDREN OF RICHARD B. SMEDLEY AND SUSANNA WOODWARD (568).

1735. Anna Amanda, born, 1831, 3, 30; died 1839, 8, 20.

1736. Philema P., born 1839, 11, 15.

1737. Mary Anna, born 1842, 4, 9. Married 1865, 11, 30, to Eli Palmer, of West Chester, son of Wilson and Julia Ann, of Concord, Delaware county. He and his brother Reese are plumbers, gas fitter, dealers in stoves and tin-ware, &c., on Market St., West Chester, Pa.

1738. Wilmer, born 1843, 8, 23. Married 1861, 2, 13, to Elizabeth Beitler, of Lionville and resides near Downingtown, Pennsylvania.

1739. Sarah J., born 1846, 1, 14.

CHILDREN OF THOMAS C. CHANDLER AND RACHEL WOODWARD (569).

1740. Rebecca, born 1833, 10, 7. Married 1854, 10, 3, at her father's, to Elijah Weaver, of Philadelphia, son of Elijah and Annie.

1741. Thomas Allen, born 1836, 4, 17. Married 1861, 11, 5, to Eliza Richards, of Wilmington, Del. She died 1868, 2, 28.

1742. William S., born 1838, 11, 19.

1743. Josiah W., born 1841, 2, 13.

1744. David W., born 1843, 7, 3. Married 1867, 11, 7, to Mary E. Henderson of Wilmington, Delaware.

1745. Jesse, born 1846, 9, 23. Married 1861, 5, 4, to Virginia Point, of New Castle, Delaware.

CHILDREN OF ISAAC CHAMBERS AND RACHEL FELL (571).

1746. Sarah, born 1123, 4, 12. Married 1841, 10, 14, at West Grove Meeting, to Asahel Walker, of Sadsbury, Lancaster county, son of Isaac and Deborah. Their address, London Grove, Chester county.

1747. Rebecca, born 1824, 10, 21. Married Preston Wickersham.

CHILDREN OF SAMUEL FELL (572) AND PATIENCE CHAMBERS.

1748. Mary Ann, born 1830, 4, 30. Unmarried.

1749. Rebecca, born 1831, 10, 10.; died 1832, 1, 23.

1750. James P., born 1835, 2, 24. Married 1864, —, —, to Sarah A. Buckley, of Rising Sun, Maryland. They resided in Port Deposit, where she died, 1865, 10, 6. She was interred at West Nottingham. James removed from Port Deposit to Royer's Ford, and followed milling until 1867, when he married Elizabeth F. Goodshall, and now resides near Springville, Chester county, and works in a wood-paper mill.

1751. Richard H., born 1836, 8, 28. Married 1867, 2, 21, to Eliza T. Garrett, daughter of Abner, of London Grove. They live on his mother's farm, at West Grove, Chester county, Pennsylvania.

CHILDREN OF JOHN J. WOODWARD (573) AND HANNAH MATTSON.

1752. Albert M., born 1839, 10, 19. Married 1865, 3, 1, to Harriet Parker, of Philadelphia. He is a provision dealer, No. 610 North 12th street, Philadelphia.

1753. Adolphus D., born 1841, 10, 28. Unmarried. Resides with his father.

1754. Theodore B., born 1843, 9, 17. Unmarried.

CHILDREN OF WASHINGTON B. WOODWARD (574) AND EDITH LAMBORN.

1755. Jacob Granville, born 1842, 10, 12; died 1849, 6, 13.

1756. Washington, born 1845, 1, 26; died 1866, 2, 13, in Wilmington, Del. He studied medicine and practiced his profession.

CHILDREN OF ISAAC WOODWARD (575) AND HANNAH SHARPLESS.

1757. Charity T., born 1841, 7, 4.

1758. Marietta S., born 1843, 1, 21.

1759. Sarah B., born 1844. 12, 26.

1760. Caroline D., born 1846, 12, 25.

1761. William S., born 1848, —, —; died 1849, 8, 2, and interred in Wilmington, Del.

CHILDREN OF GIBBONS KENDALL AND ELIZA WOODWARD (576).

1762. Philena, born 1831, 4, 21, in East Marlborough. Resides on her father's farm in Newcastle county, Delaware. Unmarried.

1763. Casper, born 1836, 8, 9, in Pennsburg. Married 1859, 3, 15, to Emily Matilda Johnson, of Wilmington, Del. Casper resides in Wilmington, where he carries on the business of building carriages.

1764. Emma W., born 1846, 1, 2, in Mill Creek Hundred; died 1851, 2, 12; buried at Hokessin.

1765. Mary E., born 1852, 8, 2,8 in Mill Creek, Del.

CHILDREN OF JACKSON WOODWARD (578) AND SIBBILLA T. ENTRIKEN.

1766. Thomas E., born 1839, 4, 15, in East Marlborough; died 1842, 3, 17.

1767. Anna Mary, born 1842, 3, 1, in East Marlborough; died 1843, 3, 29.

1768. Hannah, born 1844, 4, 11.

1769. Henry Clay, born 1848, 2, 4.

CHILDREN OF EMMOR S. ENTRIKEN AND MABEL WOODWARD (579).

1770. Anna Mary, born 1841, 10, 18; died 1842, 10, 15.

1771. Albert L., born 1843, 7, 26. Married 1866, 10, 4, to Isabell T. Williams, daughter of Lewis and Lydia Ann, of East Bradford. He is of the firm of "E. S. Entriken and Son," saddle and harness makers, West Chester, Pa.

1772. Emmarine, born 1846, 1, 12. Married 1867, 5, 9, to Westley C. Johnson, of Wilmington, Delaware.

1773. Franklin B., born 1848, 2, 15.

CHILDREN OF LEWIS B. WOODWARD (580) AND ELIZABETH S. WITSIL.

1774. Clara J., born 1851, 5, 8.

1775. Ellie L., born 1854, 10, 5.

1776. Alfred L., born 1860, 2, 27.

CHILDREN OF EDWARD M'GEE AND SARAH H. WOODWARD. (581).

1777. Elizabeth, born 1848, 9, 20; died 1863, 4, 1.

1778. Phebe Ann, born 1849, 12, 14. Married 1868, 3, 3, to James Sinclair, of York.

1779. Catharine, born 1852, 1, 1.

1780. Philena, born 1853, 8, 29.

1781. Sarah, born 1855, 1, 30.

1782. Margaret, born 1856, 10, 6.

1783. Emeline, born 1859, 11, 17.

1784. Mary H., born 1863, 10, 15.

CHILDREN OF MATTHEW SAMPLE AND SIBBILLA WOODWARD (583).

1785. Lewis, born 1846, 7, 7.

1786. Sarah J., born 1848, 1, 28.

1787. Levi, born, 1850, 1, 6.
1788. Samuel, born 1851, 9, 19.
1789. Adaline, born 1853, 3, 22.
1790. Merrit S., born 1855, 12, 1.
1791. Phebe A., born 1858, 3, 30.
1792. Isaac, born 1861, 10, 22.

CHILDREN OF SAMUEL WOODWARD (584) AND MARGARET DICKEY.

1793. Isabella R., born 1862, 8, 1.
1794. Joseph —., born 1865, 7, 28.
1795. Mary, born 1867, 9, 9.

CHILDREN OF THOMAS WICKERSHAM (589) AND PRISCILLA JONES.

1796. Joseph Allen, born 1838, 1, 17. Married 1865, 10, 25, to Elizabeth Lysle, daughter of Robert and Eliza, of Franklin township, Chester county. They reside in Philadelphia, Pa.

1797. Elmira, born 1839, 3, 24. Unmarried.

1798. Elizabeth J., born 1842, 11, 1. Married 1862, 2, 26, to Francis M. Pyle, son of Amos and Ann, of London Grove. He was born 1834, 10, 3. Address, West Grove, Chester county, Pa.

CHILDREN OF ANDREW MOORE AND SARAH WICKERSHAM (590).

1799. Phebe Ann, born 1839, 6, 22. Married 1864, 2, 17, at Sadsbury Meeting, to Truman C. Moore, son of Asahel and Ann Eliza, of Bart twp., Lancaster county. He was born 1836, 8, 3. Is a carpenter, and resides in Sadsbury, Lancaster county, Pa.

1800. Levi W., born 1841, 12, 2. Married 1867, 12, 17, to Margaret A. Caruthers. Residence, Smyrna, Lancaster county, Pa.

1801. Rebecca, born 1845, 9, 29.

CHILDREN OF PRESTON WICKERSHAM (592) AND REBECCA CHAMBERS.

1802. Rachel, born 1851, 1, 4; died 1851, 8, 5.
1803. William R., born 1855, 10, 11; died 1860, 4, 4.
1804. Mary S., born 1862, 4, 15.

CHILD OF LEVI WICKERSHAM (593) AND ANGELINE P. RUSSELL.

805. Florilla, born 1853, 9, 15.

CHILDREN OF DAVID PUSEY (598) AND EDITH G. HOOPES.

1806. Ella M., born 1858, 8, 21.
1807. Hannah Elizabeth, born 1862, 12, 31; died 1868, 8, 18.

CHILDREN OF JOEL W. SWAYNE (603) AND SUSAN CUNNINGHAM.

1808. Thomas W., born 1840, 3, 21. Unmarried.
1809. George, born 1842, 5, 7; died 1842, 7, 19.
1810. Mary S., born 1843, 12, 11, died 1846, 4, 27.
1811. William C., born 1845, 10, 28. Unmarried.

CHILDREN OF THOMAS P. HAWLEY (607) AND ANNA M. PALMER.

1812. Virginia, born 1857, 9, 6.
1813. Joseph P., born 1859, 10, 21.
1814. Howard, born 1865, 8, 14.

CHILD OF JOHN BIERLY AND SARAH WOODWARD (611).

1815. Mordecai C., born 1848, 11, 25.

CHILD OF AARON COMMONS AND SARAH WOODWARD (611).

1816. Lydia S., born 1858, 11, 3.

CHILDREN OF LEA P. WOODWARD (613) AND CLARA EVESSON.

1817. Henry C., born 1853, 7, 4.
1818. Mary F., born 1857, 10, 27.
1819. Lee P., born 1861, 9, 21.
1820. Clara E., born 1868, 9, 30.

CHILDREN OF ROBERT B. SHOEMAKER AND LYDIA WOODWARD (614).

1821. Ellis W., born 1860, 10, 1.
1822. Henry G., born 1864, 5, 18.
1823. Francis Marion, born 1867, 4, 26.
1824. William S., born 1868, 9, 18.

CHILD OF OWEN L. WOODWARD (617) AND SARAH RALSTON.

1825. Hannah B., born 1856, 7, 14.

CHILDREN OF NATHAN G. BUCKWALTER AND SARAH A. WOODWARD (618).

1826. John Lewis, born 1863, 3, 28.
1827. Mary Emma, born 1864, 4, 8.

CHILDREN OF CHARLES PLUMBLEY AND MARY ANN KENT. (622).

1828. William K., born 1852, 5, 25.
1829. Harriet E., born 1853, 10, 27.
1830. Thomas E., born 1856, 8, 17.
1831. George H., born 1859, 9, 21.

CHILDREN OF DANIEL KENT (624) AND MARGARET BROOMER.

1832. William E., born 1854, 12, 1.
1833. Henry H., born 1856, 7, 8.
1834. Robert F., born 1859, 5, 18.
1835. Lewis P., born 1863, 6, 18.
1836. James H., born 1865, 2, 13.

CHILD OF WILLIAM KENT (625) AND MARY F. KINSEY.

1837. Charles K., born 1863, 12, 8; died 1863, 12, 30.

CHILDREN OF CHARLES W. M'GEATH AND ELIZABETH SMITH (627).

Six children—three living, and three deceased in infancy. Names not ascertained.

CHILDREN OF THORBAN W. SMITH AND MARY SMITH (628).

Five children—but one living. Names not given.

CHILDREN OF MAHLON W. PICKERING AND SARAH A. SMITH (629).

Five children—but two living. Names not ascertained.

CHILDREN OF THOS. WILKINSON SMITH (630) AND RACHEL LEWIS.

Two children—both died young. By second wife, Louisa Pratt, had two children; one deceased.

SEVENTH GENERATION.

CHILDREN OF JEREMIAH BROWN AND MARGARETTA HAINES (631).

☞See Fifth Generation, under 245.

CHILDREN OF ANDREW LEWIS AND SARAH HAINES (632).

1838. Frederick W., born 1842, 1, 21. Married 1870, 11, 1, to Isadora Olivia Wilson, of Philadelphia. Frederick assisted in organizing a company in Fulton twp., Lancaster county, Pa., and was mustered with it as orderly sergeant in the 32d Regt. Penn'a Volunteers, July 31, 1861. Served in the army of the Potomac. The title of the regiment was subsequently changed to 99th Pa. Vols. In June 19, 1864, Frederick was promoted to first lieutenancy of Company B. August 21, 1864, was promoted to captain of same company. Honorably discharged from the service July 26, 1865. He entered the University of Pennsylvania the following autumn as a student of medicine, and graduated March 14, 1867. Began the practice of medicine in Philadelphia, and now resides at No. 1433, Poplar street. Since his residence in Philadelphia he was elected a member of the College of Physicians, the American Medical Association, Pathological Society of Philadelphia, etc., etc.

1839. Mabel A., born 1843, 1, 31; died 1863, 2, 12.

1840. Mary Emma, born 1844, 3, 3. Married John, son of Francis P. and Deborah Smith, of Cecil county, Md. They now reside in Iowa City, Iowa.

1841. Lucretia M., born 1845, 6, 24. Married 1871, 6, 21, to —— ———. Resides in the West.

1842. Milton T., born 1846, 10, 3. Married Isadore, daughter of Joseph and Rachel Ross, of Harford county,

Md. Milton kept store for one year at Wrightsdale and then removed to Grafton, West Virginia, where he has a position on the Baltimore and Ohio Railroad.

1843. Clara I., born 1849, 4, 13.

1844. Eva Alice, born 1851, 3, 20.

1845. Harvey H., born 1853, 7, 21.

1846. Willis O., born 1854, 9, 3. Went to Iowa, and lives with his brother-in-law, John Smith.

1847. Charles L., born 1858, 1, 16.

1848. Jeremiah B., born 1861, 9, 3.

1849. Sarah, born 1865, 5, 3.

1850. Virginia, born 1867, 10, 25.

CHILDREN OF WILLIAM P. HAINES (634) AND MARY KIRK.

See Sixth Generation, under 217.

CHILDREN OF ALBERT HAINES (636) AND HANNAH R. JACKSON.

1851. Granville, born 1857, 9, 25; died 1860, 6, 27.

1852. Eleanor, born 18—, —, —. Deceased.

1853. Milton, born 18—, --, —; died 1870, 3, -. He was killed by falling off the bridge of a barn.

1854. Infant, born 18—, —, —.

CHILDREN OF JOB HAINES (643) AND ELIZABETH DUNN.

1855. Edwin, born 1841, 1, 28. Resides at Rising Sun, and is engaged in the hardware store of Jesse A. Kirk.

1856. John Dunn, born 1849, 11, 30. Is engaged in studying law in the city of Baltimore.

1857. Sarah Askew, born 1852, 2, 23; died 1854, 9, 15.

1858. Mary Elizabeth, born 1854, 6, 9.

1859. William Sherwood, born 1857, 5, 14.

CHILDREN OF JOSEPH H. HAINES (644) AND REBECCA F. LINCOLN.

1860. John L., born 1847, 10, 21. Resides at Rising Sun, where he has been engaged in the milling business.

1861. Anna Frances, born 1849, 8, 20. Married 1870, —, —, to Basil H. (1439), son of Luke and Phebe Brown, of Rising Sun, Md. They reside in Philadelphia, where Basil is engaged as clerk and salesman in the hat store of Eli Keen, No. 62 North Second street.

1862. Elizabeth, born 1851, 10, 14.

1863. Margaret H., born 1854, 3, 11.

1864. Ida Ella, born 1857, 9, 28.

1865. Sarah Stubbs, born 1859, 7, 30.

1866. Rachel, born 1860, 12, 21.

1867. Joseph H., born 1866, 12, 27.

CHILDREN OF MARSHALL J. HUNT AND ELMIRA HAINES (645).

1868. Margaret A., born 1846, 6, 4.

1869. Emma W., born 1850, 8, 20.

1870. Rebecca E., born 1853, 2, 14.

1871. Edwin M., born 1855, 4, 4.

1872. Mary C., born 1856, 11, 1.

1873. Sarah S., born 1858, 11, 15.

CHILDREN OF SLATER B. STUBBS AND SARAH B. HAINES (646).

1874. William H., born 1852, 6, 2. Has decided to be a jeweler, and is now with "Bailey & Co.," Chestnut street, Philadelphia.

1875. Cecil Calvert, born 1854, 5, 2. Resides with his mother at Rising Sun, Md.

1876. Slater B., born 1856, 1 2.

1877. Charles Eugene, born 1858, 4, 15.

1878. Hannah M., born 1861, 1, 30.
1879. Edwin H., born 1863, 4, 18.
1880. Isaac, born 1865, 2, 21; died 1865, 12, 10.
1881. Isaac Job H., born 1867, 5, 13.

CHILD OF GEORGE BROWN AND SARAH H. HAINES (560).

1882. Virginia, born 1871, 5, 9.

CHILDREN OF WILLIAM HAINES (653) AND FRANCES M. BAILEY.

1883. Hesther, born 1862, 12, 14.
1884. Emma, born 1864, 2, 3; died 1866, 7, 1.
1885. Howard, born 1867, 12, 13.

CHILDREN OF KIRK BROWN AND EMELINE HAINES (658).

1886. Alice, born 1870, 6, —.

CHILDREN OF JOSEPH BAILEY AND PRISCILLA HAINES (659).

1887. Clarence H., born 1868, 7, 2.
1888. Infant, born 1870, —, —,

CHILD OF CHARLES H. STUBBS AND SARAH B. HAINES (661).

1889. Clarence Theodore, born 1869, 6, 20.

CHILDREN OF JOSEPH T. ENGLAND (665) AND MARY A. ALEXANDER.

1890. Isaac H., born 1853, 10, 18.
1891. Helen E., born 1855, 12, 2.
1892. Joseph L., born 1857, 3, 12.

CHILD OF REUBEN H. ENGLAND (666) AND MARGARET FIELDS.

1893. James Reuben, born 1854, 6, —.

CHILDREN OF ABNER KIRK AND MARY ENGLAND (667).

☞ See (411.)

CHILDREN OF WILLIAM CLAYTON AND DEBORAH A. ENGLAND (668).

1894. Reuben E., born ——, —, —.
1895. Charles H., born ——, —, —.
1896. John M., born ——, —, —.
1897. Irene Maria, born ——, —, —.
1898. Mary Elizabeth, born ——, —, —.
1899. Isaac E., born ——, —, —.
1900. Sherman, born ——, —, —.
1901. Joseph P., born ——, —, —.

CHILDREN OF JOHN ENGLAND (669) AND MARY SOPHIA YOUNG.

1902. Emma, born ——, —, —.
1903. Ida May, born ——, —, —.
1904. Horace, born ——, —, —.

CHILDREN OF ROBERT H. ENGLAND (670) AND SARAH H. NEWTON.

1905. Ruberta, born 1852, 1, 1; died 18—, —, —.
1906. Georgianna, born 1854, 12, 13.
1907. Zilpha, born 1857, 2, 1; died 18—, —, —.
1908. Edward E., born 1860, 7, 24.
1909. Esther J., born 1862, 5, 19.

CHILDREN OF GEORGE ENGLAND (671) AND MARY BROWN.

1910. Edward, born 1847, 11, 8; died 1853, 6, 21.

1911. Charles C., born 1849, 7, 4. Charles learned the trade of cabinet-making, and worked at the business at Delta, in Peach Bottom township, York county.

1912. George, born 1851, 2, 28. Is a farmer, and at the present time resides at his uncle's, near Wakefield, Lancaster county, Penn'a.

CHILDREN OF STEPHEN J. BROWN AND SARAH ANN ENGLAND (672).

1913. Samuel J., born ——, —, —.
1914. Ella Virginia, born ——, —, —.
1915. Esther Haines. ——, —, —.

CHILDREN OF CHARLES PARKER AND SARAH ANN (ENGLAND) BROWN (672).

1916. Sarah, born ——, —, —.
1917. Stephen, born ——, —, —.
1918. Lewis, born ——, —, —.
1919. Amanda, born ——, —, —.
1920. Lottie, born ——, —, —.
1921. Joseph. born —, —, —.

CHILDREN OF SETH ENGLAND (673) AND ELIZABETH LARRISON.

1922. William B., born 1855, 11, 7.
1923. Henry, born 1859, 12, 25.

CHILDREN OF JOB ENGLAND (674) AND MARY BOWERS.

1924. Harvey, born 1858, 3, 6.
1925. Cornelia, born 1859, 6, 9.
1926. George W., born 1865, 4, 27.
1927. Charles C., born 1867, 5, 9.

CHILDREN OF WILLIAM HAMBLETON AND HANNAH ENGLAND (676).

1928. Mary, born 1860, 8. 20.
1929. George E., born 1862, 5, 15.

1930. Olivia, born 1863, 9, 21.
1931. Damarus, born 1866, 3, 19.
1932. Esther, born 1869, 5, 4.

CHILDREN OF SAMUEL G. ENGLAND (677) AND REBECCA PIERSON.

1933. Roberta, born 1866, 4, 7.
1934. Henry R., born 1868, 1, 16.

CHILDREN OF VINCENT STUBBS (680) AND ELIZABETH PIERSON.

1935. Edward, born 1854, 3, 25.
1936. Isaac H., born 1855, 10, 25.
1937. John H., born 1858, 11, 20.
1938. Frederic W., born 1861, 8, 22.
1939. Hannah M., born 1863, 1, 9.
1940. Charles H., born 1866, 6, 27.

CHILDREN OF JACOB SWAYNE AND SARAH H. STUBBS (682).

1941. Enoch P., born 1857, 11, 2.
1942. Calvin I., born 1861, 3, 29.
1943. Mary E., born 1865, 4, 11.
1944. Townsend, born 1868, 9, 16.

CHILDREN OF SAMUEL W. PASSMORE AND EMELINE STUBBS (683).

1945. George Birdsall, born 1856, 4, 4.
1946. Oscar Fremont, born 1857, 9, 20.
1947. Mary Elizabeth, born 1859, 7, 17.
1948. Dora Vaness, born 1861, 10, 12.
1949. Phebe Emma, born 1864, 1, 12.

CHILDREN OF ALBERT STUBBS (684) AND PHEBE A. HICKMAN.

1950. George H., born 1860, 2, 21.
1951. Esther C., born 1853, 4, 18.
1952. Benjamin P., born 1866, 5, 29.
1953. Walter, born 1868, 10, 31. Died 1868, 12, 21.

CHILD OF ELI HENRY HAINES (694) AND ESTHER FURNACE.

1954. Mabel, born 1866, 9, 13.

CHILDREN OF JONATHAN REYNOLDS (697) AND ELIZABETH LINCOLN.

1955. Mary Emma, born 18—, —, —.
1956. Isaac Wayne, born 18—, —, —.

CHILDREN OF GILBERT MAXWELL AND SARAH E. ROMAN (699).

1957. A son, born 18—, —, —.
1958. A daughter, born 18—, —, —.

CHILDREN OF JOSEPH A. ROMAN (700) AND ALICE A. MILNER.

1959. Hannah, born 1865, 5, 20.
1960. Eliza, born 1867, 2, 13.
1961. Mary, born 1869, 1, 13.

CHILD OF JOHN HULL (707) AND ELIZABETH GROUNDRY.

1962. Charles, born 18—, —, —.

CHILD OF SAMUEL M. BLAIR AND SARAH HINE (710)

1963. George M., born 1847, —, —.

CHILD OF GEORGE WASHINGTON HAINES (723) AND SARAH E. COOPER.

1964. Mary Emma, born 1864, 4, 4.

CHILD OF GEORGE W. ALLYN AND ESTHER K. GAMBLE (729).

1965. Clarissa, born 1868, 12, 1.

CHILDREN OF WILLIAM T. KIRK (766) AND DEBORAH SMEDLEY

1966. Emma L., born 1850, 12, 14.
1967. Caroline P., born 1853, 1, 4.
1968. Mary A., born 1855, 11, 20. Died ——, —, —.
1969. Laura S., born 1857, 8, 12.
1970. William T., born 1860, 7, 1.
1971. Theodore V., born 1862, 12, 8.

CHILDREN OF WILLIAM J. HARLAN AND ABBEY A. KIRK (766).

1972. George W., born 1847, 12, 14.
1973. Mary A., born 1849, 5, 15.
1974. William M., born 1851, 8, 3.
1975. Theodore E., born 1853, 9, 16; died ——, —, —.
1976. James E., born 1854, 12, 30; died ——, —, —.
1977. Walter J., born 1857, 12, 14.
1978. Maria E., born 1866, 11, 9.

CHILDREN OF GEORGE H. KIRK (770) AND HARRIET CRAIG.

1979. Maria L., born 1860, 2, 25.
1980. George W., born 1862, 3, 12.
1981. Harriet A., born 1864, 3, 12.

CHILDREN OF GEORGE H. KIRK (770) AND ANN N. RUSSELL.

1982. Whitney, born 1867, 7, 6.
1983. Hughes, born 18—, —, —.

CHILDREN OF WALTER F. NEEL AND MARY AMELIA HUTTON (775).

1984. Delphine Louisa, born 1858, 7, 19; died 1858, 8, 21.
1985. Rachel Margaret, born 1859, 5, 21; died 1859, 5, 22.

1986. Laura Mary, born 1860, 4, 17.
1987. William H., born 1861, 10, 5.
1988. Clara Lucinda, born 1863, 10, 11.
1989. Thomas Neel, born 1864, 9, 17; died 1864, 10, 6.

CHILDREN OF S. B. RUSSELL (779) AND AMELIA LEVIS.

☞ See under (318).

CHILDREN OF GEORGE H. KIRK AND ANN N. RUSSELL (780).

☞ See under (770).

CHILDREN OF JACOB T. WHITSON AND MARY B. RUSSELL (781).

1990. Russell Taylor, born 1863, 12, 26.
1991. Charles Sumner, born 1866, 3, 16.

CHILDREN OF WILLIAM M. HAYES AND RACHEL H. RUSSELL (782).

1992. John Russell, born 1866, 6, 25.
1993. Jacob Carroll, born 1869, 3, 28.

CHILD OF ELWOOD SMEDLEY AND HANNAH R. RUSSELL (784).

1994. Charles, born 1869, 6, —.

CHILDREN OF AMOS COATES AND SARAH PIERCE (790).

1995. Anna H., born 1855, 11, 9.
1996. Mary P., born 1859, 5, 30.
1997. John S., born 1863, 4, 10.
1998. L. Irea, born 1361, 11, 13.

CHILDREN OF CHARLES LEWIS AND JANE PIERCE (792).

1999. Henry P., born 1857, 11, 17.
2000. Maris E., born 1861, 11, 13.

CHILDREN OF ELIAB AXTELL VAUGHN AND ELIZABETH PIERCE (793).

2001. Laura J., born 1859, 1, 10.
2002. Loretta R., born 1861, 2, 1.
2003. William W., born 1865, 3, 22.

CHILDREN OF LEWIS R. KIRK (802) AND MARY C. RICHARDSON.

2004. Infant, born 1870, 4, 22; died 1870, 7, 24.
2005. Clifford, born 1871, 5, 8, dec'd.

CHILDREN OF ISAAC S. KIRK (803) AND FANNIE LINCOLN.

2006. Jennie H., born 1861, 5, 20.
2007. Clara L., born 1866, 3, 2.
2008. Charles B., born 1870, 1, 11.

CHILD OF CHARLES H. STUBBS (805) AND SARAH B. HAINES.

☞ See under (661).

CHILDREN OF CHARLES BEAUMONT AND SARAH B. WEBSTER (814.)

2009. Walter W., born 1863, 6, 14.
2010. Samuel W., born 1855, 9, 8.
2011. Ellis I., born 1858, 2, 11.
2012. Mary, born 1859, 12, 25.
2013. Helen K., born 1862, 7, 17.

CHILDREN OF JOHN RANDOLPH WEBSTER (815) AND SUSAN NYE.

2014. Henry, born 1859, 4, 20.
2015. Infant, born 1860, 12, 11; died 1862, 10, 20.

CHILDREN OF HENRY EWING AND MARY E. WEBSTER (816).

2016. Mary E., born 1863, 8, 10; died 1864, 7, 3.
2017. Irvine A., born 1865, 4, 14.
2018. Ella —., born 1867, 2, 15.

CHILD OF SAMUEL BAILEY AND MARY D. IRVINE (822).

2019. Infant daughter, born 1867, 2, 15.

Child of Samuel I. Hodgson and Helen Johnson (824).

2020. Infant, born 18—, —, —.

CHILDREN OF CHARLES F. KIRK (833) AND SARAH KIRK.

2021. Mary Elma, born 1864, 1, 24.
2022. Slater A., born 1865, 10, 11.
2023. Ellis J., born 1868, 9, 28.
2024. Sarah R., born 1870, 4, 12.

CHILDREN OF JACOB H. KIRK (834) AND ELMINA COOK.

2025. Willis L., born 1867, 1, 4.
2026. Ella C., born 1868, 7, 8.

CHILD OF JOSIAH P. KIRK (835) AND ANNIE REYNOLDS.

2027. Walter B., born 1869, —, —.

CHILDREN OF JOSEPH SLAUGHTER AND ANNA M. COOK (857).

2028. Mildred R., born 1861, 4, 9.
2029. Julia, born 1862, 6, 29.
2030. John, born 1865, 8, 30.
2031. William H., born 1868, 2, 19.

CHILDREN OF CHARLES A. COOK (859) AND EVELYN LOWNES.

2032. Edward, born 1863, 12, 11.
2033. Susan, born 1866, 12, 19.

CHILDREN OF WILLIAM R. BROWN (863) AND NANCY A. OWENS.

2034. Estavilla, born 1856, 9, 12; died 1857, 10, 22.
2035. Susan N. born 1858, 8, 12.
2036. Margaret E., born 1861, 1, 8.
2037. Robert K., born 1865, 11, 3.
2038. Maria, born 1867, 2, 7.

CHILD OF KIRK BROWN (869) AND EMELINE HAINES.

☞ See under (658).

CHILDREN OF WILLIAM H. BROWN (872) AND SARAH REMELL.

2039. Henry, born ——, —, —.
2040. William, born ——, —, —; died ——, —, —. Interred at Penn Hill, 1867, 10, 2.

CHILD OF EDWIN L. BROWN (885) AND MATILDA FREED.

2041. Infant, born 170, —, —.

CHILDREN OF CHARLES FRANKLIN KIRK AND SARAH KIRK (886).

☞ See under (833).

CHILDREN OF BENJAMIN F. TAYLOR AND RUTH ADA KIRK. (887).

2042. John K., born 1864, 3, 29.
2043. Jane Ruth, born 1865, 9, 10.

CHILDREN OF WILLIAM PUGH AND MARY E. BROWN (897).

2044. Harold B., born 1864, 5, 28.
2045. Edwin A., born 1866, 6, 14.

CHILD OF NEEL HAMBLETON AND SARH A. BROWN (903).

2046. Infant, born 1870, —, —.

CHILDREN OF JESSE PRICE (1050) AND ISABEL RAY.

2047. Loretta, born 1846, 8, 18; dec'd.
2048. Olive C., born 1848, 6, 13.
2049. Orland B., born 1850, 7, 7.
2050. Charity, born 1852, 2, 10.

CHILDREN OF ISAAC PRICE (1051) AND JANE RAY.

2051. Lovica C., born 1844, 8, 28.
2052. Benjamin F., born 1845, 3, 27.
2053. Hester Asenath, born 1850, 11, 25.
2054. Isaac B., born 1853, 3, 25.
2055. John W., born 1858, 8, 17.

CHILDREN OF JEHIEL CON AND SARAH PRICE (1052).

2056. David, born ——, —, —.
2057. Thomas A., born ——, —, —.
2058. Ellen, born ——, —, —.

CHILD OF JAMES KELLY AND SARAH (PRICE) CON (1052).

2059. Hester, born ——, —, —.

CHILDREN OF THOMAS PRICE AND (1054) ELIZABETH WILLIAMSON.

2060. Lucretia L., born 1847, 3, 19; died ——, —, —.
2061. Oliver, born 1849, 3, 1; died 1849, 3, 3.
2062. Olive, born 1849, 3, 1; died 1849, 3, 3.
2063. Lyndon D., born 1850, 9, 5.
2064. Elma L., born 1853, 6, 17.
2065. Mary E., born 1857, 1, 8.

CHILDREN OF STEPHEN EMBREE AND RUTH COPE (1055)

2066. Elizabeth, born 1841, 4, 10.
2067. Melinda, born 1843, 3, 29.

CHILDREN OF JUSTUS L. BLANEY AND ANN COPE (1058).

2068. Edith Lucretia, born 1848, 1, 21.
2069. Joseph C., born 1849, 6, 25.
2070. Sarah Almira, born 1851, 6, 7.
2071. Isaac P., born 1854, 7, 25.
2072. John L., born 1855, 7, 8.
2073. William H., born 1858, 11, 28.

CHILDREN OF JOHN NAYLOR AND SARAH R. COPE. (1059).

2074. Nathan M., born 1842, 9, 30; died 1843, 1, 2.
2075. David E., born 1844, 2, 18.
2076. Martha E., bòrn 1847, 7, 26.
2077. George Gilbert, born 1849, 8, 16.
2078. Uriah C., born 1851, 8, 3.
2079. Ruth Ann, born 1854, 12, 18; died 1855, 3, 16.
2080. Narcissa J., born 1856, 8, 15; died 1856, 9, 24.

CHILDREN OF OLIVER COPE (1061) AND MARY H. ENLOES.

2081. Ruth Ann born ——, —, —.
2082. John Henry, born ——, —, —.

CHILDREN OF ISAAC P. COPE (1062) ANN CUMMINGS.

2083. Emma Almira, born 1849, 11, 3.
2084. Leander W.. born 1851, 5, 8.
2085. William A., born 1852, 9, 14.
2086. Evaline, born 1854, 7, 30; died 1854, 7, 30.
2087. Ella Jane, born 1856, 4, 8.
2088. Albert Henry, born 1858, 4, 2.

CHILDREN OF CYRUS BENEDICT AND HANNAH COPE (1063).

2089. Ann —., born 1846, 11, 11.
2090. David E., born 1849, 1, 6.
2091. Charles C., born 1851, 7, 21.
2092. William H. Seward, orn 1855, 5, 4.

CHILDREN OF THOMPSON M'CUTCHEON AND MARY ANN COPE. (1066).

2093. Howard F., born 1851, 10, 10.

2094. Albert E., born 1852, 12, 23.

2095. Thomson L., born 1854, 5, 25.

2096. Emily Rosella, born 1856, 10, 7.

2097. Frederick Willard, born 1858, 2, 16.

CHILD OF DAWSEY COPE (1067) AND ADELINE RIGGS.

2098. Sarah Louisa, born 1859, 8, 23.

CHILD OF JOHN EDWARD LOPEZ AND SARAH JANE COPE (1069).

2099. Mary Estella, born 1858, 12, 23.

CHILDREN OF ISAAC C. PENNOCK (1073) AND REBECCA ENLOES.

2100. Oliver C., born 1846, 6, 14. Resides at Honey Grove, Cedar county, Iowa.

2101, Mary I., born 1847, 9, —. Resides in Alliance, Ohio.

2102. Susan C., born 1849, 6, —; died 1850, 2, —.

CHILD OF WILLIAM PENNOCK AND (1077) AND ELIZA N. PAXSON.

2103. Ada M., born 1854, 5, —.

CHILDREN OF JOHN REEDER AND RUTH HAGAMAN (1082).

2104. Elizabeth, born 1845, 12, 8.

2105. Michael, born 1847, 8, 24.

2106. John, born 1851, 6, 6; died 1851, 7, 15.

2107. Jesse, born 1851, 6, 6.

2108. Sarah, born 1855, 10, 31.

CHILDREN OF WILLIAM ELLIOTT AND MARIA HAGAMAN (1083).

2109. Robert, born 1846, 5, 24.

2110. Sarah A., born 1848, 4, 6.

2111. Caroline, born 1851, 1, 13; died 1851, 7, 12.
2112. Harriet, born 1853, 1, 23.
2113. John H., born 1854, 4, 5; died 1854, 4, 6.
2114. William Henry, born 1858, 3, 8.

CHILDREN OF ISAAC C. HAGAMAN (1084) AND MARGARET ELLIOTT.

2115. Benjamin, born 1846, 12, 29.
2116. Mary, born 1849, 4, 28.
2117. Charles, born 1853, 2, 11.
2118. Ann, born 1854, 7, 30.
2119. William, born 1857, 11, 16.
2120. Walter, born 1859, 2, 28.

CHILDREN OF ZACHARY BROWN AND SARAH HAGAMAN (1088).

2121. Henrietta, born 1855, 3, 6.
2122. Ruth Elma, born 1857, 10, 15.

CHILDREN OF JOHN A. COPE (1091) AND ADA WINDER.

2123. Joseph W., born 1860, 4, 1.
2124. Alvah, born 1861, 10, 13; died 1861, 12, 1.
2125. Isaac, born 1863, 2, 6.
2126. Jesse, born 1866, 1, 7.
2127. Rachel E., born 1868, 12, 1.

CHILD OF ELLIS W. COPE (1093) AND DEBORAH FOWLER.

2128. Clara, born 1855, 5, 25.

CHILDREN OF ELLIS W. COPE (1093) AND MARY E. BLACKFORD.

2129. Emma Ordel, born 1859, 11, 27; died 1866, 9, 19.
2130. Luanda, born 1861, 8, 11; died 1866, 8, 10.
2131. Cyrus Martin, born 1866, 8, 10; died 1866, 8, 10.

CHILDREN OF DAWSEY ARMSTRONG AND LUCINDA COPE (1097).

2132. Viola, born 1864, 11, 17; died 1864, 12, 12.
2133. Oscar Emmett, born 1866, 1, 13; died 1867, 10, 14.
2134. Rosella, born 1868, 9, 1.

CHILD OF PORTER RICE AND SARAH ANNETTE COPE (1098).

2135. Nancy Annette, born 1868, 10, 18.

CHILD OF SAMUEL ARMSTRONG AND EMELINE COPE (1099).

2136. Nathan Edgar, born 1868, 7, 9.

CHILDREN OF ENOS P. VANSYOC (1102) AND PHEBE CREW.

2137. Martha J., born 1854, 1, 9.
2138. Albert, born 1855, 9, 8.
2139. Ruth Emma, born 1858, 9, 5.

CHILD OF JESSE VANSYOC (1104) AND RACHEL MORRISON.

2140. Henry Elmer, born 1858, 5, 2.

CHILD OF ENOCH BERRIER AND SARAH JANE VANSYOC (1106).

2141. Amanda Leonora, born 1858, 5, —.

CHILD OF WILLIAM BUNDY AND SARAH ANN COPE (1114).

2142. Elizabeth D., born 1858, 1, 6.

CHILDREN OF HENRY STAUFFER AND MARY ANN WINDER (1141).

2143. Walter Otto, born 1852, 5, 25.
2144. Joseph Edwin, born 1854, 9, 13.
2145. Ida Louisa, born 1857, 9, 27.
2146. Leonard Samuel, born 1860, 1, 13; died 1866, 9, 30.
2147. Elmer Ellsworth, born 1864, 5, 13; died 1865, 2, 23.
2148. Mary Alice, born 1866, 2, 18.

CHILDREN OF JOSEPH MINER AND SARAH AMELIA WINDER (1142).

2149. Amy Josephine, born 1851, 1, 20. Married 1867, 10, 17, to Jacob Stuteman. Jacob was born 1843, 12, 8.

2150. Mary, born 1855, 7, 6.

2151. Perry Stetson, born 1858, 11, 11.

2152. Ella Louisa, born 1861, 5, 15.

CHILDREN OF JOHN STAUFFER AND ABIGAIL WINDER (1143).

2153. Florence Endora, born 1855, 7, 6.

2154. Horace Raymond, born 1858, 3, 8.

2155. Wallace Winder, born 1861, 9, 3.

2156. Cora Alice, born 1868, 4, 4.

CHILD OF CHARLES WESTLEY SWARTZ AND HANNAH C. WINDER (1145).

2157. Mary Lavinia, born 1868, 12, 30.

CHILDREN OF LYMAN WOOSTER AND NANCY LUCINDA WINDER (1147).

2158. Franklin Ellsworth, born 1862, 5, 8.

2159. Frederic Luther, born 1865, 11, 5.

CHILD OF ANCIL B. MILLER AND AMY SOPHIA WINDER (1148).

2160. Ancil, born 1846, 3, 23.

CHILDREN OF ABNER K. ELLIOTT (1151) AND HARRIET A. ROCHELLE.

2161. James Wilkinson, born 1858, 8, 13; died 1863, 3, 25.

2162. Sarah Sabina, born 1859, 10, 24; died 1859, 12, 27.

2163. Elvina Belinda, born 1861, 9, 16; died 1861, 10, 22.

2164. Abner Verner, born 1866, 10, 20.

2165. Harriet Vernilla, born 1867, 10, 14.

2166. Vivian Ottomer, born 1868, 11, 24; died 1869, 2, 4

2167. Oliver Ottis, born 1869, 11, 26.

CHILDREN OF HENRY MITCHELL AND JUDITH CORDELIA ELLIOTT (1154).

2168. Mary E., born 1858, 10, 27.
2169. Charles R., born 1860, 5, 25.
2170. Abner Delmont, born 1862, 3, 4.
2171. Orpha Cordelia, born 1864, 6, 6.
2172. Rachel Florence, bo: n 1866, 11, 1.

CHILDREN OF JOHN R. SHAW AND ZELPHA ALERDMAN (1229).

2173. Mary S., born 1862, 1, 1; died 1862, 1, 28.
2174. Amos E, born 1863, 6, 9; died 1867, 6, 3.
2175. Laura E., born 1865, 7, 19.

CHILDREN OF JOHN WHITE AND MARY ANN BROWN (1352).

2176. Clinton I., born 1844, 6, 12. Married 1869, 4, 1, to Elizabeth, daughter of Samuel and Eliza Krewson.
2177. Ringgold T., born 1846, 9, 24.
2178. Thomas Jefferson, born 1848, 4, 29.
2179. John Randolph, born 1850, 1, 10.
2180. Hannah E., born 1852, 1, 22.
2181. Mary A. N., born 1854, 10, 28.

CHILDREN OF JOHN R. ABRAHAMS AND MARY ANN BROWN (WHITE) (1352).

2182. Sarah A., born 1860, 4, 16.
2183. James R., born 1862, 8, 6.
2184. Alice C., born 1864, 4, 8.

CHILDREN OF SAMUEL J. BROWN (1354) AND MARY L. CAMERON.

2185. Norville C., born 1855, 9, 23.
2186. Ida Ross, born 1857, 12, 27.
2187. Elizabeth A., born 1860, 6, 8.
2188. Annie C., born 1863, 4. 26.
2189. Charles H., born 1865, 4, 7.

CHILDREN OF ISAIAH D. PASSMORE AND NARCISSA A. BROWN (1356).

2190. Isaac Reuben, born 1858, 10, 16.
2191. Mary E., born 1861, 11, 21.
2192. Thomas W., born 1867, 8, 23.

CHILDREN HENRY BROWN AND MARY ELIZABETH ENGLAND (1359).

2193. William, born ——, —, —.
2194. Clara, born ——, —, —.
2195. Emma, born ——, —, —.

CHILDREN OF ELI ELISHA ENGLAND (1360) AND CATHARINE CLAWSON.

2196. William Granville, born ——, —, —; died ——.
2197. John Kirk, born ——, —, —; died ——, —, —.

CHILDREN OF CLEMSON BROWN AND LYDIA A. GRIFFITH (1368).

2198. Kirk, born 1845, 1. 4.
2199. Ross, born 1846, 8, 31.
2200. Elizabeth, born 1848, 2, 8.
2201. Anderson, born 1850, 1, 27.
2202. Webster, born 1853, 6, 17.
2203. Mary Ann, born 1855, 9, 29.
2204. Hannah A., born 1859, 10, 15; died 1861, 3, 27.
2205. Annie Job, born 1865, 2, 1.

CHILDREN OF WILLIAM K. GRIFFITH (1370) AND JANE C. CAMERON.

2206. Robert, born 1849, 5, 22.
2207. Andrew M., born 1852, 8, 18.
2208. Mary Ann, born 1857, 9, 23.
2209. Alice M., born 1861, 1, 28.
2210. Elizabeth I., born 1865, 5, 8.

CHILDREN OF JOB M. GRIFFITH (1371) AND MARY E. BROWN.

2211 Leon Winfield, born 1865, 2, 8.
2212. Mary Jane, born 1866, 12, 15.
2213. Ella, born 1868, 6, 24.

CHILD OF THEODORE HILAMAN AND MARY EMELINE KIRK (1384).

2214. Idora, born ——, —, —.

CHILD OF GEORGE SWAYNE AND RACHEL L. KIRK (1385).

2215. Lester, born 1867, 2, 1.

CHILD OF JOB HAINES KIRK (1388) AND ELIZABETH BROWN.

2216. Harvey, born, 1868, 12, 20.

CHILDREN OF FRANKLIN TERRY AND HELEN BROWN (TOUCHSTONE) (1422).

2217. Margaret E., born 1864, 10. 14.
2218. Luella. born 1868, 10, 17.

CHILDREN OF WILLIAM J. HESS AND ELIZABETH BROWN (1424).

2219. Emily, born ——, —, —; died ——, —, —.
2220. Franklin, born ——, —, —.
2221. Harlan, born ——, —, —.
2222. Adaline, born ——, —; —; died ——, —, —.
2223. Thompson, born ——, —, —.
2224. George M., born ——, —, —; died ——, —, —.
2225. Milton, born ——, —, —.
2226. Abner, born ——, —, —; died ——, —, —.
2227. Henry, born ——, —, —.

CHILDREN OF FRANKLIN BROWN (1425) AND ELLEN WOODWARD.

2228. Abner, born 1849, 3, 9. Resides near Wakefield. Is a farmer by occupation.

2229. Naomi E., born ——, —, —. Married 1868, 9, 17, to William, son of John and Hannah Fite. William is a farmer and thresher; he resides near Wakefield, Lancaster co., Pa.

2230. Joseph, born 1853, 5, 26.

2231. Elizabeth, born 1855, 8, 17.

CHILDREN OF WILLIAM J. TOWNSEND AND SOPHIA BROWN (1426).

2232. Benjamin F., born 1849, 6, 9; died 1849, 9, 11.

2233. Slater F., born 1851, 10, 5. Married 1871, 2, 16, to Mary Jane, daughter of Abner and Sarah Bradley. Slater is a farmer and resides south of Wakefield, Lancaster co., Pa.

2234. Alice, born 1854, 7, 11.

2235. Elizabeth E., born 1856, 6, 3; died 1857, 6, 3.

2236. Annie Virginia, born 1859, 6, 13.

CHILD OF WILLIAM K. BROWN (1427) AND MARY HARLAN.

2237. Abner Huber, born ——, —, —.

CHILDREN OF WILLIAM K. BROWN (1427) AND ELIZA PIERSON.

2238. Electra E., born 1861, 6, 30.

2239. Wilmer Lawrence, born 1863, 1, 19.

2240. Willis K., born ——, —, —.

2241. Owen, born ——, —, —.

2242. Burdella, born ——, —, —.

CHILDREN OF ROBERT JAMISON AND LUCY BROWN (1429).

2243. Sophia J., born ——, —, —.

2244. Silas, born ——, —, —.

2245. Louisa, born ——, —, —.

2246. Charles, born ——, —, —.

2247. William, born ——, —, —.

2248. Naomi Nettie, born ——, —, —.

CHILDREN OF THEODORE WHITTAKER AND EMILY BROWN (1430).

2249. Ida, born ——, —, —; died ——, —, —.
2250. William, born ——, —, —.
2251. George, born ——, —, —.
2252. Mary, born ——, —, —.
2253. Abner, born ——, —, —.

CHILD OF ANTHONY GOADONOW AND MARY E. KIRK (1441).

2254. Clara K., born 1865, 4, 18.

CHILD OF BASIL H. BROWN (1439) AND ANNA F. HAINES.

2255. Infant, born 1871, —, —.

CHILDREN OF ROBERT CATHERS AND MARY ELIZA KIRK (1448).

2256. Lydia H., born 1852, 6, 20.
2257. Florence C., born 1854, 2, 14.
2258. Delia J., born 1856, 9, 30; died 1858, 9, 11.
2259. John W., born 1859, 1, 8; died 1863, 5, 19.

CHILDREN OF THEODORE KIRK (1450) AND ———— ————.

2260. John P., born 1852, 6, 23.
2261. Alfred A., born 1854, 4, 7.
2262. Caroline, born 1856, 1, 1.
2263. Eloise, born 1861, 10, 7.
2264. Mary J., born 1865, 10, 10.
2265. Franklin, born 1868, 9, 8.

CHILDREN OF THOMAS S. KRAUSS AND CAROLINE KIRK (1451).

2266. Elam H., born 1859, 1, 21.
2267. Ida M., born 1863, 6, 21.

CHILDREN OF WILLIAM A. LOCKARD AND MARIA KIRK (1453).

2268. Mary E., born 1856, 1, 3.
2269. Anna J., born 1858, 1, 12.

2270. George H., born 1859, 8, 20.
2271. William S., born 1864, 6, 20.

CHILDREN OF JONATHAN M'CARDELL AND SARAH E. KIRK (1456).

2272. Virginia, born 1854, 5, 15.
2273. Annie, born, 1857, 4, 17.
2274. Sallie R., born 1866, 12, 31.

CHILD OF HAINES REYNOLDS AND ANN ELIZA KIRK (1457)

2275. John Haines, born 1865, 5, 9.

CHILDREN OF JOHN THOMPSON AND MARY JANE KIRK (1458).

2276. Margaret, born 1864, 3, 31; died 1866, 8, 10.
2277. Esther Reynolds, born 1865, 8, 27.
2278. William John, born 1868, 2, 26.

CHILD OF THOMAS FOSTER AND ESTHER A. KIRK (1459).

2279. Infant, born 186-, —, —; died ——, —, —.

CHILDREN OF AUGUSTUS BROOMFIELD AND MARGARET R. KIRK (1460).

2280. Ella, born 1860, 2, 16; died 1860, 4, 19.
2281. Henry, born 1862, 8, 1; died 1862, 11, 1.
2282. Francis, born 1863, 10, 28; died 1864, 2, 12.
2283. Jerome, born 1866, 8, 4.
2284. Leroy, born 1868, 2, 9.

CHILDREN OF THOMAS I. WILSON AND ADALINE H. KIRK (1466).

2285. Claude K., born 1867, 1, 26.
2286. Samuel T., born 1868, 10, 11.

CHILD OF DAVID EDWIN KIRK (1477) AND RACHEL A. HOUSE.

2287. Nicholas H., born 1867, 2, 9.

CHILD OF HANSON KIMBLE AND MARY HANNAH KIRK (1478).

2288. John Haines, born 1860, 10, 26.

CHILDREN OF EDWARD L. BROWN (1494) AND HANNAH HART.

2289. Mary A., born 1861, —, —.
2290. Annie L., born 1863, —, —; died 1866, —, —.
2291. Ida C., born 1865, —, —.
2292. Albert H., born 1868, —, —.

CHILDREN OF JOHN C. RUMFORD AND LYDIA BROWN (1495).

2293. Charles C., born 1844, —, —.
2294. John W., born 1846, —, —.
2295. William L., born 1849, —, —; died ——, —, —.
2296. Evaline, born 1851, —, —.
2297. Samuel B., born 1853, —, —.
2298. Cadelia, born 1855, —, —.
2299. Edward, born 1857, —, —.
2300. William F., born 1859, —, —.
2301. Lewis C., born 1861, —, —.
2302. Frederic S., born 1865, —, —; died 1865, —, —.
2303. Delaware, born 1869, —, —.

CHILDREN OF JAMES ROSSITER AND SARAH E. BROWN (1499).

2304. Albert P., born 1862, —, —.
2305. Joseph G., born 1866, —, —.
2306. William S., born 1868, —, —.

CHILD OF JOHN T. CHURCHMAN (1503) AND ANNIE M. STRICKLAND.

2307. William A., born 1868, 6, 14.

CHILD OF GILPIN O. HUTTON AND FRANCES M. W. WHITTAKER (1510).

2308. Clarrissa K., born 1868, 10, 17.

CHILDREN OF ALFRED KIRK (1514) AND ANNE THOMPSON

2309. Amy E., born ——, —, —.
2310. Mary M., born ——, —, —.
2311.
2312.

CHILDREN OF NATHANIEL BROWNFIELD AND ELMA MITCHELL.
(1611)

2313. Samuel M., born 1832, 8, 10.

2314. Thomas, born 1835, 4, 17. Married 1868, 2, —, to Elizabeth McLean, daughter of Alexander and Janett, of Uniontown, Fayette county, Pa. Elizabeth was born 1843, 2, 22.

2315. Elizabeth, born 1837, 2, 24. Married 1863, 6, 3, to Thomas Prentiss, son of Thomas and Isabel, of Uniontown. He was born 1825, 9, 19.

2316. Minerva, born 1838, 12, 17. Married 1864, 12, 1, to William Kinzey, son of Henry and Maria, of Fayette county, Pa.

2317. Mary M., born 1841, 5, 12. Married 1858, 12, 13, to James Hager, son of James and Rachel, of Uniontown. Joseph McLean Haddam.

2318. Susan Ann, born 1842, 11, 2. Married 1863, 6, 13, to George W. Thorndell, son of William and Mary, of Uniontown.

2319. Sarah Springer, born 1844, 10, 15.

2320. Louisa B., born 1846, 5, 8. Married 1866, 8, 5, to Joseph McLeau Haddam.

2321. William M., born 1847, 11, 17.

2322. Emma Frances, born 1850, 5, 21.

2323. Elma, born 1852, 2, 23.

2324. Rachel Seabright, born 1855, 7, 12.

CHILD OF WILLIAM C. MITCHELL (1612) AND MARY A. GOODRICH.

2325. William, born 1841 or 1842.

CHILDREN OF JESSE COLDREN AND MARTHA CAMPBELL (1613).

2326. Elizabeth, born 1847, 2, 24; died 1851, 3, 3.
2327. William H., born 1848, 4, 20.
2328. Sarah Allen, born 1852, 9, 16.
2329. Lewis C., born 1862, 5, 16.

CHILDREN OF NATHANIEL C. GRAY AND SUSAN CAMPBELL (1614).

2330. Sarah Elizabeth, born 1851, 10, 7.
2331. Hannah Louisa, born 1854, 8, 1.
2332. Emma Frances, born 1856, 5, 25.
2333. Lewis Williams, born 1862, 3, 3.
2334. James Franklin, born 1864, 9, 8.

CHILDREN OF ELLIOTT HIBBS AND MARY ANN CAMPBELL (1618).

2335. Deborah C., born 1861, 7, 14.
2336. John N., born 1866, 3, 4.

CHILDREN OF WILLIAM EYRES AND FRANCES CAMPBELL (1620).

2337. Mary R., born 1844, 12, 31.
2338. Sarah J., born 1847, 3, 5.
2339. Jonathan, born 1849, 1, 24.
2340. Loulla, born 1866, 10, 17.

CHILDREN OF S. N. WOODSWORTH AND JANE CAMPBELL (1622).

2341. Matilda A., born 1850, 6, 2.
2342. Mary F., born 1852, 2, 15.
2343. William W., born 1853, 2, 11.
2344. Verginet, born 1856, 11, 13.
2345. Rosetta, born 1864, 3, 26.

CHILDREN OF WILLIAM N. CAMPBELL (1623) AND IVIO S. EDMUNDSON.

2346. Mary C., born 1861, 7, 8.
2347. Elizabeth, born 1862, 12, 10.
2348. Della, born 1864, 10, 3.

CHILDREN OF JAMES STILWELL AND SUSANNA CAMPBELL (1624).

2349. Mary D., born 1860, 2, 22.
2350. Sarah S., born 1861, 11, 11.
2351. Bertha J., born 1863, 8, 15.
2352. Cora J., born 1866, 9, 2.
2353. Fannie W., born 1868, 11, 14.

CHILDREN OF ELLIS B. CAMPBELL (1628) AND SARAH NIXON.

2354. Rebecca E., born 1858, 4, 5.
2355. Mary E., born 1864, 3, 7.
2356. Dora M., born 1866, 1, 8.

CHILDREN OF LEWIS CAMPLELL (1629) AND MINERVA M'DOW.

2357. James A., born 1861, 2, 9.
2358. Elliott B., born 1863, 2, 28.
2359. Emily E., born 1865, 4, 28.
2360. Susan B., born 1869, 7, 8.

CHILD OF ABEL C. PRICE (1631) AND MARGARET JAMESON.

2361. Anna Snowden, born 1858, 6, 21.

CHILD OF EMELINE PRICE (1632) AND MARTHA SHEPHERD.

2362. Elizabeth, born 1866, 3, 31.

CHILDREN OF NATHANIEL STEPHENS AND HANNAH PRICE. (1633).

2363. Byron ——, born 1855, 8, 21.

2364. Mary Alice, born 1856, 12, 23; died 1863, 1, 5.

2365. Ann Esther, born 1858, 10, 4.

2366. John D., born 1859, 12, 16.

2367. William Ellsworth, born, 1861, 8, 20; died 1865, 6, 20.

2368. Elizabeth B., born 1863, 1, 14.

2369. Mary Ida, born 1864, 10, 7.

2370. William C., born 1866, 4, 14.

CHILDREN OF GEORGE MARTIN (1655) AND ANN TRIMBLE.

2371. Edith, born 1850, 10, 25, at Concordville; died 1863, 10, 28, in Philadelphia.

2372. Rebecca, born 1852, 6, 6, in Philadelphia; died 1853, 11, 27.

2373. George, born 1854, 2, 7, in Philadelphia; died 1854, 11, 4.

CHILDREN OF NATHAN S. MARTIN (1656) AND SUSAN EVES.

2374. Annie, born 1853, 7, 23.

2375. George, born 1855, 11, 8.

2376. Lydia S., born 1859, 2, 26.

CHILD OF D. O. TIMLOW AND LYDIA BRINTON (1658).

2377. William Ferree, born 1864, 11, —.

CHILDREN OF JOHN F. BRINTON (1659) AND ANNA BINNEY.

2378. Mary Emeline, born 1860, 1, —.

2379. Ferree, born 1861, 7, —.

2380. Nathan B., born 1863, 6, —.

2381. Joseph S., born 1865, 3, —.

CHILD OF WILLIAM P. BRINTON (1661) AND MARIA ROGERS.

2382. Bessie, born 1860, 9, —.

CHILD OF BRIGHAM YOUNG AND MARGARET PIERCE (1668).

2383. Brigham Morris, born 1854, 1, 18.

CHILDREN OF ELI H. PIERCE (1670) AND SUSANNA NEFF.

2384. Eli Harvey, born 1851, 9, 27.
2385. Mary Barr, born 1853, 9, 21.
2386. Leonidas, born 1855, 6, 21.
2387. Susanna Octavia, born 1857, 3, 27.

CHILDREN OF THOMAS PIERCE (1671) AND HARRIET A. GREEN

2388. Harriet L., born 1859, 7, 5.
2389. Thomas Harvey, born 1861, 3, 20.
2390. Morris Clifton, born 1863, 2, 25.

CHILDREN OF WILLIAM PIERCE (1673) AND JERUSHA SMITH.

2391. Hannah Evaline, born 1855, 9, 17.
2392. Hiram Robert, born 1857, 4, 9.
2393. Martha Lavinia, born 1860, 8, 3.
2394. Margaret Jerusha, born 1863, 1, 10; died 1864, 10, —.
2395. Sarah McKee, born 1865, 10, 20.
2396. William Smith, born 1868, 5, 26.

CHILDREN OF JAMES FISHER AND EDITH EVALINE PIERCE (1674).

2397. James Madison, born 1857, 12, 14.
2398. Robert P., born 1859, 10, 1.
2399. Joseph, born 1861, 9, 16.
2400. Clara, born 1863, 11, 8.
2401. George Washington, born 1865, 3, 4.
2402. Mary Evaline, born 1867, 3, 20.

CHILD OF EDWIN H. HANEY (1676) AND JOSEPHINE YOULE.

2403. Walter Y., born ——, —, —.

CHILDREN OF GIDEON SPEAKMAN AND ANNA MARY HARVEY (1677).

2404. Lillian, born ——, —, —.

2405. Harvey, born ——, —, —.

CHILD OF JOHN V. PAINTER (1679) AND —— ——.

2406. Lulu, born 18—, —, —.

CHILD OF URIAH H. PAINTER (1680) AND BELINDA AVERY.

2407. Ellen, born 18—, —, —.

CHILD OF EUGENE VICKERS (1690) AND MARY E. DAVIS.

2408. Correne, born 1868, 3, 10.

CHILDREN OF JESSE K. PAINTER (1692) AND SARAH EARLY.

2409. William E., born 1861, 8, 8, at Bristol, Pa.

2410. Awanna H., born 1865, 8, 8, at Jersey City, New Jersey.

CHILD OF LEICESTER M. PAINTER (1693) AND MARY E. WHITE.

2411. George J., born 1869, 7, 14.

CHILD OF BENJAMIN W. SWAYNE (1706) AND MARGARET BANCROFT.

2412. William, born 1851, 9, 16.

CHILDREN OF WILLIAM MARSHALL SWAYNE (1707) AND MARY BARNARD.

2413. Ada B., born 1851, 10, 23, in East Marlborough.

2414. Antonis Canova, born 1853, 9, 21.

2415. William Marshall, born 1855, 8, 30.

2416. Richard M. B., born 1858, 11, 11.

2417. Mary B., born 1862, 4, 30, in West Chester.

2418. Kate C., born 1865, 10, 5.

2419. Alice W., born 1869, 9, 14.

CHILDREN OF JACOB SWAYNE (1708) AND SARAH J. B. NOBLIT

2420. Mary M., born ——, —, —.
2421. William, born ——, —, —.
2422. Jacob, born ——, —, —.
2423. Elizabeth M., born ——, —, —.

CHILDREN OF CHARLES BARNARD AND ELIZABETH M. SWAYNE. (1709).

2424. Margaret B., born 1853, 9, 7.
2425. Josephine W., born 1856, 6, 14.

CHILDREN OF SAMUEL KINSEY (1712) AND MARTHA F. CUSTER.

2426. Charles F., born 1845, 1, 18.
2427. Emma Letitia, born 1847, 6, 30; died 1848, 8, 17.
2428. George C., born 1849, 7, 25.
2429. John Woodward, born 1853, 10, 21.
2430. Emma Irene, born 1856, 1, 27.
2431. William, born 1858, 10, 23; died 1858, 11, 1.

CHILDREN OF MARIS GARRETT AND ELIZABETH KINSEY (1715).

2432. Mary, born 1848, 2, 28.
2433 John Kinsey, born 1849, 8, 21.
2434. Elma, born 1851, 2, 11.
2435. Amy Ida, born 1852, 10, 23.
2436. Margaret W., born 1854, 10, 10; died 1866, 5, 3.
2437. Charles M., born 1856, 7, 22.
2438. Hibbard, born 1858, 5, 26; died 1858, 5, 26.
2439. Granville, born 1859, 6, 5.
2440. Elizabeth K., born 1860, 11, 23.
2441. George W., born 1861, 11, 4.

2442. Josephine, born 1861, 11, 4; died 1863, 9, 20.
2443. Philena, born 1863, 6, 19; died 1863, 10, 26.
2444. Walter Leslie, born 1864, 8, 11; died 1864, 12, 29.
2445. Ada, born 1866, 7, 23; died 1866, 8. 1.
2446. Laura Bertha, born 1866, 2, 26.

CHILDREN OF H. A. SLATER AND PHILENA KINSEY (1718).

2447. Theodore, born 1861, 12, 5; died 1862, 9, 26.
2448. Edward H., born 1863, 12, 17.
2449. Samuel K., born 1865, 7, 30; died 1866, 7, 14.
2450. William, born 1867, 10, 14.
2451. Serena M., born 1869, 4, 29.

CHILD OF DAVID W. BRANSON AND ANN BAILEY (1726).

2452. William E., born 1867, 6, 24.

CHILD OF BENNETT S. WALTON AND REBECCA BAILEY (1727)

2453. William B., born 1858, 1, 4.

CHILDREN OF JOEL S. BAILEY (1731) AND SARAH S. WELCH.

2454. William W., born 1866, 4, 28.
2455. Marion G., born 1868, 3, 31.

CHILD OF ELI PALMER AND MARY ANN SMEDLEY (1737).

2456. Linda B., born 1866, 11, 30.

CHILD OF WILMER SMEDLEY (1738) AND ELIZABETH BEITLER.

2457. Anna B., born 1868, 12.

CHILDREN OF ELIJAH WEAVER AND REBECCA CHANDLER (1740).

2458. Anna. R., born 1855, 10, 10; died 1856, 2, 25.

2459. Chandler, born 1858, 3, 30.
2460. Rebecca, born 1861, 6, 30.

CHILDREN OF THOMAS ALLEN CHANDLER (1741) AND ELIZA RICHARDS.

2461. William R., born 1862, 12, 11.
2462. George Waellper, born 1868, 2, 23; died 1868, 4, 29.

CHILDREN OF ASAHEL WALKER AND SARAH CHAMBERS (1746).

2463. Mary Ann, born 1843, 2, 3; died 1843, 9, 9.
2464. Deborah, born 1844, 5, 21. Married, 1867, —, —, to William H. Marshall.
2465. Rebecca, born 1846, 2, 1.
2466. Patience, born 1847, 3, 8; died 1852, 1, 21.
2467. Isaac, born 1848, 9, 30.
2468. Mary, born 1851, 5, 3; died 1851, 9, 30.
2469. William D., born 1854, 4, 21; died 1854, 6, 11.

CHILD OF RICHARD H. FELL (1751) AND ELIZA T. GARRETT.

2470. Abner G., born 1868, 5, 20.

CHILD OF ALBERT M. WOODWARD (1752) AND HARRIET PARKER.

2471. Huizinga P., born 1867, 10, 18.

CHILDREN OF CASPER KENDALL (1763) AND EMILY M. JOHNSON.

2472. Emily Matilda, born 1860, 1, 7.
2473. Florence G., born 1864, 1, 19.
2474. Lillian, born 1867, 7, 28.

CHILD OF WESTLEY JOHNSON AND EMMARINE ENTRIKEN (1772).

2475. Elsie B., born ——, —, —.

CHILD OF JAMES SINCLAIR AND PHEBE ANN M'GEE (1778).

2476. ———, born 1868, 12, 25.

CHILDREN OF FRANCIS M. PYLE AND ELIZABETH WICKERSHAM (1798).

2477. Elmer A., born 1862, 11, 29.

2478. Clarence W., born 1866, 4, 11.

CHILDREN OF TRUMAN C. MOORE AND PHEBE ANN MOORE (1799).

2479. Wilmer A., born 1865, 8, 23.

2480. Edward, born 1867, 9, 17.

CHILD OF LEVI W. MOORE (1800) AND MARGARET A. CARUTHERS.

2481. Howard C., born 1868, 10, 18.

EIGHTH GENERATION.

CHILDREN OF JOHN G. SMITH AND MARY EMMA LEWIS (1840.)

2482. Lincoln, born 1865, 5, 22.

2483. Mabel, born 1867, 6, 30.

CHILD OF MILTON T. LEWIS (1842) AND ISADORE ROSS.

2484. Infant (daughter), born 1869, 7, 4; died ——, —, —.

CHILD OF JACOB STUTEMAN AND AMY JOSEPHINE MINER (2151).

2485. Alvin Grant, born 1868, 8, 1.

CHILDREN OF THOMAS PRENTISS AND ELIZABETH BROWNFIELD (2317).

2486. Walter, born 1864, 4, 5.

2487. Mary Elma, born 1865, 11, 8.

CHILDREN OF WILLIAM HINZEY AND MINERVA BROWNFIELD (2318).

2488. Frank B., born 1865, 9, 18.

2489. Charles H., born 1867, 11, 1.

CHILD OF JAMES HAGER AND MARY M. BROWNFIELD (2319).

2490. Nathaniel, born 1859, 8, 16.

CHILDREN OF GEO. M. THORNDELL AND SUSAN ANN BROWNFIELD (2320).

2491. William, born 1863, 11, 29.
2492. Mary Snyder, born 1865, 12, 9.

CHILDREN OF JOSEPH M. HADDEN AND LOUISA BROWNFIELD (2322).

2493. Harvey, born 1867, 3, 4.
2494. Jane E., born 1868, 10, 14.

FINIS.

ERRATA.

The family of Mary Woodward (149) was unintentionally omitted from its proper place. Her children should have been placed opposite the numbers placed below.

CHILDREN OF JONATHAN WOODWARD AND MARY WOODWARD (149).

616. Margaret, born 1819, 9, 19. Married 1843, 1, 5, to Amos Davis, son of Samuel and Ann. They reside at Coatesville, Chester county, Pa.

617. Deborah, born 1821, 9, 13; died 1823, 11, 16.

FIFTH GENERATION.

618. Susanna, born 1823, 12, 2. Unmarried. Lives in West Chester with her cousin, George Hawley.

619. Evan, born 1825, 12, 15. Married 1859, 3, 3, to Matilda Supplee. He resides in West Whiteland township. Is a farmer.

620. Thomas, born 1828, 7, 21; died 1869, 8, 20. Married 1869, 7, 7, to Elizabeth A. Wright, daughter of Joseph and Eliza. He lives in Philadelphia; is a tailor.

621. Robert, born 1832, 1, 8; died 1850, 8, 16; buried at East Caln.

CHILDREN OF AMOS DAVIS AND MARGARET WOODWARD (616).

1825. Mary E., born 1843, 11, 8; died 1855, 6, 19.

1826. Henry C., born 1846, 9, 13.

1827. Samuel L., born 1850, 4, 9.

1828. Sarah E. M., born 1856, 10, 28.

A HISTORY

OF THE

EARLY SETTLERS BY THE NAME OF KIRK.

Also, a Record of Two Hundred and Nine of the Descendants of Alphonsus Kirk, who migrated from Lurgan, Ireland, and settled in New Castle county, Delaware.

WRITTEN BY RACHEL PRICE.

ALTHOUGH I have already made some short notes of the early settlement of my predecessors in this country, with some of their privations and hardships, as related by my father when I was young, yet, at the request of some of my near relations and friends to give a more full detail of occurrences that then took place, as I am the only survivor now remaining that can remember, so as to relate them, I am induced to make the attempt, though sensible of my inability to perform; yet if the simple relation of facts, according to the best of my memory (often hearing him* relate them when I was so small as to sit on his lap, listening with great interest and attention when he was conversing with his friends.)

If the recording of them may be the means of awakening

*Her father, William Kirk (12).

gratitude and love to the Great Preserver of men, in the hearts of His numerous offspring, for the many favors conferred upon us, spiritual and temporal; that we may be more fully given up to serve Him is the desire of my heart.

My grandfather, Alphonsus Kirk, son of Roger and Elizabeth Kirk, of Lurgan, in Ireland, came to America in the year 1689, and settled in New Castle county, Centre township, near Brandywine creek, about a mile in a northerly direction from where Young's Paper Mill now stands. He was married to Abigail Sharpley, of Shillpot creek, on the 23d day of the 12th month, A. D. 1692. She came from England in the ship with William Penn. They settled on a farm a half mile from Centre Meeting House, where they continued to reside during their lives. Their son Adam inherited it after them his life time. It then descended to his son Caleb, in whose possession it remained a considerable time. It is now gone out of the name.

My grandfather, it appears, had eleven children, who mostly lived to grow up and settle. My father, whose name was William, was the youngest child but one, whose name was Timothy. They had many adventures together when young, which they would speak of when they met, which they frequently did, and would in a pleasant manner rehearse, which was very interesting to us in childhood; but there was an affecting occurrence took place when they were small boys, which I have often heard my father relate, which struck my infant mind with horror and dismay. It so happened that my grandmother was left with only these two little boys with her, when there came up a large bear, and near the door before she saw it. She only had time to shut the lower part (it being a double door) before he had his fore feet upon it;

there being a pudding bag hanging on it so as to prevent her from getting it shut very quick. She pushed it against his paws with all her strength to prevent his getting in, and called to the little boys to bring her the axe, which was in the house; but they could not find it. She told them to hand her the rolling-pin, which she beat his feet with until he was willing to withdraw them so that she could get the door fastened. He then attempted to climb upon a kind of shed that was over the door and extended to a window in the second story. She, seeing his determination to get in if he could, requested her little sons to go down into the cellar and get into a chest that was there and shut down the lid, but not so close that they could not get their breath, and she would go up and try and prevent his getting in.

The shed had been made of round saplings covered over with brush, and there was snow on them. Some of them rolled as he walked on them so as to let him fall through and hurt him. She threw him some parts of beef, which he devoured with great greediness, appearing to be very hungry; then went off. They had killed a beef that day, which no doubt attracted the hungry and devouring animal.

The next morning several men set out in search of him, his feet being wounded so that they bled on the snow, enabled them to track him. They soon found him. Grandfather taking his axe, and with some stout dogs, attacked him with violence. A hard conflict ensued, in which the bear seemed likely to gain the victory over the dogs.

Grandfather went to their assistance with his axe. In the meantime his eldest son with others came riding up and observed the scuffle, but not seeing his father with them he incautiously raised his gun in order to fire; but his companion observing called to him to desist, which he did, and was preserved from doing injury. They soon succeeded in killing the bear. Oh, what cause for thankfulness and gratitude to the Preserver of men, in that He condescends to protect in many and imminent dangers!

In the early settling of the country there was much difficulty in getting their grain ground after they had raised it; there being so few mills, very slow in operation.

The inhabitants pretty widely scattered around, they, some of them, had a considerable distance to go.

They often had to wait a good while for their grists, as they had to wait their turns.

My father informed us of a circumstance which occurred with one of his oldest brothers when a lad: He was sent with a grist to a mill, and there were so many there before him and he was so long detained that he became so extremely hungry that as soon as his grist was commenced he took some meal and made himself a cake, putting it into the ashes to bake. Being urged by hunger, he took it out before it was sufficiently baked, and sunk his teeth into it while it was in a state of dough. It adhered to his teeth and gums, and was so excessively hot as to scald them and make them extremely sore for a time; but eventually this was thought to be a benefit, supposing that the heat was so severe and stuck so close about them that it destroyed the sensitive nerves in the teeth that they never decayed nor ached afterward.

When my father had arrived at an age that he thought proper to settle himself, he became attached to a young woman in the neighborhood, of respectable family, who were Baptists by profession.

She had previously become convinced of the principles

professed by Friends. Her name was Mary Buckingham. Whether she became a member amongst Friends before they married I have no recollection of hearing said on the subject. As we do not find any record* of their marriage it may be supposed they did not accomplish it through meeting, but she must have become united with Friends soon after, as I have often heard my father say that it was a great trial to her father that she should become a Quaker; but she believing it required of her, went, through much opposition. Some of her brothers-in-law were ministers (so-called) in their society, strove hard to reclaim her from her delirium, calling the Quakers by many harsh names, bringing many charges against them of unbelief or deism, and such like.

Sometime after their marriage her father was taken ill, which proved to be his last sickness. She felt it to be her duty to him to go and nurse him and do all in her power to relieve and comfort him on his deathbed—often sitting up with him and watching over him, while her anxious relatives made use of the opportunity of endeavoring to convince her of her error in embracing what they called false opinions; but she was favored to open her views with so much clearness and enabled to give an account of the hope that was in her with so much satisfaction, that, although her father joined not much in their conversation, yet it appeared that he had listened with interest and attention when they were not aware of it, as he took an opportunity with her before his death, telling her with great affection that he was then perfectly satisfied with her views and principles as he had heard her set them forth, which was a great comfort to him, and that he

*Rachel was mistaken in this one point. William Kirk, of Nantmeal, and Mary Buckingham, married at Centre, 1733, 6, 8.—*Kennett Records.*

believed that if she kept close to them, they would be the means of preserving her in her trials through life. The interview was truly consoling to her and my dear father, encouraging them to persevere in the views of religion they had embraced, and to endeavor to live up to them.

I have already mentioned that my father, when he married, settled in East Nantmeal, on a tract of land about one mile from the meeting house, where he farmed and also followed and kept the weaving business, carried on for many years. There he spent a long and useful life. He died in his eightieth year, and was buried in Nantmeal burying-ground, where his two wives and a large number of his children and descendants are laid. He left his property to his only son, Isaiah, who resided on it until the advanced age of his eighty-second year. Deceased 1835, 12 mo., 19th.

He left his property to his sons, Samuel and William Kirk. He was confined to his room one year, which he bore with resignation to the Divine will. He had a paralytic affection, so benumbing his feelings that he was not sensible of extreme suffering, though he had a cancer on his lip increasing fast.

But recurring to some circumstances which took place in their early settlement, although but trifling, they may afford some amusement at least to survivors. When my father left his father's, he took a favorite dog with him. They soon found that at whichever home he considered himself most kindly treated he preferred being at; so that when he felt himself offended at one place he would immediately go to the other and stay there until he met with an affront, and then he would go directly back again, the distance of near thirty miles, through a thinly inhabited country. As they had no post then to send letters by, they found him very convenient to carry intelligence between them.

They would their letters enclose in something which was water-proof, as he had to cross the Brandywine. They would tie them fast about his neck and then would threaten to whip or offend him in some way. He would go straight off in a few hours to his other home; thus they had great accommodation from the sagacious animal.

At one time when there were several of my father's first set of children at play, his seventh child, a little girl whose name was Rachel, a small child about three years of age, became separated a short distance from the others who were older. When they missed her they soon went in search of her and found her sitting rocking herself, saying something in a soothing voice, as though she might have had a little kitten a singing to; but when they came up close behind her they saw, to their great surprise, that it was a large garter snake coiled up in her lap, and she was stroking her dear little hand over it, saying, "Poor thing, thee has a striped gown on as well as me." It was perfectly harmless, but one of the older ones being alarmed, raised her up by putting their hands under her arms and threw it off as far as they could from them; it showed marked displeasure at them for disturbing its comfortable abode, and she not knowing what they meant did not wish to have it disturbed; literally fulfilling the declaration "that the little child shall play with the asp and put its hand on the den of the adder."

My father's eldest son, Caleb Kirk, married a widow Coates, who had three sons. She was some years older than he was. They also had three sons, and one daughter, who died young, namely: Elisha, an humble, meek, eminent minister amongst Friends; Caleb and Eli Kirk. They all lived to have families. Tamer, his oldest daughter, who lived to be grown up, manifested a desire when young to live in some newly-settled country or wilderness. When she arrived at an age that might be thought proper to marry, she was addressed by a young man by name of Phineas Mendenhall, who had a prospect of going to North Carolina to settle. Her friends thought it had an influence on her mind to induce her to accept him. They married, and very soon after, they set off to go to North Carolina; settled in Guilford county, pretty much in the woods, where, no doubt, they had many difficulties to encounter. Her youngest sister, Mary, one of the twins, also was desirous from a child to live in a newly-settled part of the country. When grown up she wrote to her sister, who had been absent about seven years, that if she would come and make a visit to her relations and friends she would accompany her home and stay and live with them.

Accordingly, Tamer came with that expectation. Our parents were very much tried in giving her up, but at length submitted. After spending a few weeks with us, they set off, after taking an affectionate and affecting leave of all of us.

I well recollect it, being the first scene of the kind that I then had ever witnessed. Impressions on the mind of children, even when young, of a striking nature, are often lasting, although but trifling incidents.

I have no recollection of my sister Tamer before she went away, I being an infant; but now remember her well. She was a good looking, portly person. She pulled my first teeth when I shed them. This circumstance, though small, impressed her more fully on my mind.

I have retained the recollections of a young man of the name of Jehu Wickersham, who was acquainted with my sister Mary. He went to Carolina, sometime after her, where they renewed their attachment and were married, and settled there for a time; but the State of Georgia opened for settlement, inducing many to move there.

My sisters, and their families, were both of them amongst those who went about three hundred miles from their settlements into the State of Georgia, to a place settled by Joseph Matlock and Mattock's Settlement.

There they lived in peaceable possession of their homes, undisturbed by the natives for a considerable time, until there was a new purchase made by Government, with which the Indians seemed dissatisfied.

My brothers-in-law, with others, bought land in it, as it was considered very good. Many were induced to make settlements on it, to clear and sow it with grain; but the frequent incursions of the Indians was cause of great discouragement to them, so that it was deemed best by many not to reside on it.

They, therefore, left, but when the grain that they had sown was ripe they thought they would go there and gather it, the distance not being far from the first settlement where they resided. Sister Tamer, her husband and three sons went for that purpose, leaving their two daughters behind at home. Early one morning sister went to milk a cow they had with them. While her hands were thus engaged a party of Indians lying in wait fired on them, and put an end to her useful life; they also killed her eldest son. The youngest they took in charge and kept in captivity about two years. They adopted him and were kind to him, and when redemption was offered him he had become so attached to them and their manner of life that it required some persuading to get him from them. The father and other son made their escape. This awfully trying circumstance made such an impression on the minds of sister Mary and husband that they came, as soon as they could get away to North Carolina, to their former settlement. In that neighborhood they lived for many years. They of late years moved with their children and their families to Indiana, where they are settled, and from the latest accounts are both living, she being now in the eighty-sixth year of her age.*

In the year 1777 my brother, Daniel Williams, (he was my mother's son of her first husband), and Mary his wife, with two little daughters and my brother-in-law, †John Williams with his wife Sarah (a twin sister to Mary Wickersham), and a little daughter, set off in company together with a prospect of seeking a place of abode. They traveled on together through some difficulties and perplexities, being in the time of the Revolutionary war. When they got to North Carolina, and the twin sisters were rejoiced to meet with a prospect which they, before they left, had of settling there. Brother D. looked toward going to Georgia, which they did.

John and Sarah were getting themselves fixed as well as they could under their limited circumstances, when, alas, sickness seized her so severe that she was taken off in a few days; often expressing her great desire to be taken out of this troublesome world, and left it as one going to sleep on the 12th day of 12th mo., 1778. Thus in less than two years were his prospects changed, showing clearly the uncertainty of all human dependence. He was then left with two children, the youngest not one year old. He struggled along with them there awhile and then came back with them amongst their relatives.

*From a late acconnt received they are near Centreville, Wayne county, Ind., with their son-in-law, William Kirk. She is now in her eighty-ninth year. This was written prior to 1847.—C. H. S.

†Same name, but not of the same family.

Brother Daniel, when they arrived in Georgia, it being about the middle of the 12th mo., went to his wife's uncle's, there being several of them settled there of the name of Embree.

After being there awhile he purchased 100 acres of good land with some impovments, within the old purchase, where they settled comfortably, except being near to the frequent incursions of the Indians, who almost every year caused some part of the settlements to break, but they were not injured by them. He spent the remainder of his life there in a place called Wrightsborough. He frequently wrote to his relatives and twice visited us, bringing his wife with him. He lived until about the year 1800, when he departed in peace, leaving behind there his widow and seven daughters. Their only son, they buried before they left Nantmeal.

In the course of a few years, the mother, with her daughters, all moved to the State of Ohio, and settled in the neighborhood of Stillwater, all near together, except one who settled in the western part of the State. When on a visit to the meeting of Friends in that part of the country, in the year 1807, I had the satisfaction of seeing them all, in their own habitations. They were then, most of them, married and pretty comfortably settled where they generally remained, to dwell. Their mother lived to a good old age and died in peace.

Sister Lydia, married William Humphreys, a brother to Mary Williams, Daniel's wife. They lived at Robinson or Forest. Had no family of their own, but Sister Sarah's daughter found them as parents to her. They took her and raised her, and in their advanced age she, in return of their kindness, staid with them as a daughter and took care of them as long as they lived. They have both been gone several years, and she, Catharine, is married to John Martin, of Uwchland.

Brother Isaiah died 19th of 12th mo., 1835, and was interred on the 20th, in Nantmeal burying-ground, after which a meeting was held.

Elizabeth Kirk, daughter of S—— Richards, his valuable companion, was removed by death, 2d mo.. 28th, 183—. She came forth in the ministry in early life, not very long after her marriage, under many discouragements and sore conflicts, but was favored to get along to the satisfaction of her friends. We once went in company together and attended the Yearly Meeting in New York, taking meetings on the way, I believe to the satisfaction of her friends. She was also interred at Nantmeal, and a solemn meeting held.

Their daughter, Elizabeth Garrettson, resided in Yorktown, Pa. She died 10th mo., 31st, 1335, after an illness of three weeks, leaving an affectionate companion and three little daughters behind to mourn their loss. The younger one died after her mother.

Their son, William Kirk, departed this life on the 27th of the 1 mo., 1837, after an illness of one week, of bilious fever, which he bore with resignation. He was interred in East Nantmeal burying-ground.

My father, William Kirk, in the first settlement of that part of the country, took up a tract of land about a mile from East Nantmeal meeting house. He put a small cabin on it and began in the woods, with a small family and limited means of subsistence. His wife, a sensible, valuable woman, united with him in the utmost endeavors to procure a livelihood. They had many difficulties to encounter at first, while in the wilderness, but were favored to succeed beyond his expectations, and were enjoying many comforts, when, alas, sickness commenced. His beloved companion was removed by death in 1752, and three of his children out of ten were all taken from him in the course of three months—a sore bereavement to be stripped and tried. I well remember to hear him speak of it with a sorrowful heart when I was young.

There was one circumstance I often remember to have heard him relate, and never without shedding tears. It was when he had a small portion of his land cleared so as to till crops, but small. A very severe winter came on, snow three or four feet deep and much drifted; traveling through the woods difficult. When their limited stock of provisions had nearly come to an end, my father set out in hopes of procuring some provisions; rode all day without obtaining any and was quite discouraged. His wife, a woman of resolution, said she would try and get some.

He being not well staid with the children. (I think they had two children and a brother of hers a little lad). She got on horsback (they having one horse and a cow), and set out early in the morning through deep snow as high as the fences. She got with great difficulty as far as Ashbridge's Mill before she could obtain any. Here she met with it. She informed him of their situation; that she had no money, but they had a crop of grain in the ground and she had a piece of home-spun linen—she would pledge that. The friend said he wished for no other security than her word, and furnished her with as much flour as she could take with her, and offered to supply them until harvest. It took her all night to get back to their cabin. Father was anxiously looking for her. The children had been crying with hunger, and he had nothing to give them. He thought of her kneading bowl. He took it and scraped it, washed the small portion of flour off it, and boiled the water and made porridge of it to satisfy their hunger, so they went to sleep. When she arrived in safety their hearts were filled with gratitude for the favor.

In the course of time feeling great difficulty in struggling along with a family of small children, he thought best to marry again to a widow with one son. Her name was Sibbilla Williams. They had nine children of us—the most of us lived to the age of maturity.

I* was married in the year 1784, on the 20th day of 10th month, in the 22d year of my age, to Philip Price, Jr., and went to reside with him near Darby, in the house with his father and mother—Philip and Hannah Price. We stayed with them near three years; they then purchased a small farm for us at West Nantmeal, seven miles from the meeting which I was raised a member of. The place was a pleasant one and good land, but the distance from meeting, with very few friends near us and the people generally dissipated in their habits, it was not desirable to bring up a family in such a neighborhood. My husband heard of a place for sale in East Bradford, went to see it, was pleased with it and desired to purchase it. He went to consult his parents about it and get his father to go with him to see it, expecting to be from home a week. It was on first day. We attended our meeting and went to our mother's afterwards. She and her youngest daughter, Sister Sibbilla, lived together in the same house with our brother, Isaiah Kirk, and family. My father having lived to 78 years of age, died 2d of 3d month, 1787.

My dear mother went home with me to bear me company in my husband's absence. We passed the week very comfortably. She was as well as usual for her to be, but was taken

*Rachel Kirk.

sick about nine o'clock that night with a very severe pain in her arm, which struck through to her breast. I gave her some camphor and bathed her with it, after which she seemed a little easier, and lay till daybreak, when she arose and dressed herself, and prepared to go home before meeting. Upon my telling her that she was not well enough to go, she replied, "If I should not live, I have a desire to be at my own home." I told her we would do all we could for her. She said she knew that, "but I have a great choice in being at home if I can get there."

She grew worse fast. My husband set off immediately to let our brother and family know. He and Sister Sibbilla came to see her as soon as they could, but she was past conversing much—mentioned some property which she said ought to have been attended to before being laid on a sick bed. * * * * * * * * * *

Her remains were conveyed to her house and buried from there, at East Nantmeal burying-ground, after which a solemn meeting was held.

My friends of the Monthly Meeting of Concord, thought it right to acknowledge and recommend me to the Quarterly Meeting of Ministers and Elders as an appropriate Minister. A minute to that import was furnished the Select Quarterly Meeting in the fourth month, 1802.

A SHORT ACCOUNT OF THE ANCESTORS OF ALPHONSUS KIRK.

[According to tradition,* it being by no means a historical fact, we have the following: Dr. Robert Church, a native of England, soon after his marriage, joined the English army as a surgeon, and was in the Scottish rebellion of 1556; after which he settled in Scotland. Here he took the name of Kirk, which in that language signifies Church. He had a son, Thomas, who had three sons, Robert, Roger and Timothy, all of whom returned to Ireland in the year 1631.

Assuming that the above, so far as the first and second generations are concerned, is altogether traditional, we commence with the third, existing in the British Islands, which is a starting-point in the genealogy of this family of Kirks that can be relied upon with as much certainty as any other historical fact, based on documentary and corroborative evidence.]

FIRST GENERATION.

1. Roger Kirk resided in the town of Lurgan, Province of Ulster, county of Armagh, Ireland. He was a Friend, and, in the year 1675, was fined, with many others, because he would not swear as a juror (see Besse's Sufferings of Friends, 480). His wife's Christian name was Elizabeth. Roger died on the 24th of the 1st month, 1698. He had a son, ALPHONSUS, who migrated to America.

---

*The names have been arranged in the same order as those in the previous part of this volume. Wherever we have deemed it necessary to add anything we have enclosed it in brackets. C. H. S.

SECOND GENERATION.

CHILD OF ROGER AND ELIZABETH KIRK, OF LURGAN, IRELAND.

2. Alphonsus, born in Ireland, 16—. Migrated to America. Proud groups him with Friends who arrived in 1682, and settled on the Brandywine creek and "about Center," that is west of the Brandywine (see Vol. 1, 218); but there are family documents which show that his arrival was a few years later.

Alphonsus took passage from Belfast on the 11th day of 11th mo., 1688, landed at Jamestown, Virginia, on the 12th of 1st mo., 1689, and arrived in Pennsylvania the 29th of 3d mo. following. He brought with him certificates, copies of which follow. They were (1864) in possession of Sibbilla Embree.

"*Whereas*, the bearer hereof, Alphonsus Kirk, having an intention to transport himself into the Province of Pennsylvania, in America, at the request of the said Alphonsus, we think it our duty thus to certify concerning him. That he hath lived with his father from his infancy until now, and for aught we know, hath been subject and obsequious to his parents; and since his convincement he hath belonged to our Meetings, and hath behaved himself quiet and honest in his deportment and dealings here, and for anything we do know, or now understand, we having made inquiry concerning him, and he saith himself, is free and clear of all women here, on the account of, or concerning marriage or anything relating thereto. We leave him, and advise him to the measure of the grace of God in his own heart, to which if he would submit, it will teach him to deny all ungodliness.

From our Meeting at John Robinson's, the 9th of 10th month, 1688.

Robert Hoopes,	John Webb,
John Robinson,	Mark Wright,
William Porter,	Thomas Wainwright,
Timothy Kirk,	James Webb,
Jonathan Hoopes,	William Williams,
Robert Kirk,	Jacob Robinson,
William Cook,	Thomas Walker.

Alphonsus was furnished with a certificate by his parents, to wit:

"This is to certify that we are willing our son, above named, should take this journey herein mentioned; desiring the Lord to be his preserver, and leave him to the disposal of the Almighty. And if it be his fortune to marry, we give our consent, providing, it be with a Friend in unity with Friends, according to the order of truth.

"ROGER KIRK,
ELIZABETH KIRK."

On page 25, of a small volume, entitled "The Family," written by Hon. Eli K. Price, we find the following:

"It was the good 'fortune' of Alphonsus Kirk to marry, and that in accordance with the condition imposed by his parents; therefore, with their consent; for on the 23d of 12th month, 1692–3, he did marry Abigail Sharpley, a Friend and daughter of Adam Sharpley, according to the order of truth, at the house of her father, on Shilpot Creek. The marriage certificate describes Alphonsus as being of Brandywine Creek.

Proud mentions Adam Sharpley's arrival under date of 1682, and as a settler on the east side of Brandywine creek, Newcastle county.

Alphonsus Kirk died 1745, —, —. His wife Abigail died 1748, —, —.

Timothy Kirk, of Sandy Springs, Md. (1852), has in his possession an old Bible with a title page containing:

AT LONDON.

Printed at John Day's, dwelling over Aldergate.

Anno 1581.

Among other entries on the record is—

"Alphonsus Kirk is my name and with my pen I write ye same. 1729."

THIRD GENERATION.

CHILDREN OF ALPHONSUS KIRK (2) AND ABIGAIL SHARPLEY.

3. Roger, born 1694, 1, 21; died 1762, 1, 19. Married 1726, 12, 9, at Nottingham, Md., to Jean Bowen, daughter of Henry Bowen, of Cecil county, Md. Jean died 1752, 7, 28. [Roger resided somewhere near Brick Meeting House, Md. One account says that he was named "long Roger," to designate him from Roger Kirk, who resided on North-east Creek, the ancester of those contained in the former part of this work. It will be perceived that they were about the same age and died within a few years of each other.]

4. Elizabeth, born 1695, 4, 23; declared her intentions of marriage before Newark or Kennett Monthly Meeting 1717, 3, 4, and was married to Daniel, son of James and Honour Brown, of Nottingham.

5. Jonathan, born 1697, 11, 15; died 1735, 9, 1.

6. Mary, born 1698, 8, 31; died 1699, 1, 29.

7. Debrey, born 1699, 11, —; died 1704, 7, 23.

8. Abigail, born 1701, 7, —; died 1704, 7, 29.

9. Timothy, born 1704, 3, 6; died 1704, 8, 19.

10. Alphonsus, born, 1705, 8, 2; died 1732, 1, 1. Married.

11. Adam, born 1707, 3, 1; died 1774, 10, 8, and was buried at Center grave-yard same day. He was married at Kennett, 1744, 9, 14, to Phebe, daughter of Moses and Alice Mendenhall, of Kennett. Adam was a resident of Christiana Hundred, Delaware. [Of him little is known. In the year 1740, the citizens of Willingtown (now Wilmington) petitioned to Hon. Thomas Penn, one of the proprietors, to incorporate their settlement into a borough or town. Among the petitioners we find the names of Adam and Alphonsus Kirk.—*A History of Original Settlements on the Delaware*, pp. 207 : *by Benjamin Ferris.*]

12. William, born 1708, 1, 4; died 1787, 3, 2. Married at Center Meeting, New Castle county, Delaware, 1733, 6, 8, to Mary Buckingham, of Birmingham, Chester county. She was interred 1753, 3, 11. William's second marriage was to Sibbilla Williams, daughter of John and Elizabeth Davis, and widow of Edward Williams. William Kirk settled in East Nantmeal, Chester county. He was a farmer and weaver. He died at an advanced age, and was buried at East Nantmeal burying-ground. [For further history, see the account of the trials and hardships of her ancestors, by Rachel Kirk (57).]

13. Timothy, born 1711, 5, 1; died 1786, 5, 2. Married "ye 2 day of 3d mo., 1734, to Sarah Williams. She died ye 27th 9 mo., 1796, being eaged 82 years old."

FOURTH GENERATION.

CHILDREN OF ROGER KIRK (3) AND JEAN BOWEN.

14. Abigail, born 1727, 9, 5; died ——, —, —. Married ——— Corbally.

15. Rachel, born 1728, 2, 22. Married John Sergeant.

16. Henry, born 1730, 3, 9.

17. Margaret, born 1731, 9, 5.

18. Jean, born 1733, 12, 1.

19. Timothy, born 1734, 2, 22; died 1824, 3, 4. Married 1762, 3, 13, to Lydia Shepherd. She died 1785. Timothy married again 1787, 3, 1, to Elizabeth, daughter of Benjamin and Lydia Wilson, of East Nottingham, Cecil county, Md. Elizabeth died 1831, 3, 20, in her 78th year.

20. William, born 1736, 2, 10.

21. Elizabeth, born 1738, 12, 17.

22. Mary, born 1740, 12, 27.

23. John, born 1742, 12, 17.

24. Hannah, born 1744, 12, 10.

25. Sampson, born 1746, 12, 18.

26. Sarah, born 1720, 12, 13.

CHILDREN OF DANIEL BROWN AND ELIZABETH KIRK (4).

27. Elizabeth, born 1718, 1, 22.

28. Rachel, born 17—, 12, 18.

29. Abigail, born ——, —, —. Married 1743, 10, 8, to William, son of John and Hannah Churchman. He was born 1720, 11, 29, and died 1798, 4, —. Abigail died 1793, 2, 14.

30. Timothy, born ——, —, —; died 1808, 4, 4, in Berkley county, West Virginia, a member of Hopewell Monthly Meeting. He was married to Mary, daughter of John and Mary Jones, of Cecil county, Md.

31. Daniel. Married 1759, 12, 27, Miriam, daughter of David and Lydia Gregg of East Nottingham.

32. Jeremiah, born ——, —, —. Married 1765, 11, 14, Anna, daughter of Samuel and Catharine Wilson.

CHILD OF ALPHONSUS KIRK (10) AND —— ——.

33. Hannah, born 1730, 12, —. Was married 1749, 8, 11, at London Grove, to John, son of William Hayes, of East Marlborough.

CHILDREN OF ADAM KIRK (11) AND PHEBE MENDENHALL.

34. Lydia, born 1746, 1, 8; died 1793, 2, 2.

35. Hannah, born 1747, 5, 31; died ——, —, —.

36. Adam, born 1749, 6, 13. Married at Center Meeting, 1774, 3, 30, to Esther, daughter of Joseph Wilson of Newcastle county, Del. Had five children, viz.:

37. Phebe, born 1751, 7, 28.

38. Abigail, born 1753, 11, 29. Married 1780, 5, 10, to Daniel, son of Francis and Mary Windle of East Marlborough.

39. Caleb, born 1756, 3, 30. Married 1779, 4, 29, at Centre Meeting, to Sarah, daughter of Smithen Chandler, of same place.

40. Deborah, born 1758, 19, 12; died 1764, 12, 2.

41. Betty, born 1761, 10, 27; died 1764, 11, 7.

42. Joshua, born 1763, 11, 6; died 1777, 11, 7.

43. William, born 1765, 9, 13; died ——, —, —.

CHILDREN OF WILLIAM KIRK (12) AND MARY BUCKINGHAM.

44. Caleb, born 1734, 5, 4; died ——, —, —. Married at Caln, 1756, 9, 30, to Elizabeth Coates, widow of Samuel Coates and daughter of Ann Mendenhall, of East Caln.

45. Ruth, born 1736, 7, 16; died 1753, —, 12.

46. Tamer, born 1738, 8-2, 8. Married Phineas Mendenhall; removed with him to North Carolina and from thence to Georgia, where she resided a few years. was massacred

by some Indians. She had two daughters. They removed finally to near Stillwater, Ohio.

47. Hannah, born 1740, 10, 21; died young and was buried 1753, 4, 13.

48. Othniel, born 1742, —, —; died young.

49. Rebecca, born 1744, 3, 31; died 1753, 2, —.

50. Lydia, born 1748, 12, 11; died 1823, 8, 23. Married William Humphrey. Had no children.

51. Mary, born 1751, 1, 1; died 1837, 10, 6. Married Jehu Wickersham and removed to Georgia, from thence to North Carolina, and finally to Ohio and Indiana.

52. Sarah, born 1751, 1. 1; died ——, —, —. Married John Williams. No children.

CHILDREN OF WILLIAM KIRK (12) AND SIBILLA WILLIAMS.

53. Isaiah, born 1754, 12, 9; died 1835, 12, 19. Married Elizabeth Richards. She died 183–, 2, 28, and was interred in East Nantmeal burying-ground.

54. Elizabeth, born 1756, 11, 24. Married John Meredith.

55. Joshua, born 1759, 12, 12.

56. Ruth, born 1761, 4, 16.

57. Rachel, born 1763, 4, 18; died 1847, 8, 6. Married 1784; 10, 20, to Philip Price, son of Philip and Hannah Price, of Darby, Pa. She was a minister, being furnished by the Meeting with a minute to that effect in the 4th month, 1802. She and her husband resided for many years in the borough of West Chester, and established a well known Seminary, for the education of young ladies. Philip Price was born ——, —, —, and died 1837, 2, 26.

Rachel possessed considerable literary attainments, and to her, the descendants of Alphonsus Kirk are indebted for the genealogical tables of their ancestors.

58. Adam, born 1766, 5, 12.

59. William, born 1769, 1, 23.

60. Sibbilla, born 1771, 10, 23. Married Joseph Brinton.

CHILDREN OF TIMOTHY KIRK (13) AND SARAH WILLIAMS.

61. Jacob, born 1734-5, 12, 19; died 1782, 7, 16.

62. Alphonsus, born 1736, 12, 16. Married at Pikeland, 1762, 7, 6, to Mary, daughter of James and Elizabeth Pryor, of Kennett. Alphonsus died 1763, 4, 17. New style.

63. Rachel, born 1738, 12, 18; died ——, —, —.

64. Adam, born 1740, 12, 16; died ——, —, —.

65. Joseph, born 1742, 3, 5; died ——, —, —.

66. Thomas, born 1744, 9, 26.

67. William, born 1746, 12, 21.

68. Timothy, born 1749, 1, 8.

69. Sarah, born 1750, 10, 19.

70. Ezekiel, born 1753, 12, 19; died 175-, 7, 27.

71. Ezekiel, born 1755, 11, 29.

72. Jonathan, born 175-, 3, 25. Never married. Went to Nova Scotia.

FIFTH GENERATION.

CHILDREN OF TIMOTHY KIRK (19) AND LYDIA SHEPHERD.

73. Hannah, born 1763, 12, 3.

74. Jane, born 1766, 1, 14.

75. Lydia, born 1768, 3, 28.

76. Joshua, born 1770, 8, 20. Married, 1794, 11, 6, to Mary, daughter of Abraham and Charity Sidwell.

77. Elizabeth, born 1772, 2, 17. Married, 1791, 12, 8, to Samuel Foster, of East Nottingham.

78. Mary, born 1774, 5, 15, Married, 1801, 3, 12, to Levi, son of Samuel and Isabella Reynolds, of Coleraine, Lancaster county, Pa.

79. Catharine, born 1777, 3, 14. Married, 1800, 7, 6, to Job, son of Samuel and Ellen Coppock, of Little Britain.

CHILDREN OF TIMOTHY KIRK AND (19) LYDIA WILSON.

80. John, born 1787, 11, 25; died in infancy.

81. Lydia, born 1789, 5, 2.

82. Esther, born 1792, 2, 4. Married Abner White. He died 1847, 1, 1. [Esther still lives; and, of late years, has resided in Ohio. In the fall of 1870, we saw her while on a visit to her daughter. She was a "hale, hearty" old woman, being in her 79th year.—C. H. S.]

83. Abigail, born 1796, 11, 16. Married James Hartley. Both deceased.

CHILDREN OF TIMOTHY BROWN (30) AND MARY JONES.

84. Rachel, born 1760, 2, 18.

85. Jesse, born 1762, 5, 9.

86. Timothy, born 1764, 9, 22.

87. John, born 1767, 3, 30.

88. Mary, born 1770, 5, 15.

89. William, born 1773, 1, 25.

90. Catharine, born 1776, 4, 24, in Virginia.

CHILDREN OF DANIEL BROWN (31) AND MIRIAM GREGG.

91. Abigail, born 1760, 11, 19; died 1769, 9, 6.

92. Joel, born 1762, 5, 2.

93. Joseph, born 1763, 9, 13; died 1769, 9, 3.

94. David born 1765, 4, 24; died 1765, 7, 24.

95. Miriam, born 1766, 6, 14.

96. Elizabeth, born 1768, 3, 3.

97. Daniel, born 1770, 3, 4.

CHILDREN OF JEREMIAH BROWN (32) AND ANNA WILSON.

98. Abner, born 1767, 4, 20; died 1804, 10, —, in Virginia.

99. Catharine, born 1769, 2, 5. Married William Rogers.

100. Rebecca, born 1771, 1, 21; died same day.

101. Jeremiah, born 1772, 12, 14; died 1773, 7, 8.

102. Anna, born 1774, 10, 23. Married Jeremiah Rogers.

103. Jeremiah, born 1776, 11, 25.

104. Rachel, born 1779, 9, 16.

105. Ezra, born 1781, 9, 9; died 1804, 4, —.

106. William, born 1784, 11, 1. Married Esther, daughter of Eli and Susanna Kirk of West Nottingham. William was a farmer and resided near Brick Meeting House, Md.

CHILDREN OF ADAM KIRK (36) AND ESTHER WILSON.

107. Isaiah, born 1775, 2, 27; died ——, —, —.

108. Hannah, born 1776, 10, 22.

109. Rebecca, born 1778, 3, 30.

110. Benjamin, born 1780, 4, 4.

111. Ann, born 1782, 6, 17.

CHILDREN OF CALEB KIRK (39) AND SARAH CHANDLER.

112. Joshua, born 1779, 6, 27.

113. Phebe, born 1781, 2, 2. Married at Center, 1803, 6, 29, to Joel, son of Amor and Mary Hollingsworth.

114. Samuel, born 1782, 8, 25.

115. Caleb, born 1784, 11, 11; died 1785, 9, 27.

116. Abigail, born 1787, 8, 11; died 1790, 10, 26.

117. Ann, born 1789, 5, 31.

118. Caleb, born 1792, 4, 16.

119. Sarah, born 1793, 12, 28; died 1803, 8, 18.

120. Lydia, born 1796, 12, 30; died 1803, 8, 13.

121. Hannah, born 1799, 10, 20.

CHILDREN OF CALEB KIRK (44) AND ELIZABETH COATES.

122. Elisha, born 1757, 12, 25; died ——, —, —.
123. Caleb, born 1759, 8, 3; died ——, —, —.
124. Beulah, born 1762, 4, 7; died ——, —, —.
125. Eli, born 1764, 4, 13; died ——, —, —.

CHILD OF ISAIAH KIRK (53) AND ELIZABETH RICHARDS.

126. Elizabeth, born ——, —, —. Married, ——, —, —, to ——— Garretson, and had three children.

CHILDREN OF PHILIP PRICE AND RACHEL KIRK (27).

127. Martha, born 1785, 11, 3; died 1852, 9, 11. Married Nathan H. Sharpless.

128. Hannah, born 1787, 3, 26; died 1861, 1, 10. Married David Jones Davis, M. D.

129. William, born 1788, 9, 17; died 1860, 1, 27. Married Hannah Fisher. "He was one of the early Westtown scholars, and left home, before he was of age, to teach a school for colored children, under the care of Friends, in Philadelphia.

"His ideas soon became enlarged and changed, and he studied medicine with Dr. Joseph Parrish, whom we remember not only as the best of physicians, but as the kindest and blandest of gentlemen, who always acted on the most liberal, sincere and humane convictions.

"William graduated at the University of Pennsylvania, when its chairs were filled by the eminent names of Rush, Physick, Wistar, James and Coxe. He made a voyage to China as surgeon of the Lancaster Robinson, one of the first of Thomas P. Cope's ships, and escaping capture, returned to a good market after the war of 1812 had commenced. He attempted another such voyage before the war ended, in the brig trader Donalson; but she being capsized in a gale and disabled, returned to port to refit, and while detained the news of the peace of 1815 arrived, and, sailing soon after, carried the first news of it to China. He spent about three years in Paris, in assiduous attention upon the lectures and hospitals of that great seat of medical science, returned to Philadelphia and commenced practice with the best qualifications and brightest prospects. But after a few years he allowed himself to be diverted from the regular pursuit of his profession to other occupations, changed his residence from place to place, and hence failed to acquire that wealth that otherwise would have crowned his professional services and placed his family in affluence. After years lost to the profession, part of the time in the Ohio legislature, he resumed its practice in Cincinnati, and pursued it with conscientious devotion until his death, and always won the attachment and confidence of his patients.

"His disposition was most kind and social, and his manners always gentle and without affectation, were the most polished and attractive. He had known much of the world and its philosophy, but lived to acknowledge the faith of his mother to be the most truthful and beautiful that the world had ever received, and in that faith had the belief of our reunion in immortality."—(*The Family, page* 37–38, *by Hon. Eli K. Price.*)

130. Sibbilla, born 1790, 2, 19; died 1853, 8, 6. Married John W. Townsend.

131. Margaret, born 1792, 4, 19. Married Jonathan Paxson.

132. Benjamin, born 1793, 12, 17. Married Jane Paxson. "He remained upon the farm; has always been a farmer,

though sometimes engaged in teaching, and preserved through life the simplicity of dress and manners in which he was educated in his youth. He was a son after the heart of his parents; and only ever differed from them, or seemed to, when the Society of Friends in this country was rent in twain in 1827 and '28, but this separation estranged them not in affection nor individually in faith. If the life of early Friends was a return to the simplicity and truthfulness of apostolic days, then that of our brother is like unto theirs."—(*The Family, page* 38, *by Hon. Eli K. Price.*)

133. Sarah, born 1795, 11, 6. Married Caleb Carmalt.

134. Eli K., born 1797, 7, 20. Married Anna Embree. Being fond of reading went into the counting-house to escape the farm. He had a full mercantile education in the shipping house of Thomas P. Cope, and for a year with J. C. Jones, Oakford & Co., to prepare especially for the China trade. That trade becoming greatly depressed when he became of age, he decided not to waste his time, and to gratify a different aspiration, studied law with John Sergeant, from whom he ever received the kindest treatment. His profession he has uninterruptedly pursued to the present time. He was at first best prepared in mercantile law, which he began to read in the counting-room; but the people identified him, after his admission, more with real estate, and to land titles he has most devoted his professional life. In 1853 the old city, as it was under Penn's charter, of two miles square, demanded reforms in the fire department, and from the evils of the disconcert of action of about a dozen municipalities, with differing laws, into which Philadelphia was divided. He was put upon the Senatorial ticket, against his own remonstrances, and Mathias W. Baldwin and William C. Patterson upon the House ticket, and they were elected over the regular candidates of both po-

litical parties. The Consolidation Act was the result, and during the three years E. K. Price remained in the Senate of Pennsylvania he legislated with a special view to the security of titles to real estate; to regulate charitable and religious uses and trusts, so as to place all religious societies upon one equal platform before the law; to put the rights of women upon a better footing, and to repress legislative corruption.

With the same object of security of title to real estate, he wrote and published a professional work, and prepared acts of Assembly at other times. He wrote, and with the aid of his brother Philip, printed and circulated the Memoir of Philip and Rachel Price, which was reprinted at Glasgow in "The British Friend;" and wrote and printed for our relatives the Memorial of "Rebecca," his daughter, and of her mother, and now presents them this contribution toward their family history.—(*Volume entitled "The Family,"—By Hon. Eli K. Price.*

He ceased to be a member with Friends by the best act of his life, that which gave him one of the best of women to be one of the best of wives. This was at the period of the separation; a circumstance that made each division less attractive to those who did not sympathize with the controversy. Having no unity with the disunity, and wishing the society not to be responsible for his acts or writings, he has remained in isolation, but honoring and loving the good in whomsoever he finds it.

Professionally, he has had much to do with questions of property growing out of the separation; always giving his counsels in favor of peace, and it is with great satisfaction that he bears the testimony that no religious bodies, so much at variance, were ever more governed by pacific counsels in favor of peace; so that forbearance and *time* rather than litigation have composed legal rights, and generally left the property with the greater local number having it in charge. He has often queried to himself whether the sages of the Society of the last century would not have weathered the storms of this without shipwrecking the unity of the Society; and is inclined to think they would.

One near and dear to the writer always seemed to him more than others deeply centered in that true wisdom which alone could have averted the catastrophe; and that came by her deep affections and true parental instincts, and also from Him whom she watched as her constant guide from early infancy. His mother, then at Westtown, and in the Select Meetings, was a constant, but nearly silent witness to much that was passing; and as became her position as a minister of the Gospel, preserved her wonted serenity, and in the deep recess of her soul heeded only the guidance of that Light which the winds of controversy could not reach, nor cause its constant flame to flare or flicker, or prove delusive to her steadfast mind. Silence and resignation, during this period of severe trial, she felt to be her allotted portion, "endeavoring to know the Divine will,* * * * on leaving all to Him that hath the key of David; He that openeth and no man shutteth, and shutteth and no man rightly openeth." Memoir 128. (*The Family, page* 40, 41, *by Hon. Eli K. Price.*)

135. Isaac, born 1799, 11, 30; died 1825, 8, 25. Married Susanna Payne.

"He died in his twenty-sixth year of an attack of fever, obscure in its symptoms; was faithfully attended by Dr. Darlington, and by our brother William, who devoted all of many days and nights to be with him, to soothe and allay suffering. For the few years he was in business, farming at this homestead, Isaac evinced unusual enterprise and capacity.

Had he lived to continue as he began, he would have been successful and prosperous. He adhered while he lived, to the faith, practice and example of his parents; and though, in his youth, very playful and highly humorous in his disposition, and irresistible in his power to provoke mirth, he never did aught to give his parents pain. He died in the faith and hope of the righteous.—(*The Family, by Hon. Eli K. Price, page* 41.)

136. Philip M., born 1802, 7, 7. Married Matilda Greentree. Was the youngest son of Philip and Rachel Price. He had the most prolonged and best school education at Westtown; was fond of mathematics and general reading. Studied medicine with his friend, Dr. John D. Godman, and graduated in medicine in the University of Pennsylvania.

He practiced his profession for a time; but to the exposure and labors of a country physician, he preferred the office of Surveyor of Spring Garden, which he held for many years, and laid out the streets and made the plans of that district. His interest in building and railroad, and other improvements, amounted almost to a passion, sometimes pursued to his own injury and at the imminent risk of health and life. He was active in starting the Pennsylvania Railroad, and it may be said that the Erie Railroad, which at this day sees its completion, would not at times have lived without him. And now tributary roads also claim his attention. May he long live to be useful in that tempered moderation that insures safety and happiness!—(*The Family, page* 41–42, *by Hon. Eli K. Price.*)

137. Rachel, born 1808, 7, 10; died 1808, 9, 25.

SIXTH GENERATION.

CHILDREN OF ABNER WHITE AND ESTHER KIRK (82).

138. Alvin, born 1811, 11, 22. Married —— ——. No children.

139. Eliza, born 1814, 1, 1. Married Walter Moore, M. D.

140. John, born 1815, 10, 18. Married Hannah King.

141. William T., born 1817, 9, 28. Married Matilda Springer.

142. Abner, born 1819, 8, 15. Married Miriam King, daughter of Joseph and —— King.

143. Elisha, born 1821, 3, 1. Married Esther Richie.

144. Thompson, born 1823, 1, 18. Married Mary Simpson.

145. Margaret R., born 1825, 4. 9. Married first to James Paxton and second to Edward Moore.

146. Timothy K., born 1826, 9, 18. Married Susan Smith. Timothy learned the trade of blacksmithing with Milton Blake. Afterward removed to York, Pa., where he opened a Commercial College. He still resides at that place.

147. Esther J., born 1828, 3, 23. Married Samuel Brogan. Samuel is a farmer by occupation, and resides in Fulton township, Lancaster county.

148. Hughes, born 1829, 12, 10. Married Theresa DeHavert.

149. Joel S., born 1831, 12, 25. Married Susan Shaw.

150. Robert I., born 1834, 3, 26. Married Almeda Simpson.

151. Lydia M., born 1836, 6, 24. Married Eli Coulson, M. D. They have four children living and the same number dead.

CHILDREN OF NATHAN H. SHARPLESS AND MARTHA PRICE (127).

152. Hannah S., born ——, —, —. Married to Edward B. Darlington. Edward deceased.

153. William P., born ——, —, —. Married Anne G. Pennell. She is deceased. Married second, Sarah J. Leedom.

154. Philip P., born ——, —, —. Married Mary A. Paschall.

155. Henry P., born ——, —, —. Married Harriet Price.

156. Anna S., born ——, —, —. Married Stephen Paschall.

157. Alfred, born ——, —, —. Married to Elizabeth Sharpless.

158. Samuel E., born ——, —, —. Married Martha S. Ash.

CHILDREN OF WILLIAM PRICE (129) AND HANNAH FISHER.

159. Emelia, born ——, —, —. Married David P. Marshall.

160. Sallie R., born ——, —, —. Married Ludwig Hanan

161. Caroline F., born ——, —, — ; died ——, —, —.

162. Henrietta P., born ——, —, —. Married Robert K. Wright.

163. Helen G., born ——, —, —. Married Charles P Mulinier.

164. Josephine, born ——, —, —. Married John A. Bigelow.

165. Annette M., born ——, —, —. Married Rudolph Lawler.

166. William Redwood, born ——, —, —. (Not married).

CHILDREN OF JOHN W. TOWNSEND AND SIBBILLA K. PRICE (130).

167. William P., born ——, —, —. Married Anna Mary Kirk.

168. Anna M., born ——, —, —. Married George Thomas, M. D.

169. Rachel P., born ——, —, —. Married J. Lacy Darlington, of West Chester, He is a son of Dr. William Darlington. Has been identified for many years with various Agricultural Societies formed in Chester county.

170. Charles M., born ——, —, —; died ——, —, —.

171. Henry C. Married Georgiana L. Talman.

172. Edward Y. Married Henrietta M. Truth.

173. Philip P., born ——, —, —. Single.

CHILDREN OF JONATHAN PAXSON AND MARGARET PRICE (131).

174. Philip P. Married Phebe Speakman.

175. Henry. Married Helen Harlan.

176. Hannah.

177. Rachel.

CHILDREN OF BENJAMIN PRICE (132) AND JANE PAXSON.

178. Paxson. Married Jane Jackson.

179. Mary. Married Josiah Wilson.

180. Isaiah. Married Lydia Heald.

181. Philip.

182. Jacob. Married Rachel L. Thomas.

183. Edward.

184. Joel.

CHILDREN OF CALEB CARMALT AND SARAH PRICE (133).

185. Hannah, born ——, —, —. Deceased.

186. Jonathan, born ——, —, —. Deceased.

187. Sibylla. Married John C. Morris.

188. Philip P.

189. Samuel F. Married Anne E. Woolsey.

190. Rachel T. Married Rev. Elisha Mulford.

191. William Henry, M. D. Married Laura W. Johnson.

192. James Edward. Single.

CHILDREN OF ELI K. PRICE (134) AND ANNA EMBREE.

193. Rebecca E. Married Hanson L. Withers.

194. John Sergeant. Married Sallie B. Baker.

195. Sybil E.

CHILDREN OF ISAAC PRICE (135) AND SUSANNAH PAYNE.

196. Rachel born ——, —, —; died ——, —, —.

197. James M., born ——, —, —. Married Sarah Lightfoot.

CHILDREN OF PHILIP M. PRICE (136) AND MATILDA GREENTREE.

198. Helen F. Married T. S. Yardley.

199. Hannah P. Married H. Barton, M. D.

200. Mary.

201. Anna.

202. Philip M.

203. Charles S.

SEVENTH GENERATION.

CHILDREN OF SAMUEL BROGAN AND ESTHER J. WHITE. (147).

204. Mary Emma, born 1849, 10, 18. Married Franklin Leek. He is a carpenter by occupation.

205. Edwin J., born 1852, 5, 17.

206. Gilpin S., born 1853, 9, 1; died 1866, 8, 23. He was killed by a roller, while rolling land on the farm of Gilpin Stubbs.

207. Alice A., born 1855, 8, 23.

208. Samuel M., born 1862, 8, 13.

209. Lydia Ann, born 1864, 2, 7; died 1864, 8, 1.

CPSIA information can be obtained
at www.ICGtesting.com
Printed in the USA
LVHW100607210323
742065LV00002B/191